Hi Bathurms,

Thanks so much for your support.

Enjoy

Dan Myers

Fero Scitus Publishing

6115 Boulevard East

West New York, NJ 07093

Visit our website at www.publishersdilemma.com

First edition: November 2019

The characters and events in this book are fictitious. Any similarity to real persons, living or dead is coincidental and not intended by the author.

Printed in the United States of America

DARIUS MYERS

In Memory of:

Jo Jo Myers,

Ted Walker,

Robert Tassie,

Carl B. Clark

THE PUBLISHER'S DILEMMA

Acknowledgments

I am a Man of God, so let my acknowledgments begin with me showing love and thanks to my creator, my Lord, and Savior, Jesus Christ. I know I don't get to this place without you. It's been a fantastic journey that's been fruitful and made safe through your grace. I give you all the glory and praise.

I also acknowledge my parents, Joe and Betty Myers, who for 63 years of marriage and 85 years of life, continue to the best example of Pure Love I know. I thank you for showing me how always to put God first and to chase my dreams.

Thanks, are owed to the Fabulous Sisterhood of Laguna Niguel and Dana Point. To Deborah Meyers, Brenda Sessley Mason (RIP), Sheila McDaniel, Pamela Lathan, Delores Thomas; Visiting with you guys and your feedback was a Masters Class, I thank you for your time and care when this project was still in incubator stage.

To my longtime and dear friend Linda Gill Anderson, thank you so much for the introduction to Monica Harris Mindlovich, who said, "Darius, this was a fun read, now put quotations around all that beefy narrative, let it go and get on to the next one." If you are looking down Monica, I have a ton of excuses for not doing it while you were around, but I finally all these years later, I am letting it go and moving on to the next one. Thank you so much for your kind words and support. Rest In Power Monica.

To my ace of a friend, Steve McDonald, my enthusiastic first reader, thank you, my Brother, for the encouragement.

To my good friends Wanda Bolton, Andre Jackson, and Robert Lanza, I thank you for your encouragement and a fresh set of eyes, especially when it all became blurry to me. I'm blessed to have people in my life, like you, who are best of the best and kind friends and supporters.

The Publisher's Dilemma characters, especially the good guys and gals, are all composites and built from countless wonderful interactions from amazing people in my life. Creating these characters was a blast and made easy because of these many great relationships. Thank you all for being bright lights in my life.

Darius

Part One

THE PUBLISHER'S DILEMMA

Chapter One

An elderly white man led by a young African American woman exit Gill Harris's office and hurriedly made their way to the 39th-floor elevator bank. They did so silently. As they waited for the elevator, the woman hit the down button repeatedly. It's a sign of her anxiousness.

She broke the silence and asked him, "My God, what did you do?"

The Old Man shrugged his shoulders with a confused look on his face. He then stuttered as he tried to speak.

"I, I, I told him."

The woman looked at him with a perplexed look. She's in disbelief as to what just happened. She interrupted his stuttering and said sternly, "Don't say another word until we get out of here. Not another word, do you understand me?"

"Yes, I do, I understand," he said without a stutter.

"Okay, I will get us out of here, and then we'll figure this out. The elevator will be here in seconds and when it does follow my orders."

When the elevator arrived, she whispered as they boarded, "Keep your head down, there's a camera in here. We can't let the camera see our faces."

It took the elevator seconds to reach the ground floor. The woman then pointed to a private exit reserved only for the executives of the 39th floor.

"We are going to the private exit. Do you understand me? I need you to move fast, okay?"

"I understand. I will move as fast as I can," the old man said.

She didn't wait for him to move. She was nervous and scared. She grabbed him by the arm and pulled him to the private exit that lets them out the building and into the city streets.

Just minutes earlier, while the old man and woman waited for the elevator, Donald Alexander dialed the extension of Kwame Mills.

Mills was working late in his office on the 37th floor. He recognized Alexander's extension and picked up the call right away.

"Hey Donald, what's up?"

"Kwame, can you come upstairs? I'm hurt bad and need help. Please come, immediately." Donald dropped the phone, and after he did, Kwame heard him moan in pain.

Without another a word, Kwame hung up his phone and sprinted from his office and up the two flights of stairs. He made it to the 39th floor and missed by seconds the elevator with the assailants as its doors closed and began to descend.

He ran full tilt to Donald Alexander's office with no idea what he just missed and what lied ahead.

Chapter Two

Nurse Anna Dulany's cell phone is ringing. She is the head of the Emergency Room crew at City Hospital. The call is from Johnson, the lead paramedic in the ambulance racing to her emergency room. When Johnson's name flashed on her phone's caller I.D., she answered it immediately.

"Dulany here, what's up Johnson?"

"Hey Dulany, this is not a catch-up call. I am bringing in a big one from Harris Simmons, the media company. He is one of the top executives and has lost lots of blood. You may want to secure the premises."

"Oh my, Johnson, thanks for the heads up. How long will it take for you to get here?"

"We're hightailing it and should be there in five to ten minutes. Please be ready. This guy is in bad shape."

"Thanks Johnson, I'll be ready. Got to go," Dulany said. She ended the call and jumped into action.

"Crew, let's gather around," she yelled out. In seconds her team of E.R. nurses and attendants have gathered, in front of her, ready for action.

"Listen up everybody, we've got a VIP shooting, and the paramedics are on the way. We've got about five minutes, and this may be a long night, so run to the bathroom if you need to go. And let's clear a treatment area and be ready. We don't know what's ahead, but I just got a call from Paramedic Johnson, and he said it is serious."

Dulany's crew was experienced with VIP admittances but hadn't received one in a while, so she reminded them of the protocol.

"Let's focus on the patient and remember no one is to talk with the police. They will likely arrive shortly as well and will be itching to get any news they can about the victim and the shooting. Let's also be aware of the press. If they find out we have a VIP, we'll have a dozen or so newspaper reporters wanting to get the scoop on what will be tomorrow's big headline story."

"Remember," she continued "once the patient arrives, the only people who will be working without any ulterior motives will be the doctors and us. So, we must be on our A-game."

She then took a step back and inspected her team. They had the intense game face on that she liked to see during emergencies. They were ready and she was too. She then shouted, "Okay, you all know the code. So, let's hear it."

Dulany then roared "Nobody," and the team shouted with her even louder in unison, "and I mean, nobody gets in the way of us saving lives." They then broke off to get ready for the incoming patient.

As the ambulance raced through the city streets, Paramedic Johnson was having a similar conversation. He yelled to the driver Lucas, who was only on the job for a couple of weeks. "Lucas, when there's a high-profile shooting, the uniformed police officers want to crack the case as it is a sure-fire way to a detective's promotion. And that goes for the press as well. For the local newspaper reporters who hang out in the emergency room parking lots, high-profile shootings don't happen very often anymore in New York. The shooting of this guy is going to be a big story, maybe even a career-making one. Everyone is going to try and make a name off it. So be ready as this admittance may be crazy."

The newspaper reporters that Johnson was referencing call themselves the Celebrity Press Patrol. The E.R. crew, paramedics and cops call them the Celebrity Hack Patrol.

Johnson didn't like the Celebrity Hack Patrol. He continued to gripe about them as they made their way to the hospital, "We've got to be particularly aware of the Celebrity Hack Creeps."

He had long stopped calling them by their favored moniker. "These

THE PUBLISHER'S DILEMMA

Hacks, they get in the way of us saving lives, that's why I despise them. They spend most of their days hanging out in the parking lot at City Hospital. They hang around, hoping to catch a story with a celebrity spin that will capture the next day's headlines. Most of the time, they end up drinking coffee and playing low-stakes poker and blackjack until it's time for them to head back to their newsrooms to put together a story for the day."

"Celebrity Creeps, that's funny," Lucas said and laughed.

"Well, we don't need them in the way of things. We have precious cargo in here, a life is on the line, so I need you to be sharp. Got it, Lucas?"

"Roger that Boss," Lucas said to his Johnson, who was also his supervisor.

Johnson then recalled the last big VIP shooting. "These kinds of VIP shootings are pretty rare nowadays. I worked the last high-profile Celebrity shooting five years back when Yancey Stuart, the Manhattan real estate tycoon, was shot and killed by his wife, Dawn Davis Stuart."

"Five years seems like a long time ago," Lucas said.

"Yeah, Lucas, it does, but it was a big one. Dawn Davis Stuart, man oh man, she was something else. That woman shot her husband to death for cheating on her. The truth is he was a real cad and probably deserved it. She caught him, literally, with his pants down in a VIP booth with a prostitute at a strip club. The story is she was alerted by a friend, went to the club packing a gun, found him and shot him dead."

"Damn, that's gangster stuff right there," Lucas said.

"Indeed, the Celebrity Hacks nicknamed her Madame Hot Temper. She was so notorious for her snobby, boorish, and belligerent demeanor in New York City society circles that nobody felt bad for her. She wore out friendships easily, so much so that her character references at her trial were limited to immediate family. She ended up getting three years in jail."

"Wait, hold up," Lucas's voice rose with excitement." Did you say,

DARIUS MYERS

Madame Hot Temper? I remember that story. I was in college. All the guys in my dorm followed the shooting, the arrest, and the trial. It was such a crazy tabloid, only in New York news story."

"You got that right Lucas. Only in New York does a wife, in this case, a real hot wife, go into a strip club with guns blazing and then become a celebrity," Johnson said and smiled in remembrance of Madame Hot Temper.

"I have to admit though we loved us some Dawn Davis Stuart," Lucas continued. "She was so glamorous. Man, we all thought she was a babe. Stupid Yancey Stuart had it coming. He married her, so he should have known better, but I guess he didn't know just how hot-tempered she could be."

"No doubt, that was a fatal mistake. Yancey should've gone home that day. A bad decision on his part," Johnson said, shaking his head.

"Well, she's out of jail now," Lucas said. "She was featured in an article about "Criminal Wives Who Have Served Their Time." Her story said that it had been a couple of years since she fulfilled her sentence. She was a model prisoner and led a tutoring program in the prison GED program. She has quietly remarried and moved on from New York City society and public life."

"Good for her, but before prison, she was something else," Johnson said. "Anyhow, as far as the New York City gossip circles are concerned, an incident such as tonight's shooting at Harris Simmons is way overdue. I know the City's gossip whores are ready for another high-stakes murder involving New York Society. These are the true-life tales that the New York press covet. They sell newspapers."

Johnson was right. Five years had indeed been a long time, but based on tonight's event, the news, gossip and society pages of New York were about to get a murder story that rivaled the Yancey Stuart murder.

Chapter Three

"I forgot how loud this city could be," Kwame muttered to himself. It's 6:00 am, and he can hear from outside that the City is already in fast forward. His friend, Tom's apartment, is on the fourth floor of a luxury doorman building but far from sound-proof. Kwame is regretting that it's not this morning.

He turned over in the bed and said, "It'd be great if I can steal another 15 minutes of shut-eye, I'm going to need it with this big day in front of me."

His thoughts are for naught as the noises from car horns blaring, motorcycles revving, and the churning of a compactor in a garbage truck, pierced his early morning grogginess.

"Next time I am staying in a hotel. After all, I am here on business, and Tom was at a record industry party, so I didn't even get to see him last night."

As he laid in bed, the fight for 15 more minutes of sleep lost, he began to think about the big meeting, the reason for his trip to New York.

"I've got to be on today, if these guys don't like me, it will be a great opportunity lost."

He then decided to pray.

"Lord, thank you for waking me up this morning, healthy and clear-headed. I ask you to be with me today for my meeting with Donald Alexander, President of Harris Simmons. I want this job, Lord, you know I do, and I ask that you stay in charge. May you guide me and take over my judgment and lead me through this meeting. I thank you, God, for all that you do for me. In your name, I pray. Amen."

"Thank you God, take away all this stress and leave me blessed," he said to himself following the prayer.

Kwame knows that he needs all the help he can get today, the opportunity is too big. The position at World Media will make him one of its top executives. He'll also become a leader at Harris Simmons, the most highly regarded and coveted place to work in the media industry.

His good friend, Steve Ryan, worked for seven years at Athletes Week, Harris Simmons's top-selling sports weekly. Ryan raved about Harris Simmons as a first-rate company. "Look man, for starters, if you can get in here, you'll be able to retire in twenty years with two homes and two country club memberships."

Kwame was doing well, but his current company Trident was not the kind of place where you could retire with multiple homes and country club memberships. The possibilities of a great future at Harris Simmons excited him. He wasn't thinking about sleep or the noise anymore, mentally he began to gear up for the day ahead. He sat up in bed and recited aloud his rehearsed career highlights.

"I am now the Chicago Head of Sales for NewsInc, a 10-year-old digital news magazine that is owned by Trident Newspapers, a national digital news and media company. NewsInc was Trident's first foray into digital media publishing. I was a key member of the start-up team. We became profitable in only six years, and I was promoted to run the Chicago office. In my four years in this role, I increased sales for the office by 75%. This success has earned me a great total compensation package of $300,000 annually."

Going through the rehearsal calmed him. He knew what he had to say and that his pitch was solid. His thoughts returned to Steve Ryan and his

THE PUBLISHER'S DILEMMA

advice.

"Kwame, I know that the Chicago market has treated you well, but this is a great way to return to New York. You'll be back in the mix here with the hottest company in the business. You'll also get away from those dreaded Chicago winters."

He also said, "And let me emphasize that it's not often that you'll get a call from the President himself. I tell you Don Alexander is the real deal. He is an amazing executive and an even better person. He asked you to come in and talk about this role. You should feel honored and do whatever you can to get this job."

Steve Ryan was a great friend. He could have been envious of Kwame's opportunity and not helpful. Instead, Ryan was the ally he needed. Like Kwame, he knew how rare it was for African Americans to rise to senior executive levels in the business. Ryan was cheering hard for him.

"You deserve this, Kwame. I know you will reach back and pull us up once you get going, just as Donald Alexander is doing with you."

To have his good friend rooting so hard was encouraging. It also inspired him to be even more buttoned-up. He jumped out of bed and headed to the bathroom to shower and shave.

"Let's get this day started and get this thing done," he said out loud as he walked to the bathroom.

By 7:00, he is dressed and ready. He then decides to take a walk and get a cup of coffee, "I can kill a little time by going go to the corner store and pick up a coffee and say hello to Juan."

It's a five-minute walk to the store, and he begins to think about how much he enjoys New York City and how excited it would be returning in this prominent role at Harris Simmons. He's also eager to visit with Juan, the store owner.

Juan's store is a neighborhood hangout. Even for the corporate suit types, they all come to gossip and trash talk. Tom loves the place, and after Kwame's first visit, he did too. It's nothing fancy, and if you didn't know better or Juan, you might find it a bit grimy. But the coffee is good, cheap, and Juan, the owner, is one of those New York guys that is friendly with everyone. Since his departure from New York, Tom's place had been Kwame's New York home, and he had gotten to know Juan. As they became friendly, Juan and Kwame developed a witty New York versus Chicago banter.

When Kwame walked into the store, Juan sees him and smiles brightly. He then shouted out, "Well, alright now, hey everybody, it's Kwame, my man from Chicago."

It may be early in the morning, but Juan is full of energy and excited to see a familiar face and talk trash.

"Good to see you, my man. What are you doing here? How's the Windy City and those Barons, they still got a good basketball team?"

There are three other customers in the store. They noticed Kwame's smile in recognition of Juan's early morning energy. They smiled as well.

Kwame walked over to the self-serve coffee station. He picked up a large coffee cup and said, "Good Morning Juan, what in the heck are you yapping about so early in the morning? Is it because the Barons suck? And by the way, you still owe me $40 for that jersey. Don't make me call the Goon squad to get my dough."

A few years back Kwame gave Juan a jersey for the all-time Chicago basketball great James Strachan. Juan offered to pay for the Jersey, but Kwame refused it.

"What Jersey? I burnt that darn thing. I hate James Strachan. Besides, Carl B. Gainey and C.J. Strong were the best players on that team." Juan knew that this comment made no sense, given that James Strachan was a professional hoops legend. He only said it to get a rise out of Kwame.

THE PUBLISHER'S DILEMMA

Kwame kept pouring his coffee. He didn't take the bait, he was accustomed to Juan's trash talk by now. Instead, he turned to him and asked, "You forgot to take your medicine this morning, right? You better call home and get your pills, because you need to be medicated talking that nonsense."

Laughter filled the store as Juan and the other customers burst out in laughter.

After the laughter subsided, Kwame walked to the cash register to pay for the coffee. Juan then asked him, "So what are you doing in town Poppi?"

"I'm here for a job interview with a big media company."

"Nice Bro, so it means you may be coming back if you get it?"

"Yes, indeed Juan, if I get it, I'll be coming back."

"That's good for you, my friend. You look like you are ready for today with that million-dollar blue suit and tie. You are ready for today, right?"

"You know I am, but just the same, it's not a good thing to be too confident. So, say a prayer for me."

"Of course, I will. I always pray for my friends, especially when they ask. And coffee is on me today, another way of me throwing some good vibes your way."

"Thank you, I appreciate it, Juan. I hope to get it and if I do I'll see you a lot in the future."

"That's a bet Brother, that would be awesome."

Kwame then walked to the door and right before he stepped outside, Juan yelled, "Hey Poppi, I almost forgot, I see your ex-wife, Carrie Sinclair, has made quite a name for herself. She's some woman, Poppi. Can I ask her out?"

Kwame turned back to Juan, smiled, and said, "Go ahead Poppi. But you know what they say, be careful what you ask for, you just might get it."

"Si Poppi Si. I know all about that, Kwame. I suck at love, and I got two divorces as proof."

Juan then gave himself the sign of the cross and said, "I take back what I just asked for. Jesus help me for I know not what I ask."

And then he said to Kwame "But you know Carrie is special. She's smart, successful, and smoking hot."

"Yes, she is Juan, she is, you don't have to tell me. I'll see you soon my friend."

As he walked back to Tom's, Kwame smiled as he thought about Juan's fascination with Carrie. Everybody was fascinated by Carrie Sinclair. But that part of his life was over.

Kwame made it back to Tom's at 7:20 and it's quiet as Tom isn't up yet. But as he looked throughout the living room he quickly realized that he might be wrong. The door to Tom's bedroom is closed. There's a purse on the love seat and below it on the floor, a pair of expensive-looking lady's shoes.

Kwame had seen this before, so many times that it was beyond counting. This morning he just smiled.

Tom Wilson is his best friend, he is also a babe magnet. Women adored him, and Tom relished the attention. Tom's magnetism was so unique that to Kwame it seemed as if he had a Superpower. Facetiously, he would tell his buddy, "Besides being six feet six, smart as hell, articulate, broad-shouldered, lean and muscular with chiseled facial features and a glowing mocha skin, brother you've got nothing on me."

Tom would often say back,"Bro, you are doing quite fine on your own. You are six feet two, and the girls love your chocolate skin tone, thick head of curly hair, and that dimpled, white perfect smile. And besides, most of the girls I meet when we hang out are asking about you. They are all interested in meeting Kwame."

Kwame knew that Tom liked having him as a wingman; they looked out for each other. He also knew that Tom was the guy who could walk into the room, engage the prettiest girl in conversation, and by the time the evening was over, she would ask for his number. He was on a whole other level.

So, as he was seated on the couch in the living room drinking his coffee, he grew quite curious about who was in the bedroom. Was it someone he knew or somebody new. He then heard from the bedroom what sounded like a hushed conversation and a giggle. He strained to listen to what was going on when the door suddenly swung open.

Kwame recognized her immediately. A tall, slender, breathtaking, dark-skinned African-American woman walked out in front of Tom and wearing a form-fitting, black mini dress. She was Danielle Jackson, the fashion industry's latest supermodel. Her face was everywhere, including the cover of the leading fashion magazine, SOVO just two months back.

Tom spoke first. It was a good thing because seeing Danielle left Kwame momentarily speechless, "Kwame, my man, you made it in," Tom said as he rushed past Danielle to hug his buddy.

Kwame stood up to greet them. Tom, dressed in a tee-shirt and warm-up pants, bounced across the room in two huge steps and hugged Kwame heartily. He then took a step back to look him over as it had been months since they last saw each other.

"Look at you, Mr. Media Mogul. You look great and thumbs up on the nice suit," he said as he admired Kwame's royal blue custom-made suit. "Sorry, I wasn't here last night, another one of those industry parties."

"That's cool, brother," Kwame said, and it was a response purely by rote. He was still mesmerized by Danielle, who had yet to move from the bedroom doorway.

"Talk to her, you fool," he thought to himself. He then was able to turn his focus from Tom to Danielle, "Hello, Ms...."

DARIUS MYERS

Tom quickly cut him off. "Oh, my bad, meet Ms. Danielle Jackson, my interior decorator."

Danielle, fitting in an earring, scowled at Tom's attempt at humor.

Tom knew better and quickly corrected his bad joke, "Just kidding Kwame, Danielle, and I are doing the dating thing. She's wonderful," her smile then returned, broader and brighter.

"I know who Danielle is," Kwame said and turned to Danielle a bit more relaxed, "So what are you doing with this thug?"

"Slumming," she said without missing a beat. She then looked at Tom and smiled.

"You're so right," Kwame said. "You can do much better, let me give you my number."

"Hey, hey, watch your manners, brother. You wouldn't be trying to steal my woman, would you?"

Kwame nodded his head up and down rapidly. "Yes, uh-huh, absolutely, you're darn right I am."

"I like this guy," Danielle said with a big smile. She then excused herself, "Pardon me Kwame. I have to go to the restroom."

As Danielle exited, Tom turned his attention to his buddy. "It is good to see you. How are you, bro?"

"Life is pretty cool. Work is fine, Mom and Dad are good, Chicago's still cold, you know. And yeah, I'm very excited about today's meeting."

Kwame was still in awe of Danielle Jackson. Tom always dated well, but she was on a whole other level. He nudged his buddy.

"You hit the jackpot buddy. She's a star. I hate to say it but she might even be out of your league."

"I know man, and I won't argue that. She's a superstar but way more than just a pretty face and a nice body. Danielle is genius-level I.Q. smart. I'm serious about her, and I hope it works out."

THE PUBLISHER'S DILEMMA

"Well, it's about time Bro. You say it's serious, huh? Give it to me straight. You know I know you. How long have you guys been together?"

"Two, two and a half months."

"Tom," Kwame rolled his eyes in exasperation, "I know you man. You're right, she is special, no doubt, but talk to me in six months."

"I'm serious, Kwame," Tom's voice rose as he protested. "We just started dating, but I've known Danielle for nine months, and we're taking it slow."

"Eleven months," Danielle yelled as she opened the bathroom door. Tom and Kwame knew then that she was listening to Kwame's cross-examination.

"And he better be serious." She then gave Tom a penetrating sister-girl stare.

Tom shifted into damage control and quickly changed the subject. "Baby, you know I am serious. Now let me make you some coffee."

"Thank you honey. But I can't have any coffee. I have an audition this afternoon, but I will have some herbal tea."

"Herbal tea? I don't have any herbal tea Danielle, sorry."

"Yes, you do. It's in the right cupboard. I bought it last week, and there's some honey in the cupboard too. I also bought a teakettle. It's in the left cupboard."

She looked and smiled at Kwame before saying, "Your Boy is a hardcore bachelor. I've got to bring my own stuff with this Dude."

"True that," Kwame said, nodding his head in agreement. "But, he's coachable."

"Yeah, I suppose you're right. I think I can work with him and smooth out those rough edges."

As Tom was in the kitchen making the coffee, Kwame learned from Danielle that she had been living in New York for the past seven years and

DARIUS MYERS

was quite familiar with the fast life that surrounded Tom Wilson in the record industry. It was something they shared in common.

"We're both out here in these glamour jobs trying to stay grounded. It's not easy, but I pray for guidance all the time and try to let God direct my path."

"As a supermodel, I know first-hand the temptations and challenges of being pursued constantly by rich, powerful men. Dating without purpose sucks Kwame, and it's nice to be with someone who understands your world. And besides, don't tell him I said it, because I have to keep your Boy humble, Tom is hot. Much hotter than all those rich guys."

Their short conversation pleased Kwame, he learned from it that Danielle was far more than just a pretty face. She could have her pick of pretty much any man in New York. She still sought love, and for now, she was hitching her saddle with sound reasons to Tom Wilson.

Tom, unaware of their chat, yelled from the kitchen, "Kwame, I should have left you a note to tell you that I finally broke down and bought a coffee maker."

"Wow," Kwame said teasingly. "Welcome to the 21st century, my brother. So, I guess you don't get to see Juan much anymore."

"No, not true Brother, I see Juan all the time. That's where I have my meal plan. I still go there sometimes just for the laughs, as you know Juan is funny as hell."

Danielle smirked and said, "Can you believe that? This brother needs help. That place is a dump."

Tom walked back in with three cups, two for coffee, and the third one for tea. He placed the cups on the coffee table. He then sat next to Danielle on the sofa and said. "Hey now, give me some credit. I've got a coffee maker and now a teapot and you. You all a package deal, right?"

"Yes, we are a package deal and don't you forget it. If I leave you, I'm taking my teapot with me."

"You are never leaving me, honey. I need you and your teapot. I'd be lost without you both," he said as he leaned over and gave her a kiss on the cheek.

Danielle smiled and then stood up and walked to open the shades in the living room. The bright light of the morning's sunshine lit up the room. The natural light so early in the morning was also unnatural for Tom.

"Whoa, I can't recall the last time that I've been up this early on a weekday. I think I come in more times than I wake up at this hour." He then returned to the kitchen to get milk, sugar, and lemon for the coffee and teacups that he set up on the coffee table.

"Welcome to the real world," Danielle yelled to the kitchen. She then returned to her seat on the sofa, and the sunlight showed off her features even more. She was more beautiful in person without makeup than she looked on her SOVO cover.

Kwame and Danielle hit it off tremendously. He sensed from their short chat that she had a good heart. He could also tell from their banter that she was strong enough to keep Tom in check. He liked her and had high hopes that they continued to date.

After only one cup of tea, Danielle said, "I've had enough, I can't get bloated. Got to keep this tummy flat."

"Don't worry," Tom reassured her. "You're looking fine, baby."

"Thank you Baby," Danielle said.

She then announced that it was time for her to leave. "Kwame, I've got a busy day ahead. I've got to get home to shower and change for my day. I've enjoyed meeting you."

"The pleasure has been all mine Danielle. I've enjoyed meeting you as well."

As they all stood up, she walked over to Kwame and gave him a hug and kiss on the cheek.

"Good luck. I hope everything turns out well today."

"Good luck to you too," Kwame said as he released Danielle from the embrace. "My day has already been great. I started with a hug and a kiss from a supermodel."

"Oh, thank you Kwame, so sweet of you to say," she said and smiled.

Tom walked Danielle to the door, and they kissed goodbye, passionately, like new lovers.

Once the door closed, Kwame began to cross-examine Tom about his intent with Danielle.

"So, what's up Boy? This babe's off the hook, all I want to hear you say is that I hope your playboy days are behind you."

"I know this is not going to mean anything to you Kwame because you know my past, but she could be the one Bro."

Kwame was hopeful for his buddy. He knew Tom was terrible in relationships, so he didn't buy into this declaration of intent. Instead, he gave his buddy a tongue-in-cheek lecture.

"Good for you, my man. I like her too. But what does that mean, she could be the one? Does that mean the one right now? Talk to me in six months. Remember Sharon?"

"Ah, see, I know you were going to pull that one."

"What? You know this list is pretty long." Kwame then ran off a list of Tom Wilson's ex-girlfriends, "And Gabriella, Susan, Linda, Debbie, Shelby, Maggie, Judi, Kimberly, Carla, Kawanne and oh, yeah, I almost forgot, Chari."

"Okay, okay." Tom realized that he had to prove his commitment to his best friend.

"Time will tell, Kwame. But enough about me, you know if you get this gig, you're going to have to deal with her. Have you given any thought to

THE PUBLISHER'S DILEMMA

that?"

Kwame, who was now sitting on the loveseat, crossed his legs and looked to the window. The sun was bright and made him squint. The squint seemed to heighten his concentration on the subject of her.

"I am so over Carrie, and I'll tell you what. If there is one thing that I enjoyed about being in Chicago, it was not having everyone in my business. Being the subject of everyone's gossip is not fun at all."

"I hear you on that."

Tom was now lying on the sofa and was trying to contort himself into a comfortable position.

"You can count on the wolves to come out of the woodwork on that one for sure. If there is one thing that will never die in this town, it's gossip."

"Man, are you right."

Kwame then looked at his watch and realized it was time for him to leave.

"Alright, you need to get up and go to bed, your butt's too big for this sofa anyhow," he said as he watched Tom still struggling to get comfortable on his sofa. "Besides, I've got to get going, it's 8:15 now, and although it's just a 10-minute subway ride, anything could happen. You know, these New York subways. I don't want to be late."

"Yeah, you're right. You'd better get going."

Two minutes later, at 8:17, Kwame Mills was on his way to Harris Simmons.

Chapter Four

Kwame Mills knew a little about Donald Alexander from press reports, but when he did his due diligence to prepare for his interview, he learned that he was an industry wunderkind.

Steve Ryan emailed a pretty thorough download on Alexander. He shared in his notes, "By the age of 30, Alexander had already been Publisher of two media properties. He was named Publisher of Tennis World, the world's top tennis media property when he was just 27. His tenure at Tennis World was short and fruitful. In just three years at the helm, he was able to turn the property around by posting net revenue returns averaging 40%. After the untimely heart attack and death of the legendary Mulliken Laschever (M.L.) Zellweger, Athlete's Week's long-time Publisher, Alexander was rewarded for his success at Tennis World and named to succeed him. M.L. Zellweger, a media industry maverick, was the heart and soul of Athlete's Week."

Ryan's email continued, "When Alexander assumed the Publisher's position, Athlete's Week was the industry's top sports weekly. In his five years at the helm, Alexander posted annual net revenue returns of 20%. The industry average for the same five-year period was only 8%, and many media properties suffered even worse fates as the industry was in heavy transition during the mid to late 2000s."

THE PUBLISHER'S DILEMMA

He concluded, "Gill Harris took an immediate like to Alexander, as did many of the heads of top publishing firms. Three years ago, when the media industry rumor mill grew with talk that Alexander was being courted to take over the top job at key competitor Spring Communications, Gill Harris responded by relinquishing the title of President and naming Alexander to the post."

Kwame also learned that Donald Alexander was born and raised in Cleveland, Ohio. He was the oldest son of Jake Alexander, the renowned jazz bass guitarist. Jake was a keyboard player and member of The Missionaries of Jazz, the 1980's jazz supergroup. His mother, Margaret, a schoolteacher, was, according to Alexander, "a non-divorced single parent."

In an article in the Cleveland Gazette about the Alexander family, Donald said about his mother, "She raised us pretty much by herself. It did have a benefit for us, though. In the summer, we got an opportunity to travel with my dad to some exciting places in Europe and South America. We were always meeting interesting and famous people."

That same article noted that "Alexander's younger brother, Rick, lived in New York, and chose to follow in his father's footsteps as a jazz musician. Although he personally never pursued a career in music, Donald Alexander shared the family's musical inclination. An accomplished guitarist and saxophone player, he still, from time to time, sat in on local gigs with Rick's group, The Jazz Hummers."

A graduate of Calvary College in Ohio, Donald Alexander completed a double major in music theory and business. In a recent interview, when asked how he got into the Media business, Alexander said, "I thought I would move to New York and pursue a career in artist management with a record label. Although my dad warned me, I quickly found the business not to be palatable. I guess this was something I had to find out for myself. It took me a couple of years to figure this out. I then started to talk to some friends in the media business who helped me get in over at Tennis World. The rest of my story has been the result of hard work and good luck, mostly lots of good luck."

Kwame also learned that Donald Alexander was unquestionably a huge success in New York. He lived in a 3,500 square-foot penthouse apartment in the Sanchez Palace, one of the most exclusive addresses in Manhattan's SoHo District. And just recently purchased the three-acre Dryden Estate, owned by the late oil tycoon, Clark Dryden, in the exclusive Southampton enclave of Willow. He counted politicians, business leaders, actors, and musicians as friends, and as President of Harris Simmons Communications, earned an estimated $5 million a year.

In the Cleveland Gazette article, Alexander said, "when I reflect on my success, I often pinch himself and think, not bad for a brother man from Cleveland. I guess I've done all right for myself."

What Kwame Mills's due diligence did not reveal was that as well as he had done, Alexander felt like his life and success was to some extent, compromised. He was a solitary success as an African-American in the media business. This guilt increased after a recent employment report on ethnic minorities in the industry. The story, completed by the trade magazine Media Monthly, revealed that no other African-American had come close to his level of success. The report went on to show that no African-American or Latino held the post of Chief Revenue Officer or Executive Vice President of Sales in the top media 50 brands nationally. When he shared these findings with friends, both black and white, they often placated his guilt by telling him that his success was unique and rare and had progressed well beyond racial or ethnic lines.

True he thought, "there are very few top jobs, there are only five major Media publishing companies, but what about mid-to-senior level jobs? And if I agree with that nonsense, I let corporate America and those who

THE PUBLISHER'S DILEMMA

have the power off the hook."

Even before the report, Alexander often chided himself for not doing more, "I need to find the courage to use my power. My company owns and operates 15 Media Properties, and we don't have a single African-American, Latino, or Asian in the operating positions of Publisher or Head of Sales."

Equally disheartening was that there was no better news coming from their competitor companies. This solitude further confirmed his despair as there was no other person of color at his competition that he could even lament with and potentially build a strategy.

"I am in this seat alone. I've got to do something." Finally, in his despair to get some guidance, he picked up the phone and called Ron Cherry.

Alexander's closest confidant is Ron Cherry, an African-American investment banker at The Century Bank. Cherry, as a senior managing director, had been around long enough to see African-Americans integrate the top levels at investment banks. He knew full well the solitude Alexander was experiencing.

Cherry's secretary, Claire Jenkins, picked up the phone call on the second ring, "Ron Cherry's office. How can I help you today?"

"Claire, this is Don Alexander."

"Well, how are you, Mr. Alexander?"

Claire is a professional secretary. She always answered Ron Cherry's office with a happy greeting. Alexander enjoyed talking with her. He always kidded her that if she wanted to leave the rough and tumble world of investment banking and stop making inordinately insane amounts of money that she could come up and work at Harris Simmons. Claire would also tease him by saying that she was almost ready for a pay cut.

DARIUS MYERS

Today, she was as warm and as cheery as ever, "I'm great today, Claire, are you ready to take that pay cut?"

"I'm almost there, Donald, a couple of more years and I'm headed your way. Don't you dare pull back this offer."

"I won't Claire, we need you. But don't tell Ron. It's our secret."

Donald heard another phone ring and got to business, "Sounds busy over there. Is my main man Ron around today?"

"You are right. It's crazy around here today, and we just put the finishing touches on a deal. Ron is coming up for air, so your timing is perfect. He just got off his other line. Let me connect you."

"Thank you, Claire," Donald said as she connected his call.

Ron Cherry is gregarious, intelligent, battle-tested, strongly opinionated, and could always be counted on for good advice. He picked up the phone and without waiting for a hello, started speaking, "Don Alexander, my pal. I'm glad you called. You were on my list today. Marcia and I are having a small dinner party next week, uh, next Thursday." He is making his way through his Calendar, looking for the right day. "Nope, next Saturday, at 6:00 pm, cocktails, can you make it?"

Alexander turned to his Calendar, and while he checked on his availability, asked Cherry, "Does Marcia have any surprises for me?"

"You know Marcia. She wants to go down in history as the person who helped New York's most famous and eligible bachelor jump the broom. What can I say? You should feel fortunate to have a personal Date manager."

Alexander had grown accustomed to Marcia's efforts to match him with her girlfriends. While she could be over the top in her attempts, he also realized that she meant well, so he kept a good-natured attitude about it, and besides, he liked Marcia and Ron. They had become important friends.

THE PUBLISHER'S DILEMMA

"Well, who is it this time, Ron?"

"Can't tell you buddy, you don't want me sleeping on the sofa, do you?"

Alexander had found the next Saturday in his calendar. He sees that his day is busy. He had locked in with two stars from "6 to 10 pm, Titans baseball game." Two stars meant that the engagement was significant to Donald.

"Sorry pal, I've got Titans tickets for next Saturday, and I haven't seen them all year. They're playing the Scouts, my home team. I was going to ask you to join me. Let's blow off this dinner stuff. We'll go, have a few beers, hot dogs and watch some baseball. You can get Marcia to reschedule cocktails and dinner, can't you?"

"Don, if I go to that baseball game, I may as well move in with you. You know how Marcia is about these dinner party things. I tell you what, if you come, we'll put the game on in the television in the home theater."

He contemplated his choices for a few seconds before realizing that if he blows the Cherry's off, it would be a mistake Marcia would never let him forget. He conditionally agreed to attend.

"Only if you make that game in the home theatre a promise?"

"My word is my bond. Now, what's up?"

"Ron, I just got finished reading another of these industry reports that said in my industry, not one of our media properties has an African-American or Hispanic publisher or Head of Sales. And we don't have one here at Harris Simmons. Not one."

Ron Cherry sighed audibly before saying, "That's terrible."

"I know. Let me ask you? Why do you think your business has been able to integrate?"

DARIUS MYERS

Ron Cherry knew the answers, while it had taken the investment banking world generations to get their business practices correct, they finally had. His industry had linked integration to performance, specifically good deal-making. In Ron's firm, they operated under the credo that a good deal was honest, legal, and green. At The Century Bank, race was a non-issue if you were a good deal maker. He shared this philosophy with Donald Alexander.

"Donald, there are two reasons. One is that we go after the very best people. Dealmakers, we call them around here, and if you're a good dealmaker, the only color that matters is the color green. Second, we realize that in today's business world, decision-makers in the marketplace have changed. New markets are opening up every day, and the decision-makers aren't just white males anymore. Therefore, it makes sense in our business to train and develop smart and talented ethnic minorities and women. They will bring to deals a cultural understanding and rapport that the old guard frankly was never interested in developing. Quite simply, it just makes good business sense."

Cherry continued, "Donald, my friend, I'm afraid that if bringing in more African-Americans is important to you. It will have to be your legacy. That's your dilemma as the leader of your media company. Just know that you occupy a crucial role in your firm and your industry. You will have to be the trailblazer. Don't be afraid of this challenge and remember," he said as his other line rang, "it makes good business sense. That's my other line. I'm expecting an important client call, and this might be it. Can I expect to see you next Saturday?"

"Yeah, 6:00. I'll be there. And oh yeah, the dress?"

"Thanks, I almost forgot a sports jacket and no tie. Got to go now. See you next Saturday."

THE PUBLISHER'S DILEMMA

Alexander hung up the phone with grim resignation. He agreed with Cherry that if this disparity bothered him enough, he had to be the change agent. This was his dilemma as the President of the world's largest privately-owned media company. The challenge was staring him right in the face.

"Can I go on living fabulously and not enforce what I know to be morally and ethically right, and also do the best thing for my company?"

He picked up the phone and called in his long-time Chief of Staff, Wanda Howard.

On the second ring, she answered her line, "This is Wanda Howard."

"Wanda, this is Don."

"Yes, Donald, what can I do for you today?" Wanda asked.

"Can you come in for a few minutes? I've got a project that requires your help."

"I'll be right in."

As an officer of the company, Donald often had special projects that required the help of a Chief of Staff. Wanda was Donald's. Often in the media business, the Chiefs were young, inexperienced MBAs who got the job as a favor or courtesy to a power-wielding, well-connected parent. Donald couldn't afford the development time for a young MBA. To keep his star bright, he needed someone who knew the business and someone he could trust. Wanda had 20 years in the industry, was a media marketing genius, and had been a star salesperson at Harris Simmons. She was also his first and only choice.

Wanda entered Donald's office stylishly dressed in an elegant hunter green pantsuit. She had a notepad in hand. She took a seat in a large leather chair opposite Donald's desk.

"Hi there, boss."

DARIUS MYERS

"Hi there, back at you. Wanda, I've got a top-secret project for you."

When she heard top-secret, Wanda perched up in her seat. Donald then began to speak. "I've been in this job what three years now?"

Wanda corrected him, "Three years, three months."

"Well, I think it's time we shake things up a bit."

Wanda looked at him with a puzzled look on her face.

"What I need you to do is find the names, phone numbers, biography and dirt on every African-American, Latino, and Asian holding the job of sales manager or category manager in this business."

"In New York?"

Donald looked at the window and paused a moment, he then looked at Wanda and said, "No, my friend, in the country. Make this a national search. It's time we got some folks of color in this company. I also want you to find out every opening we have here for mid to senior-level sales directors. I want you to give me as complete a report as you can in five business days. That's next Tuesday. Don't let me down."

Wanda smiled as she finished her notes and contemplated her bosses request. She understood his isolation. They talked about it from time to time, especially after these reports would come out. She understood the intent of his marching orders.

As she prepared to leave the room, Donald picked up the phone and dialed the extension of Gill Harris. His long-time secretary, Theresa Harkin, answered the phone.

"Mr. Harris's office, Can I help you?"

"Hi Theresa, this is Don Alexander. Is Gill in today?"

"Oh yes, Mr. Alexander. Let me get him for you."

THE PUBLISHER'S DILEMMA

Theresa Harkin was one of those old-fashioned, formal, solicitous style secretaries that served her boss's every need. Gill Harris needed that kind of service, and Theresa Harkin could subjugate herself to manage these kinds of affairs for Gill.

When Gill picked up the line, he spoke into the phone with the energy and enthusiasm of a five-year-old at Christmas, "Donnie Alexander," he said gleefully. Gill was always happy, and why not, he was rich and powerful, "how are you today?"

"Just fine, Gill. And, how are you?"

"I am doing just great, let me put you on a video call, I got an awesome story to share."

Before Alexander could respond, Gill put him on a video call so they could see each other. He then began to talk about his weekend round of golf.

"Man, I've got a story to tell you. I went to the Club yesterday." Gill belonged to The Centurion, the country's first 100-year-old golf club. The Centurion was in Old Greenwich, Connecticut, where Gill lived.

"I snuck out of the house to try and hit a couple of buckets. I told the wife that I was going to get the oil changed at the dealership for one of my vintage cars. Anyhow, I run into Clark Winchester on the driving range, he's a member you know, and he twisted my arm to play nine holes."

Alexander nodded his head and says, "Uh, huh. Winchester, oh boy, that had to be fun."

Clark Winchester is the Publisher of Celebrity Profiles, Harris Simmons's weekly gossip property. Gill Harris was a great storyteller, and Donald always enjoyed listening to him talk. After three years working closely with him, Donald knew when he had no choice but to listen to one of his stories, and now was one of those times. He didn't mind because most of

DARIUS MYERS

these stories were good.

"Well, I agreed to play nine holes, and at the eighth, we are both three over par, and there's $150 on the line."

As Donald looked at Gill, he could see that he was bursting with excitement. "At the ninth hole, I'm 190 yards out, and he's just 145 yards away. I took out my four-iron and hit it perfect. I put the ball five feet past the pin."

Gill was ecstatic and incredibly pleased with himself. "That shot took the legs right out from under him."

Donald smiled. He knew Winchester was such a suck-up that he probably would have tanked his shot to score brownie points. He wanted to hear if he had the guts to make a good shot under pressure.

"Did Winchester choke? What did he do on his approach shot?"

"Yeah, he choked, he shanked his approach and went wide left. He missed the green totally and went into the sand trap. He blasted out to within four feet, though on his third shot. He showed a little spunk. I was glad he came out of the sand well because, as you know, he's such a coward. My goodness, that guy is spineless."

He then broke into a huge smile that piqued Donald's interest in the outcome of the story, "Why are you smiling so?"

"Because I drained the putt, and besides the bet, we doubled down when we tied at the 8th hole and agreed that the loser would have to pick up the other's monthly club minimum for the next six months."

"Oh my, now that sounds like an expensive round Gill. What's your monthly minimum?"

"$900.00," he said with a huge smile on his face.

Donald was impressed. This innocent $150 bet had just turned into a

THE PUBLISHER'S DILEMMA

$5400 9-hole round of golf. It was costly and as cheap as Winchester is, he probably didn't sleep that night thinking of ways to recoup the $5400 that he was going to pay to cover Gill's minimum.

"Yes, it was. But you know Donald he's not going to pay it from his own money. I bet you that he'll pass it on through his expense account."

"Good point," Donald said, and as usual, Gill was right.

Clark Winchester was the standard-issue privileged, entitled, blue blood corporate manager. He was prep school educated in New Hampshire, Ivy League, Mayflower descendant, etc., he had all the stuff on paper except a soul. He was devoid of spirit.

Winchester, in Donald's mind, was a wimp, a suck-up, an aristocratic, self-entitled whiner, and a cheap ass too. He was particularly proficient at passing $8.00 cab receipts with expense accounts. It drove the guys in accounting crazy. The guy makes $700,000 a year, and he can't eat an $8.00 cab. Donald wondered how Gill got him to agree to a bet that fat.

In Donald's eyes, the bet was a great sales job, and he wanted to know that story. However, he knew that if he asked, he could be there a couple more minutes listening to another excellent but long story.

"Gill, I need to get some time with you next week. I want to talk to you about some strategic directions that I think we need to consider."

His calendar was right in front of him. He glanced quickly and could see that he was pretty wide open for the week.

"I'm here all next week. Tell me when you need me, and I'll block out as much time as necessary."

"How about next Wednesday, 11:00 am, for an hour?"

"I just locked you in. I'm on my way to L.A. today, I'm going out there to do a few lunches and dinners with the editorial and advertising teams, but I'll talk to you later in the week. Smile at Winchester when you see him for me, will you?" He laughed as he ended the video call.

As Donald Alexander's video screen went black, he smiled in recognition of the fun Gill Harris was having.

"What a happy guy," he said out loud.

By Tuesday, Wanda Howard had compiled an impressive list of ethnic advertising sales leaders for Donald Alexander.

"This is a great list that I'm excited to share with you, Donald. Included are fifteen people at the category manager level and only three more senior at the office manager level. You know some of the names on the list."

She was right. Donald already knew some of the names at the category manager level, including Steve Ryan at Athlete's Week. Ryan had been one of his star performers.

"I like Steve Ryan a lot and have plans for him, but for this project, I want to bring in an outsider. I need to expand our talent and bring in fresh blood."

"I agree that makes sense."

After further studying the list, Donald turned to Wanda, "Let's start with the more senior office managers first. Who is Luisa Mendoza at Verve?"

"She's been at Verve for six years and has been the New York manager for just six months. She's smart, well respected by advertising agencies and clients. She's a real workhorse."

"Okay, who is Hermann Fairborn?"

"Hermann has been at Sultry Press for seven years."

"What's Sultry Press?" Donald asks and quickly corrected himself. "Not the porno-skin media property?"

THE PUBLISHER'S DILEMMA

"Yes," Wanda nodded, and as Alexander sighed, she continued. "Wait now. This guy has turned around their lead property, Sultry Star. They have good numbers for liquor, packaged goods, and auto advertising."

"Last? He may be good, but I need someone that everyone around here will see as a peer. Coming from a skin magazine would put a lot of bullseyes on him as too many folks see these properties as second-rate."

"Okay, I hear you. The last guy is Kwame Mills. He's the real deal. He's been the Chicago office manager at NewsInc. the last four years, and he's got business flying in the door there."

"Tell me more?"

Wanda referred to her notes. "Let's see. He helped start NewsInc here in New York and got the Chicago office manager's job as a reward, his clients love him, he graduated from Blakeney Business School, and he's, um, single and handsome." She chuckles, Wanda just re-entered the dating world after recently breaking off a five-year relationship.

"I like what I hear. Except for that single stuff."

He knew that Wanda was being mischievous, and he played along, "Who cares that he's single and um, handsome? Do you?"

"I do, why shouldn't I? Oh, I forgot I'm talking to one of the ten most desirable men in New York. I forgot my manners."

Donald rolled his eyes, and Wanda giggled. He often was named to one of the most eligible or most desirable bachelor lists. Wanda got a bigger kick out of it than he did. It gave her a chance to look at a list of good looking guys and tease her boss about being objectified. Wanda was hardworking, but she also knew how to have fun, and she didn't have any hesitation about giving Donald a hard time.

"Now, for the second half of your assignment. Do we have any

DARIUS MYERS

openings?"

Wanda again looked to the sheet briefly and put it down, "Yes, we do. And this one is not a surprise. The Head of Sales job at World Media is still open."

Donald leaned back in his chair and looked at the ceiling before muttering, " World Media. That's right? I forgot, that Wynne Shields's property. He's a real nut job, though. How long has it been open again?"

"Six months, and God bless whoever takes that job."

Donald scratched his head. He knows that Wanda is right. He turned to her and asked rhetorically, even though he already knew the answer, "What's taking Wynne so long to fill the job?"

"Come on Don. You know the deal, Wynne's a maniac. That guy is trouble. He keeps telling H.R. that it's their fault, that they are bringing him the wrong candidates. And you know you're going to have to give someone hazard pay to work for him because the Val Tolliver story ain't exactly a secret."

Wanda then reminded Donald of the cruelty and the costly firing that took place while Donald and Gill were in Germany.

"Have you forgotten that Wynne Shields had Val Tolliver escorted from the building by security?"

"No, how could I?"

"Donald that was not only embarrassing to a rock star executive but it was also a costly perp walk. I don't know anyone who would want to subject themselves to that kind of ridicule."

Alexander closed his eyes and rubbed his temples as he thought for a second. "You're right, Wynne Shields is a maniac, reckless and heartless."

He always wondered what kind of blackmail Wynne had on the Harris

THE PUBLISHER'S DILEMMA

family. It had to be juicy because, in a fair world, he's fired and in a much more shameful way than Val Tolliver.

As he thought about Wynne's crap over the few years, Donald got agitated and right then decided to take him on.

"Well, I think you may have found the right candidate for Wynne Shields' opening. I'm not going to mess around with this. If Kwame Mills is our guy, let's find out. Let's get him in here next Thursday. I'm going to talk to Gill tomorrow and get his okay to fill this job at World. If this guy is as sharp as you say, he's got the job."

Donald raised his right hand to Wanda and gave her a thumb up. "This is great work Wanda, exactly what we need."

"Thanks boss," Wanda said as she put together her files in a pile. She rose from her seat and said, "For the record, I want you to know that this is a good thing that you're doing. I'm proud of you."

"Thanks Wanda. I feel like it's a good thing. I don't know if it's a smart thing. We both might be looking for jobs if this doesn't work out."

"No, we won't. You are too important here, and this is the right way to use your power."

"I appreciate you saying that, Wanda."

Her words gave him confidence, especially as they mirrored Ron Cherry's. Donald knew they were both right. Now it was time for him to use his power.

Alexander knew that Wynne Shields would not take well to him, making the call on this slot. Wynne was an obstinate and dogmatic leader, a style that left him with few allies at Harris Simmons. He ran World as if it was his empire, as an entity that existed outside of Harris Simmons, and for that reason, Donald knew that he would not be pleased with someone else naming a senior executive to his team. There would be resistance to get Kwame Mills onto Wynne's staff. He had to get Gill Harris's support. Suddenly, their meeting tomorrow took on even more significance.

On Wednesday, Donald got to the office a half-hour early. He was in by 7:00 am and used that extra time to take care of some paperwork and to prepare his strategy for his 11:00 meeting with Gill. At 10:55, he looked at his watch and decided to pray.

"God, I ask that you order my voice and my thoughts this morning. I need you to be in charge. I need your favor. In your name, I pray. Amen."

He then walked down the hallway to Gill's office. When he arrived, Theresa Harkin waved him in.

"Good morning Donald. He's expecting you. Go right on in."

Gill's office was the typical large office of a big-time CEO. The executive floor on the 39th floor of the Harris Simmons building faced the north side of Manhattan and afforded Gill and Donald breathtaking views of Central Park. The office was museum-like, filled with souvenirs of his life's work and his family members before him.

Hanging throughout the room were also original oil paintings of all the Harris leaders of the firm, Oliver, Sr. & Jr., Cornwall and Horace Simmons, the long-departed co-founder of the company.

Oliver Harris Sr., his Harlowe University classmate and best friend Horace Simmons started the company 75 years ago. They worked together as partners for 40 years until Simmons, under doctor's orders, was forced to retire due to a rare heart condition. Horace Simmons sold his share of the company to Oliver Harris Sr., $50 million, moved to the Florida Keys, and died five years ago at age 92.

Since the departure of Horace Simmons, the company leaders have only been direct descendants of Oliver Harris, Sr. Alexander was the first non-family member to hold a President's role and the odds-on favorite to succeed Gill.

"Good morning Donald," a cheerful as ever Gill said to Alexander.

"Good morning, Gill," Donald said as he sat down on one of the large oversized chairs opposite Gill's desk.

As usual, Gill was fawning over one of the novelties of his existence.

"Donald, I just got in this blend of coffee from Chile, it's a special dark roast blend called Kohoron. Can I offer you a cup?"

Gill had just taken a sip and appeared to be pleased. "Sure, I'll have a cup."

He pulled out another cup and began to pour Donald a coffee. Alexander got up and walked over to the wet bar.

"Milk and sugar?"

"Just milk Gill, thanks."

After Gill finished topping Donald's cup of coffee, he handed it to him and walked to the large floor to ceiling window overlooking Central Park. He looked outside, took in the view, and gasped as if he had never seen it before.

"What a view. You know this is one of the best benefits of this job. To see this daily is something I don't take for granted. How do you like this coffee?"

Donald, took a couple of seconds to assess its flavor and was pleased with the taste, he answered, "Its good stuff. I like it a lot."

"Great. I'll have some sent to your office. It'll be my treat. Now, what's up?"

Donald knew that he was on Gill's A team. They liked each other, but he wasn't 100% sure if Gill would take kindly to the request he was about to make. Was his gut instinct about Gill all wrong? If so, he would be putting his career on the line.

He could easily give Gill a revenue report on the two start-up properties that were recently green-lit or make some suggestions on some acquisitions they had been considering. But he stiffened in his resolve and put the power he thought he had on the line.

"Gill, I need your support."

"Of course, what do you need Donald?"

"Let me give it to you straight. I've taken a look at our staff numbers at the senior levels for African-Americans, Latinos, and Asians. And these numbers are reprehensible. I mean embarrassing, and just so you know, it's not just us, the rest of the industry sucks too. This inequity is beyond terrible. I want to change this disparity."

Gill looked down into his cup of coffee. He appeared to be thinking as Donald continued to talk.

"What I'm referring to specifically are our employment numbers on the sales side, the business people who are the face of our business. We operate 15 world-class properties here, Gill. We have a small number of category managers that are African-American, Latino, and Asian. Beyond that, we have not one, and by that, I mean zero, people at the director level. As I'm sure you know, the same thing goes for Publisher level."

Gill said nothing. Donald was in deep now, so he continued.

"Gill, I'm President of this company, and as such, I've got to be responsible for our long-term strategic direction. With that, I've noticed that our client base has changed. No longer is it limited to white male decision-makers. We now have decision-makers from all different ethnic backgrounds."

THE PUBLISHER'S DILEMMA

Gill shook his head up and down and said, "You're right."

This comment empowered Donald, "Thank you. Therefore, I've decided that we should expend some energy on getting ready for this changing marketplace."

"What do you have in mind?" Gill asked. He was still very stoic.

"This is my plan. I've compiled a list of the top ethnic advertising sales directors, office managers, and category managers across the country. When opportunities arise in this company, I want these people to have every opportunity to interview for them."

Gill looked down into his cup of coffee and began to comment, "Well, Donald let me say."

"Pardon me Gill," Donald interrupted. "Before you comment, let me conclude and say that I want to start this process now. We've got a major position open at World Media. Wynne Shields has had this job open for six months. I think I've got the right guy, and if so, I want to place him, and I don't want Wynne trying to block this or make it impossible for this guy to succeed."

Finished, Donald walked from the wet bar to the chair and sat down. He let out an anxious and silent sigh.

Gill, realizing that Donald had finished, turned back again to face the window. He looked out at the view once again and downed the remainder of his coffee.

Without saying a word, he walked to the front of his desk, leaving him a short distance from Donald. He sat on the front of the desk and rubbed his chin. Donald knew he was thinking, but the suspense of his silence was nerve-racking. Finally, he spoke.

"Donald. Once again, you've made me proud. You've just displayed the kind of leadership I'm looking for."

Donald breathed a massive sigh of relief. "It's true, our record for senior-level executives with ethnic minorities as you said, has been deplorable. Quite frankly, in the past, the old men, I mean the guys in the oil paintings you see here, didn't think about African-Americans, Asians, Latinos, or women as senior leaders in this company." He said as he turned around and pointed to the photos of his Uncle, Father, and Grandfather hanging on the wall in his office.

"That doesn't mean they were bad people. They were just more representative of their times, I guess. And they certainly didn't have a force like you in their face pushing for change. For the record, I always hated the fact that all the property heads looked alike around here if you know what I mean."

Gill looked at Donald and shrugged his shoulders with a shameful look, as if to suggest it's not my fault. Donald smiled back to reassure Gill that he understood.

"This has always troubled me. Donald, besides you being a great talent, that's one of the reasons why you're in this position now."

He continued, "When Spring tried to steal you a few years back, you may have forced my hand a bit. I thought you might have been a little young for the position, but because I had been watching you for a while, I knew you were bright and talented. And you know what, you've done far better than I ever imagined. Never have I regretted my decision. For the record, I want you to run this company one day. If we keep things going, you will be my successor, and this is the kind of leadership we must have to keep this company progressive and world-class."

"Thank you Gill. I appreciate you saying that and your support."

"No, thank you Donald. You are a star and the best thing we have going here. I am behind you 100%. You let me handle Wynne. I still owe him an ass-kicking for that Val Tolliver incident. You proceed on the search, and you won't get any trouble from Wynne. Otherwise, you'll be hiring his replacement, as well. I'll make sure he understands."

Chapter Five

"Daddy, what were you thinking?" The black woman was anxious to find out why her father just went on a shooting rampage.

They were now two blocks away from Harris Simmons's headquarters and passing a small building. She looked in and saw that the lobby was empty.

"Let's go in here and keep your head down in case there are video cameras. We can't take a chance on being seen. I need you to explain this to me and to try and make sense of what just happened."

The man looked her in the eyes. Although he was quite old and his posture stooped over by age, they seemed now to be the same height. They were both close to six feet tall. As she looked back at him, she could see he still looked angry, with a scowl and without fear for what just happened.

"Sammy, I warned him to stop treating me that way. Gill has never respected me. He's always been chomping at my heels, with that stupid ass smile."

"What do you mean? He was so kind to you and me," she said.

"You just don't understand Sammy."

She shook her head and said, "I guess you're right. I don't understand this at all. Shooting people, I don't. Not one bit."

She then patted his jacket pocket, "Daddy, where is it?"

"Where is what?"

"Give me the gun, please?"

He slowly began to reach into his pocket, and as he started to pull the gun out, she looked up to see if there were any cameras.

"Stop, wait. There is a camera here. Let's just go to the subway that's two blocks from here. We can't take a taxi or call a car. And we can't be spotted. Don't speak to anyone, do you understand?"

"Yes, Sammy, I do."

"Okay, when we get outside, I am going to reach into your jacket and get the gun and put it into my jacket pocket. Does it belong to you?"

"No, uh, yes. I can't remember," the old man stuttered as he strained to remember. "I have a gun collection, but I got this one from a guy I know."

"A guy you know? Do you mean illegally? Jesus, Dad, what is wrong with you?"

"Are you mad at me? I was protecting you." The old man said as his face turned to a sad and confused look.

"Protecting me, from what? You just shot two people with a gun that might be illegal. Two powerful people and one was a member of your own family. Let's get to the subway and hope we don't get noticed."

THE PUBLISHER'S DILEMMA

The woman named Sammy then ushers the old man out of the empty lobby with the same caution she used to get him out of the Harris Simmons headquarters.

"Okay now, I am going to take the gun." She said as she hugged him and pulled the gun from his jacket and calmly slipped it into her pocket.

He then said, "I'm sorry. I shouldn't have done this to you Sammy. I've dragged you into my drama."

"We're family Dad, and so is Gill. Let's get you home and hope and pray for the best."

Sammy then led him quickly to the subway. They made it to the platform without being seen. As they stood waiting, she said, "Let's hope we don't see anyone we know."

As she looked around nervously, her father began talking and pleading to God, "Jesus help Sammy and me, I'm so confused, and I need you. Help Gill and Donald. Please, God, please God."

Suddenly they could hear the screeching brakes of an incoming train. Sammy reminded him again, "Remember, be careful now, speak to no one on this train."

They were able to board the train without a sighting of any friend or associate. Once aboard, they rode the train silently.

Sammy spoke as they approached their subway stop, "Okay, Dad, we've been lucky so far. Now when we get off on our stop, you will have to enter your apartment building by yourself. I need you to pull yourself together, so the doorman will not suspect anything."

The old man finally seemed to be getting his wits about him and acknowledged this request by his daughter.

"I can do that Sammy. I'm good."

"Great Dad, just stay cool."

Sammy still looked cool on the outside, but her nerves were a wreck.

She muttered to herself, low so that her Dad couldn't hear. "What in the hell have I gotten myself into? and why would my rich estranged Father, Cornwall Harris, who I have just reconciled with shoot his nephew and another man?"

Chapter Six

Kwame Mills arrived for his interview at Harris Simmons twenty minutes early. He noticed a shoeshine stand in the lobby of the Harris Simmons building with an empty chair. He decided to kill a few minutes and get a shoeshine.

The attendant was a short, older silver-haired black man with a nametag that read Abe. Kwame sat in his booth, and as Abe began to work on his shoes, he engaged Kwame in conversation.

"How are you this morning, young man?"

"I'm great. How about you, Sir?"

"Man, I couldn't be better. Life is good, living a dream. Wife's happy too, got my bills paid. God is good young Man. Lots to be happy about."

"I hear you Sir, good for you. I'm happy to hear that all is well for you."

THE PUBLISHER'S DILEMMA

Old Abe's optimism made Kwame smile. It also made him think about how happy he was to see his good buddy, Tom, his new lady Danielle, as well as the excellent conversation he had with Juan, and, Juan's final comments about his ex-wife.

As Kwame smiled, old Abe curiously asked, "You've got some reasons to smile too young Man?"

"You know, I do, life is good. It's been a pretty good morning so far. I just caught up with a couple of old friends, and I'm here for a big job interview."

"Well, all right then. Congratulations on the good start to your day. And you know you've come to the right place right before your big interview." Old Abe then took a step back and took a hard second look at Kwame.

"Young Brother, what's your name?"

"Kwame Mills, sir."

"Nice to meet you, Kwame Mills. My name is Abe. Now I just gave you the once over, and you're looking ready. Hair is appropriate, right suit, shirt, tie, and you did right by coming in here to see Old Abe and get your shoes tight before you head upstairs."

Then Abe says, "Pardon me, I don't want to be too familiar, can I ask you a question, make a statement?"

Kwame could tell Old Abe was also an old soul, and he was eager to hear his question and statement. "Sure, you can. I can always use some good advice and guidance."

"My Man," Old Abe said and smiled. "All right then, you look good on the outside. Ready as far as the eye can see, but are you ready on the inside?"

DARIUS MYERS

"I think so, Mr. Abe. But I am always open to take advice from an elder."

"Excellent Kwame. You're right, I am your elder, and now it's clear from that answer alone that you've been raised right."

"Thank you, Sir."

"You're welcome, Kwame. Now, do you believe in a higher power? I prefer Jesus, but do you have a higher power that in a time of need you call on?"

"I believe in Jesus too, Mr. Abe."

"You call on him for guidance and ask him to order your steps today?"

As Kwame tried to gather his thoughts, Old Abe beat him to the punch. "Don't worry, God ain't mad at you. He can only help you if you ask him. Give him a quick shout-out while I'm doing my thing."

Kwame smiled, Old Abe didn't give him a chance to say that he had prayed this morning. Kwame believed that there is no such thing as too much prayer, and so he did as Abe asked.

"Lord Jesus, I'm walking into here today, and I need you to be with me. I ask that you order my steps. Give me the confidence, grace, and humility to represent you and do my best today. Bless me in my meeting with Donald Alexander, and thank you for the blessing of meeting my new friend Mr. Abe here today. I ask you all these blessings in your name, Amen."

"Amen," Abe said. "You did great Kwame. I know God heard you, and I'll keep you in prayer as well."

Abe continued, "I love me some Donald Alexander, he's a Man of God too in case you didn't know. Great sense of humor also. You remind me of him, just a younger version."

THE PUBLISHER'S DILEMMA

"Well, that's a high compliment, Mr. Abe. Thank you."

"You're welcome Kwame. What else can I help you with today? You married, got a good woman in your life?"

The directness of the question startled Kwame, and he began to struggle again for the right words. Old Abe jokingly interrupted before he could answer. "Oh Boy, that sounds like another prayer request. Is it because you have too many to choose from, or is it the one that got away?"

"Well, uh, Mr. Abe," Kwame started laughing as he watched Old Abe snicker in amusement of his discomfort.

"Hey young man, you don't have to answer that one now. I'm praying that you'll get this job and we'll see each other a lot and talk about it another time. How's that?"

"I don't mind answering. For the record, its not about a flock, but if I get this job, I'll have to move back from Chicago, and I'll have to deal at some point with the one that got away."

"Are you with someone now in Chicago? And if so, is she a keeper?"

"Yes, and Yes. Mr. Abe"

"Then it's all good Kwame." Abe then patted his shoes lightly to let him know that he had completed the shine. "Like these shoes, you are good to go. Don't look back, look forward."

"Thank you, Mr. Abe, I appreciate your kind words and thoughtfulness this morning. You are a real blessing to me." Kwame gave him a five-dollar tip.

"Well, thank you Kwame, and I also appreciate this big tip. You're going to do great this morning. I know you will."

As Kwame walked away from his excellent shoeshine conversation, he thought about his love life and how sordid it had been over the last several years. It made him realize that getting this job was not his only major worry. He began to think that if he did leave Chicago, he would have to confront his love problems. Kwame still had issues with his ex-wife, Carrie Sinclair. If he was to move back to New York, he didn't know how he would handle his first encounter with the tall, dark, modelesque, freelance photographer and writer.

Carrie Sinclair was educated at the elite Hinton College and independently wealthy from her first and short career as an investment banker at The Minnion Company, a powerful Wall Street bank. She had risen by the age of 28 to the position of Managing Director at Minnion, gaining worldwide notoriety as the youngest person to reach that position in the firm's 175-year history. By the age of 33, with an eight-figure net worth, she had enough of the investment bank business and quit to become a graduate student at Harlowe University's world-acclaimed School of Journalism. Always a high achiever, Carrie graduated from the Harlowe J-School program with top honors and for the last four years, had been traveling the world developing a reputation as a top-rated photographic journalist. Her reputation had risen so fast that she had become a top stringer for several major news bureaus, including the Tinkerton Press, Monster Bivens News Service, and Harris Simmons News Service.

Carrie's success as an international photojournalist was assisted tremendously by her dynamic personality, smarts, and stunning looks. Carrie could walk into a room, turn the heads of men, married and single, and gain the admiration of women, young and old, plain and beautiful. People would flock to her; their gaze locked on her every word and movement. Besides being rich, famous, intelligent, charming, and beautiful, she spoke five languages, was a gourmet cook, and played golf to a two handicap. When playing with guys, she played to a six, from the men's tees.

Kwame cared tremendously about his ex-wife, but he had fallen in love with Michelle Nubani, and he was anxious about their future. Michelle Nubani taught economics at Sheraton University.

He met Michelle Nubani at a cocktail party at the home of Brian King, a Chicago venture capitalist. Michelle, the daughter of the world-renowned soccer player Will Nubani, was never a serious competitive athlete, but thanks to a generous gene pool, possessed the graceful, athletic frame and gait of one. Besides some competitive tennis as a teenager, she had no interest in sports.

Michelle stood at 5 feet 7 inches tall with a light brown skin tone, a hybrid mixture coming from the deep dark brown complexion of her father and ivory white hue of her mother. Also inherited were the large brown eyes of her father and the high cheekbones and radiant smile of her mother. Michelle Nubani grew up to no one's surprise, and everyone's expectation to be a stunning beauty with brains.

When Kwame Mills first saw her, he was drinking a vodka gimlet. Her looks stunned him so much that he swallowed a bit too fast and began to choke.

Brian noticed his friend's choking episode following his first sighting of Michelle Nubani. He walked over to Kwame to heckle him.

"What's the matter, my man? Something, uh, I mean, is someone bothering you?" He asked with a teenager's mischievousness.

Brian was a busybody, and now that he noticed Kwame's reaction to Michelle Nubani, he set his sights on playing matchmaker.

"Nope, I mean no," Kwame said and turned to face the wall as he continued to dab the cocktail stain off his jacket and shirt.

"Well then, brother, is it normal to involuntarily choke like you've got a piece of ham stuck in your throat?"

DARIUS MYERS

Kwame said nothing. He just smiled and continued to focus on the wet spots on his clothes.

Brian wouldn't let the moment pass, "Look, Kwame, look Man, she's beautiful." He pulled Kwame from facing the wall so that he could see Michelle as he continued his matchmaking pitch.

"Check her out Kwame, she's so beautiful man."

Kwame looked at her. It was clear to him that she was beautiful. Brian meanwhile continued with the matchmaking.

"Oh Man, you have to rescue her. She's now stuck in one of those crazy boring cocktail party conversations. They all are over there yapping and name-dropping about famous people they know. She's over there and probably won't leave because it's rude. Come on Dude, step up free her from the madness."

Kwame looked at her again, and Brian King continued to egg him on.

"Look at her Man. She is standing there, beautiful, pleasant, smiling, taking in all of the obnoxious chatter, laughing lightly on cue, but obviously, she is above it all. I bet you she is bored as hell."

Across the room, Simone, Brian's wife, and the leader in the group of name-droppers turned to her and asked, "Michelle, you've lived in Paris and New York. And your father is an international soccer icon. I know you must have hung out with some cool international jet-setters?"

"Oh no Simone, not me, I don't have any stories unless you count Academics. There is this Nobel prize-winning economist at The University of Connelly, Kaiser Rulebread, you would only be impressed if you like my work in economics."

Simone considered this Nobel prize stuff boring and quickly changed the subject. "Did you see the concert last night on cable with the Soul

THE PUBLISHER'S DILEMMA

Superstars? Brian and I had dinner with them after they played here in Chicago."

While Simone's namedropping story earned her a chorus of oohs and aahs, Michelle looked across the room. She saw Brian and Kwame, smiled, and winked deceitfully. She had intentionally come up with a boring namedrop as she was not interested in that conversation.

Brian saw this and waved to Michelle, it was the moment he needed. He said loud enough to interrupt Simone who was busy talking about the concert, "Simone, excuse me honey, we need to steal Michelle for a second."

Michelle jumped at the chance to get away, "Excuse me folks, the man of this house, our host for this evening, beckons. I must go."

Now with Michelle walking across the room and towards them, Brian warned Kwame, "I will embarrass you if you don't say anything. Look man, this woman is beautiful. You are single, successful, and divorced from Carrie for more than two years. You better not choke up."

Brian was right. He had not been involved with anyone since his breakup with Carrie Sinclair. Brian King continued, "I'm only doing this because I know you have avoided woman altogether for so long that you probably can't remember when you last have been with one."

When Kwame first broke up with Carrie, he had a couple of dates, but no girlfriends or relationships that he would consider substantial. Occasionally, he found himself at a cocktail party with a friend like Brian. These were the situations in which he felt most comfortable. Now was one of those times. But he wasn't, and with Michelle Nubani walking towards them, he found himself more nervous than he should. Adding to his pressure was Brian standing at his shoulder, prodding him to talk. As she neared, Kwame loosened his collar, took a deep breath, and hoped he wouldn't make a fool of himself.

DARIUS MYERS

When she arrived, Brian broke the ice, "Michelle, what kind of nonsense is Simone talking about over there?"

"That's not a nice way to talk about your wife," Michelle answered in an attempt to defend Simone. "She's just trying to make conversation."

Kwame was immediately awed by Michelle's beauty. Brian King, on the other hand, was having a ball taking shots at his wife.

"Yeah, but I'll bet you it's some boring, ostentatious crap."

"Brian, stop. That's not right." She then playfully elbowed him.

"Hey, you know we can send you back over there if you like. I thought I was saving you."

"No, thank you, I'll stay over here. Thanks for saving me. I was dying over there."

"Good. I thought you'd see it my way."

"Now meet my friend, Kwame Mills. He's originally from New York, the poor soul. He lives in Chicago now and sells advertising for that rag media property, NewsInc."

Kwame turned to Brian with a bit of a baffled, embarrassed look, and said, "Thanks for that great introduction, Brian."

He then looked at Michelle and smiled while Brian continued the introduction. Michelle looked at Kwame, returned the smile, and then turned to Brian because she didn't know what he was capable of saying. He had her unnerved too.

"Now Kwame meet Dr. Michelle Nubani, professor of economics at Sheraton University. Michelle is a citizen of the world. She grew up in France and New York. Her Dad is from Ghana, and her mom is from New York. That makes her a true African-American." He laughed at his attempt at a joke.

Kwame and Michelle also both laughed, but sarcastically. They also were relieved by Brian's introduction and jokes as they knew it could be worse. Seizing an opening, Kwame turned to Michelle and stuck out his hand, "Hi Michelle. It's a pleasure to meet you."

She returned his smile and while shaking his hand said, "It's a pleasure to meet you too."

Michelle then asked, "Now, why were you standing over here by yourself?"

She wanted to get into a conversation before Brian started up again. Michelle knew that he was highly combustible, and at any moment, could start up again with trash talking.

"I don't know any famous people." He was pleased that she noticed him standing alone.

"Come on brother, don't be so low-key."

Brian turned to Michelle and said, "Don't let this brother play the low-key game. What about Phaethon Malone and Rote Tunz?"

"I don't know if you know pro basketball, but Phaethon Malone is the star forward for the New York Kings, and he is a childhood friend of Kwame's from Long Island. Rote Tunz is the Front Man in the Beat Boys, the top hip-hop group. Rote is Kwame's college roommate at Grande Point College."

Michelle's face lit up, "You know Rote Tunz? I love his music. How do you know him?"

"I'm his producer," Kwame lied, he was beginning to feel a bit more relaxed.

"Really?" Michelle said excitedly, before catching on to Kwame's fib. "Wait, I thought you were in the Media business? What are you trying to pull here?"

Kwame laughed, "Very good. I'm glad you're paying attention. The truth is Rote, and I were roommates in college. I was a history major, and he majored in marketing. I knew him before he even thought about hip-hop when soccer was his passion. He fell into hip-hop, he won a poetry jam in college on a lark and then he won a national hip-hop rap off and has been all hip-hop since."

"Is that so? He sounds like a talented guy."

Brian, sensing that Kwame didn't need him anymore, chose to exit gracefully and let them talk alone.

"Look. Simone is still over there, and she's in rapid-fire bragging mode. I've got to save those poor souls. You guys behave over here."

"Good luck Brian," Kwame said.

"Kwame," Michelle exclaimed, "Don't encourage him; he's bad enough."

Brian King then walked away, smiling and feeling satisfied in his role as cupid.

Kwame wasn't bothered at all with Brian's departure. After they said goodbye to Brian, Kwame turned to Michelle and noticing that she had finished her drink and that he needed another one himself, offered to get her a refill.

"I'm on empty. Can I get you another cocktail?"

Michelle looked at her glass and recognized its empty contents, "Sure, I'll have tonic water."

"Are you driving?"

"Yes, I am. I also don't like to get drunk, and besides, I'm enjoying our conversation."

"Well, thank you Michelle, I'm enjoying our conversation too. I'll be right back."

THE PUBLISHER'S DILEMMA

After he arrived at the bar, he turned around and saw Michelle looking in a mirror near where they were standing. She checked her hair and then reached in her purse, pulled out a tube of lipstick, and began to put it on. She had just finished applying her lipstick when Kwame returned with the drinks.

"You look great," Kwame said. He didn't feel the least bit uncomfortable anymore. Michelle blushed again.

"Thank you, Kwame."

He handed Michelle her drink and with his newfound confidence, proposed a toast. "To you, Ms. Michelle Nubani here's to getting to know you."

As they clicked their glasses, she said, "Here's to getting to know you too."

Kwame and Michelle talked all night. They spoke more about Rote Tunz. "I edited his English papers while at Grande Point, and later before he had an agent, I helped to negotiate his first record deal. We'll get tickets the next time they're in Chicago."

"I'm going to hold you to that Kwame."

"No problem at all."

They also talked about Phaethon Malone, the best-paid player and most high-profile player in New York King's history.

"Phaethon is a good dude. Probably a first ballot hall of fame basketball player, but a better guy off the court. He is a very civic-minded athlete, donating much of his free time and lots of money to charities. He completed his undergraduate degree at State University and has been taking law school classes at Harlowe University during the off-season for the last five years. He is soon to graduate. He hopes to pursue a career in politics once his playing days are over."

"Wow, he sounds like a great guy Kwame."

"He is Michelle. I'll get tickets when they come in to play the Barons. I'll set it up for us to have dinner with him when they come to town."

"Hey now, that's two sets of tickets you've promised. Don't go overextending yourself."

"I don't see it that way. I see it as two more ways to be guaranteed to see you again."

Michelle blushed, grabbed Kwame's hand, and said, "That's sweet." They also talked about Michelle's upbringing, growing up in Paris and New York.

"My family has quite a complicated history, with my Father being so famous, but he's a great guy, and he and my mom are deeply in love and committed to each other."

Kwame talked about his family, his respect for his parents, and his wishes to someday become successful enough to get his father to retire.

"My Dad is one of the most tireless, relentless guys, I know. I hope to one day make enough money to be able to buy out his business, so he can relax and enjoy the things that he likes to do."

"Like what?" asked Michelle.

"He likes to golf and fish. He's 70 years old now, and he's never had a vacation longer than a week. Never traveled abroad for a vacation, there's so much he hasn't done."

"That's admirable that you would like to do so much for your Dad."

Michelle and Kwame hit it off. Here they were, the first time they met, sharing meaningful family stories and dreams. They talked all evening. Before they knew, it was 1:00 am, and everyone had left the party except

THE PUBLISHER'S DILEMMA

for them. Brian, Simone, and the caterers were cleaning up.

Brian approached them, "You guys come up for air?"

"We're just getting to know each other," Kwame said.

"Well, good. All I want is a finder's fee. Remember who hooked you guys up. My standard rate is ten percent of your annual salary, and that'll be coming from you Kwame, Mr. Big Money ad sales guy."

Kwame rolled his eyes, "Here we go again."

Brian then continued, he was as big a personality as his wife, Simone. He couldn't help himself. "Okay, all right. You want a discount. Look how about this? Because I know and like you both and Kwame, given that you're such a special case, I'll take only five."

Kwame and Michelle, both a little embarrassed by Brian's comments, just blushed.

"Now, if you want to work off a little of your debt, you can pick up some of these glasses."

Kwame and Michelle then helped Simone, Brian, and the caterers tidy up the house. At one-thirty, they prepared to leave.

As Brian walked them to the door, he said, "Thank you both for coming, and don't forget my finder's fee."

"Bye Brian, good night Simone," Kwame said.

"Goodnight Brian and Simone, I had a great time," Michelle said. Neither of them acknowledged Brian's talk of a finder's fee.

"I'm serious," he yelled as they walked down the front walk and closed the door, leaving them outside and alone for the first time.

"Five percent!" he yelled one last time and shut the door.

Kwame was thankful for Brian King. The truth was that his antics were a terrific icebreaker, and it helped him gain confidence and have a great conversation with Michelle Nubani. Now that they were out of the house, he wanted to make sure he was going to see her again.

"Can I walk you to your car?"

"Thank you, I'm right over there," Michelle pointed to a black sedan parked directly across the street from Brian King's house.

Kwame walked her across the street. She drove a fancy black late-model convertible, which she started remotely.

After she started the car she said, "I like this feature, especially because it lets my car warm up, it beats sitting in the cold and freezing."

"That's a nice car, Michelle, and good idea, let me start up my car, too." Kwame remotely started his car, which was about 20 yards behind hers.

"Thank you. But I think it might be a little pretentious for a college professor. I may trade down for an SUV."

It took them only seconds to reach Michelle's car, and when they arrived, Michelle opened the door. She then turned around to face him, "It was nice meeting you, Mr. Kwame Mills, you made my evening really special."

"Thank you for making my evening a pleasure too, Michelle." He wasn't nervous anymore, to his surprise, he was very confident. "Can I see you again next weekend?"

"Yes, I'd like that very much." She blushed again. She reached in her purse for a pen, pulled out a business card, and wrote her number on the back. She gave the card to Kwame, moved close to him, kissed him on the cheek and gave him a warm hug. Kwame was taken aback by how nice she smelled. It increased his desire to see her again.

THE PUBLISHER'S DILEMMA

Michelle then slowly and a bit seductively slunk into the driver's seat of her car and said, "I'll be waiting for your call."

She closed the door and with a glowing smile, waved to Kwame, put her seatbelt on, shifted the car into gear, and drove off.

He felt the pitter-patter of his heart as he walked to his car. "Wow. She's special, and she smelled so terrific."

Kwame's relationship with Carrie Sinclair ended poorly. He met her in New York during his third year at NewsInc. She was a friend of Kurtis Van Weston, a golf buddy of Kwame's and a business school buddy. Carrie and Kurtis worked together at the Minnion Bank.

"I think you and Carrie will get along well, why don't we have you over to dinner at my apartment. She's just graduating from Hinton Business School and is new to town. I think you'll like her."

Kurtis Van Weston continued, "you both like skiing, hoops, jazz, and cooking. You both have promising and challenging careers, and besides, she's beautiful. Trust me Man, once you meet her, you'll be smitten."

He was right. When Kwame met Carrie, they began dating immediately, and six months later, they decided to move in with each other. After another six months, Kwame called Kurtis Van Weston and said, "Man, I proposed to Carrie."

A year later, they were married.

"We may have moved too fast," Kwame told Kurtis Van Weston after they broke up. "I don't think we gave our marriage a chance to blossom."

"I think you may have been right," Kurtis said. "It didn't help that Carrie was a star and was moving fast through the ranks at Minnion." She was only an associate at Minnion for two years, and shortly after they were married, promoted to Vice President.

DARIUS MYERS

"You are right Kurtis" Kwame said. "She was a rocket. At just age 27, she was named a principal, and the next year at 28, she became the firm's youngest Managing Director ever. That never happens, especially to black people. I had to let her do her thing."

"I know it had to be hard, but what else could you do Kwame? She was your wife, and you loved her, you couldn't hold her back."

"Yes, having a career was important to Carrie. I guess I know now how tough it is for both partners to have very demanding and challenging jobs."

"But it didn't help that you were on your grind as well," Van Weston said.

"That is true. I was working on the startup of NewsInc., I found myself traveling to see clients all over the U.S., and she was also working long hours and traveling for work. All of a sudden, we were spending long periods apart, and only after a year of marriage. Do you know we once looked back over one six-month period and counted only four weekends we had spent together? If she wasn't traveling, I was. If I was in town, she was out of town or in the office working day and night on a deal."

"That's not a marriage, that's having a roommate," Van Weston said.

"I know, I woke up one day and realized that I was married to a Managing Director at one of Wall Street's best firms. That was great, but then, I couldn't remember the last time we made love after a romantic dinner and evening together. The worse part of it all was when I had this revelation, I wasn't even at home. I was in Dallas and hadn't slept in my own bed in eight days."

"That had to be tough Kwame. You guys were too young and should have been making time to have fun and enjoy each other."

"You are so right Kurtis. When I returned home, I told Carrie about my revelation in Dallas. She admitted that she too was troubled about our relationship and marriage. As a Managing Director, she had a better paying job and enjoyed her work. I couldn't ask her to quit, that would have been selfish of me, but I couldn't quit my job either. We were just too young and hard-charging."

"I had worked long and hard at NewsInc. The property was now getting close to profitability, and I knew if I could hang in there until NewsInc made it, I would get a payoff in the form of a better paying job with less travel. We agreed to try to make more time for each other, but it didn't work. We were both a little too selfish and still made our hard-charging careers the priority."

"So, neither of you were ready to sacrifice for the other. That's a tough place for a young marriage," Van Weston said.

"Exactly Kurtis, we were at an impasse, Carrie was 28 and a superstar. I was 32 and a rising star. We planned to have kids eventually and move out of the city, which meant that I couldn't walk away from my career. And although Carrie was a managing director, she was a brand-new managing director. She still didn't have a major payday and couldn't afford to walk away until she did. And who could blame her? And it was going to take several of those paydays before I would give up my career to become Mr. Mom."

"Finally, we woke up one day and realized that we did not know each other very well anymore. We had been so caught up in our individual lives that we didn't care about the relationship, and we weren't in love anymore, then things became very strained at home."

"Yeah, but you do realize moving in with Tom was a big mistake. She was a wreck at work because of that."

"I agree. That was pretty stupid of me. Carrie was furious about this move. She never liked Tom's womanizing style, and because our sex life had long ago ceased to a halt, she was fearful that I was out chasing women along with Tom."

"That was a bad call Bro," Van Weston said, "he's a playboy for sure and the girls just throw themselves at him. Not a guy to be hanging with if your girl has insecurities."

"You're right again. But what Carrie didn't understand is that I was lost too, I just needed a change of scenery. I didn't chase girls with Tom. Instead, I dove even more deeply into my work, but Carrie suspected otherwise. She demanded that I move out of Tom's place. She was right, living with Tom was not helping matters."

"That was smart. I thought you guys were going to make it then."

"Me too, at least I hoped once I moved back home, but the real problem to the relationship remained, our two challenging careers didn't relent. We tried relationship counseling, and it didn't help. We went to our Minister for advice, and that didn't help either."

"Wow, I didn't know. You guys were trying hard." Kurtis was surprised, Kwame rarely shared with his friends other than Tom Wilson how hard he worked to save his marriage.

"Shortly after moving back, I was offered the Chicago sales directors job at NewsInc. I couldn't afford to turn it down. If I did, I would have lost my stature in the company. As you know, I accepted the position. For a short time, we tried to manage a long-distance relationship, but the damage was done. Maybe if I met had her another time in our lives, we would have worked better together, but in my heart, I knew once I accepted the job in Chicago, it was over."

Kwame was right. Nine months after he moved to Chicago, Carrie filed for divorce.

Chapter Seven

The morning following his meeting with Donald Alexander, Gill Harris arrived at the office at 8:00 am. At 8:15, he called the office of Wynne Shields. Wynne was in the office by 7:30 and already on his second cup of coffee. He answered his phone as he could see from the internal caller ID that it was Gill.

"Wynne Shields," he answered in the curt, no-nonsense tone that he created to intimidate people.

"Wynne, this is Gill. I need to see you this morning."

Wynne didn't want to see Gill. He knew he was going to press him about business or the hiring of a Head of Sales.

He attempted to blow him off, "Gill, I'm crazy today, can we push it back until tomorrow afternoon?"

Gill was silent for a moment, then he snapped. "I want to see you in my office now."

Wynne's heart raced, he was arrogant but not stupid, and he was smart enough to know that he just pissed off the boss. He dropped what he was doing and headed for the elevator to the 39th floor. Two minutes later, Wynne walked into Gill's office. Their relationship had been strained for a while, long before Gill picked Donald Alexander to be President of Harris Simmons. Their difficulties go back more than twenty years ago when Wynne joined Harris Simmons, and Gill was the publisher of The Male Life, the firm's monthly men's property. Wynne was a protégé of Gill's uncle, Cornwall Harris. Cornwall liked him because he appreciated Wynne's regal bearings and the superior attitude and arrogance that he had coming from old school money.

The truth was that Cornwall Harris wasn't a nice guy and had the same negative personality traits of Wynne. Several years ago, the Post did a story on the Harris family empire and portrayed Cornwall as an insensitive buffoon, known in the industry for having the worst people skills of all the Harris family members.

Cornwall was good friends with, Monroe Shields, Wynne's Dad. They were both members of New York, Hampton, and Aspen, Colorado society circles. Monroe was the longtime president and CEO of the Minnion Company, the investment bank. The Minnion bank had a longtime and vigorously enforced nepotism clause for senior executives that precluded family members of middle to senior-level executives from joining the firm. The press reported that upon graduation from college, Monroe asked Cornwall as a favor to find Wynne something to do at Harris Simmons.

Cornwall not only found a job for Wynne, but he also became his caretaker. Wynne Shields joined Harris Simmons at age 24, following a two-year trek throughout Europe following graduation from Caesar College. His first job, thanks to Gill's Uncle, Cornwall, was Director of Marketing at World Media.

Wynne Shields' rise through Harris Simmons was meteoric. After two years as the marketing director at World Media, he moved to London as World's European Head of Sales. Two years later, he moved to Canada and did a one-year stint as publisher of the Canadian edition, after which he was summoned to New York and was named Worldwide Business Development Director. He held this position for three years before being promoted to publisher of World Media, a position he has held for the last ten years.

Gill and Cornwall often feuded over Wynne. Gill told Cornwall "that Wynne was a prima donna, a self-serving despot, with terrible people management skills. I don't get your rabid devotion to this nut job."

Whenever they fought about Wynne Shields, Cornwall would say, "Don't touch him, he's off-limits. I will fight you tooth and nail, leave him alone."

Gill never understood this loyalty and thought it must have been some pledge that Cornwall had with Wynne's Dad, and he would often raise it with Cornwall, "what do these people have on you?"

Cornwall would repeat his order, "Don't mess with Wynne."

Adding to Gill's disdain for Wynne was how Cornwall Harris publicly endorsed Wynne Shields to be the first non-Harris to head the company.

Shortly before his retirement and tenure as CEO Cornwall Harris said to Media Monthly, the industry trade Media, "Gill has come along well, but he still lacks the fire and intensity of his grandfather, father and me. Wynne Shields has that fire, that spirit, that presence. I would like to see a progression plan that will have Gill as Chairman and CEO and Wynne as President. After Gill's departure, Wynne Shields will likely be the first non-Harris to run this firm."

Gill was profoundly embarrassed and wounded by these comments. He told his Father, Oliver Harris, Jr., "I took that as a public flogging from Cornwall and don't understand their origins, particularly given my strong performance as the publisher of Male Life."

"Has he forgotten that I was the founding publisher of Male Life and in its first five years, guided it to profitability? Has he forgotten that by the time I replaced him as CEO that it had become the number one property in its category and the third most profitable Media property in Harris Simmons's portfolio, behind World Media and Athletes Week?"

This public statement infuriated Gill's father, Oliver, Jr., who said to his son, "I privately confronted him and asked why he would choose to dress down a family member in the press? He knows we have a long-held family code that prohibits any of us from making disparaging comments about the family to the media. If he wants this fight, I will give it to him. My dad and your grandfather came up with this rule. Cornwall knows better."

By defying this code, Cornwall started a family rift that was never fully resolved. Publicly, Oliver, Jr. rallied to his son's support. He advocated his son's readiness and competence in a later article in Media Monthly that chronicled the three generations of Harris Simmons leaders.

He said, "Gill has been a spectacular leader at Harris Simmons. He is a man of his times, a much different leader than my dad, my brother, and me. He has changed with the industry and the world. His record at Male Life is proof. I'm confident that he is prepared to lead this company into its next stage of greatness."

Cornwall Harris's endorsement emboldened Wynne Shields. His surly, deprecating manner became even more of an issue with his managers at World.

Gill told his Father, Oliver, Jr., "Our top managers at other properties walk around the building in fear of having to report to him eventually, and worst of all, his property, World Media, has become a revolving door. Over the last five years, he's had four Head of Sales, with not one lasting more than a year. He fired the last person, the highly regarded industry veteran, Val Tolliver, after only eight months and last fall just before the holiday season and peak advertising selling period. She had the property in great shape and was poised to break the down cycle that World had been under for the last two years. Frankly, I believe that he may not have wanted her to succeed. It has been six months since her departure, and he still has not been able to fill the job."

The memory of these events and conversation ran through Gill's mind as Wynne Shields' walked through his door. It made him seethe, yet he allowed himself a gentleman's greeting.

"Good morning Wynne," he said as he was seated at his desk.

"Morning," Wynne answered with a tone of irritation.

As Wynne prepared to sit down on the sofa opposite Gill's desk, Gill stopped him, "Don't sit down, you're busy, so I don't want to hold you up too long."

Wynne straightened up and moved behind the sofa, which created an additional buffer between the two of them. He then said, "Thank you."

"What I have to tell you will be short and simple."

"Excuse me?" Wynne interrupted, again, his voice suggested irritation, but he did not know yet that this was a bad day to act a fool.

Gill looked sternly in his eyes, it was a look that startled Wynne, and then he repeated himself.

"What I have to tell you will be short and simple. You've had this Head of Sales position open for the last six months, and I want it filled."

Wynne attempted to interrupt him, "I know, I'm..."

Gill's jaw tightened. He banged his right fist, angrily onto his desk, and then yelled at the top of his voice, "Shut Up."

DARIUS MYERS

Wynne recoiled in surprise as Gill continued. He had never seen him snap. It was a fit of anger that unnerved Wynne. Gill, with his voice still at its highest levels, continued to yell, "Your time is up. I've asked Donald Alexander to take over the search for this position. He now has responsibility for finding the candidate."

Gill lied about this to give Wynne the impression that it was his idea for Donald Alexander to take over the search.

"What?" Wynne shouted back, his voice rising as he was stunned and realizing that he was being forced to take an order. His face began to turn red. He then stood looking at Gill with his mouth shut, his jaw tight and his teeth grinding.

"That's right. You've had six months to handle this search, and you have not been able to come up with the right candidate and that my friend is hurting our business. My business."

He then stood up and walked around his desk. Now, all that separated them was the sofa. He looked hard at Wynne, who looked back. He could now see the anger in Gill's eyes. "You know this ass-kicking has been a long time coming."

These words shocked Wynne again, and he recoiled once more.

"Over the last five years, you haven't brought on anyone who could stay in the job for more than a year. That has hurt the leadership of your property, and that is also hurting our business. I'm concerned about your ability to find the right person."

"But Gill, I'm close to making a decision," Wynne protested.

"No, you are not. It's over as far as you are concerned. Donald Alexander is in charge of this search. He will find the candidate and make the hiring decision. You will accept his choice and do all that you can to ensure the success of the next person who takes this job. Is that

THE PUBLISHER'S DILEMMA

understood?"

Wynne did not respond. He just turned away from Gill and began to walk to the door.

Turning away as he did was not a good move. As he walked towards the door, Gill yelled even louder, "Stop, you better stop right there."

Wynne turned back to face his boss, his facial and body language suggested that he didn't care at all about what Gill just said. Gill knew that, so he ripped into him even harder than before.

"Wynne, this is the deal, just in case you forgot it. I am the boss here, not you. It's my name on the door, not yours, and I have decided that we have to be very careful about the eventual levels of transition, as well as ensuring that we maintain high-level managers in this company. You're doing an excellent job of messing that up. So, if you don't like that, you can find another place to work."

Wynne Shields' face was beet red now, and furor was in his eyes. "What does that mean, Gill? Are you telling me my job is in jeopardy?"

"It means that you have demonstrated an inability to be conscious of our need to develop and maintain top-notch management. Therefore, I can no longer be a witness to activity that weakens the competitive advantages of this company."

Gill stopped suddenly, closed his eyes, and raised his hands to head, and rubbed his temples for about five seconds. And then he let it out, he hadn't had a good fight in years, and Wynne got the brunt of some pent-up anger.

"Hell yeah, you selfish bastard, you will lose your job," Gill yelled loudly. "You better watch your ass. You mess with me on this one, and I'll drag your ass out of the building myself. I should have fired your ass after the Val Tolliver debacle, which was a clear act of insubordination of both Don

DARIUS MYERS

Alexander and me. You have no executive talent at your property, and you're not making any money. Now go ahead and try me on this one if you think I'm playing. I will have you perp-walked out of here at lunchtime in front of everyone in this building and way worse than you embarrassed Val Tolliver if you test me on this one. This guy will work out. Am I understood?"

Devastated, Wynne backs up to the door. He had never seen Gill lose it like as he just did. Gill had made it clear who was in charge. He also knew that he hadn't faced any consequences because of the Val Tolliver incident, and today could be that day. That realization and Gill's look of anger punked him. Wynne's face of rage had turned to fear and surprise. He looked meekly at Gill and asked, "Is that all?"

In his fear, he had forgotten to answer Gill's mandate that Donald Alexander's choice would work out.

"Answer my question, dammit. Do you understand that this person will succeed?"

Wynne realized that he had no choice and better follow Gill's order that the candidate succeed.

"Yes, I understand," he said meekly.

"Great. Now I'm done with your selfish ass. Do you have anything else to say?"

"What should I do with the candidates I have lined up for the job?"

"You can pass their names and resumes on to Alexander."

And then Gill added a comment that made Wynne Shields' knees buckle.

"Wynne, just in case I need to say this, this deep dark family secret that you want to keep holding over our heads, those days are over. You either do your job right, follow my rules, and Donald Alexander's, or its over.

THE PUBLISHER'S DILEMMA

And if you think I'm joking, I'll be the first one to go public. So, go ahead and try me, all you'll end up doing is messing up your life, and everyone else's involved."

"Remember friend, I'm rich, powerful, and living my best life. You can't do anything to hurt me. Now, you can leave."

Wynne Shields had just suffered his most significant professional defeat. Without saying another word, he turned around and walked out of Gill Harris's office.

As he walked to his office defeated, he thought to himself, "My significant blackmail story that granted me the excessive favoritism and leniency I've enjoyed here is now no good. His threat to go public with the blackmail news meant that my most powerful chit is now useless."

When he returned to his office, Sandi Williams, his secretary, had arrived.

"Good morning, Wynne."

He walked by her, ignored her greeting, and stormed into his office and slammed the door behind him. Devastated, he sat at his desk and contemplated what just happened.

"I have been relegated to a mere symbolic head."

This thought challenged Wynne's privilege and arrogance, however it took only few moments for him to revert back to his normal cantankerous state.

"I will not have my power usurped by that idiot ass. Who does he think he is?"

"Sandi," he yelled, "get me Humphrey now."

Two floors above, Gill sat in his office. He was still steaming, but he felt good about the meeting.

DARIUS MYERS

"I should have taken that pompous asshole down a long time ago."

He then walked down the hall to Donald Alexander's office. He knocked on the open door, entered, and stood in the doorway. Donald had just arrived at the office and missed the yelling from showdown of a few minutes earlier. He was hanging up his suit jacket when he turned to see Gill.

"Hey Gill, how are you today?"

Gill smiled and said while still standing in the doorway, "I'm great Don, I don't have a lot of time. I won't even sit down. I want you to know that I just got through with Wynne. He understands very clearly that you will be in charge of the search, and he will be responsible for ensuring that your candidate succeeds."

Before Donald could respond, Gill continued with details of the meeting as he was still charged up.

"Hey, Don?"

"Yes, Gill?"

"I showed him who the boss is around here too, that asshole will keep his head down and mouth shut for a while. Listen, I've got to go. I just wanted you to know that you've got the green light. Good luck," he said as he turned to walk back to his office.

"Thanks for everything, Gill," Donald said. He was interested in knowing what happened between Gill and Wynne, but since Gill had to go, he would save it for a later conversation.

"It's my pleasure, Don."

Gill walked back to his office, a bounce to his gait, and with a feeling of contentment. He felt great about this long-overdue fight with Wynne. He knew he had done something right.

THE PUBLISHER'S DILEMMA

Donald Alexander was relieved that Gill had finally had a showdown with Wynne Shields. Donald knew enough about the history of the company and old Man Cornwall's allegiance to Wynne that he couldn't personally take Wynne on. If someone was going to fight Wynne Shields, it had to be Gill Harris as the CEO. What Gill Harris did not tell Donald Alexander was that there was a deep and dark family secret that he was willing to make public, and it was this secret that was likely behind Wynne Shields' bad behavior.

Gill Harris didn't keep any secrets from Donald Alexander, except this one. And it wasn't because he didn't want to tell him. In Gill's mind, Wynne's blackmail could turn from a dark secret to a great story. He was working covertly on a plan to bring it to the public. But he needed some time, he only found out about this secret six months ago, right after the Val Tolliver firing, and he was still piecing it all together.

Chapter Eight

At 8:50 am, Kwame Mills took the elevator to the 39th floor for his interview with Donald Alexander. He was still ten minutes early. Selma Jones, Donald Alexander's secretary, greeted him at the elevator.

DARIUS MYERS

"You must be Kwame Mills."

"Yes, I am. And you are?" He suspected the woman to be Donald Alexander's secretary, and he was correct.

"I'm Selma Jones. I am Donald's secretary."

Selma Jones was an older woman, African-American, and Kwame guessed probably in her late 50s to early 60s. He guessed because she wore the granny-styled reading glasses that his Mom wore. Her look was of a highly respected, extremely competent, professional secretary.

"Let me tell him that you are here."

She directed him to two large sofas right near the elevators on the 39th floor.

"Have a seat here. I'll be right back."

Selma walked away and returned a minute later, holding a couple of print copies of the magazines.

"You're early, would you like to use the phone or bathroom? Or do you need anything before you meet with Donald? You could be in there for a while."

Kwame thought for a second. He was ready and was eager to meet with Alexander.

"I'm okay, but thank you anyhow for asking."

"Okay, then, hold on for just one more minute," she said and handed him the latest issues of World Media and Athlete's Week. "Here's a little something for you to read while you wait."

Selma then walked down the hall to Alexander's office to announce Kwame's arrival.

The waiting area offered a splendid view of the executive floor. There were two large offices on opposite ends of the floor. They were separated by a humongous conference room. Kwame assumed that Selma Jones headed to Donald Alexander's office and that the other large office was Gill Harris's, the CEO of Harris Simmons.

After reaching the far corner office, Selma Jones knocked on the door, hesitated for a second, and walked in. When she disappeared, Kwame continued his review of the executive floor. Its contents were all modern designed leather chairs, exotic vases, and standing art sculptures. The walls were mahogany-paneled and filled with framed issues of the various Harris Simmons publications.

"There's a lot of history housed on these walls." He then stood up to take a closer look at some of the historical magazine covers when Selma walked out of Donald Alexander's office.

"Kwame, come on down here, please," she said as she stood at the doorway of Donald Alexander's office.

"Okay Selma. I'm on my way, let me grab my stuff."

He went back to his chair to pick up his briefcase and the magazines she just gave him. He then looked at his reflection in a framed photo that was above the chair, pronounced himself fit, and walked down the hallway to Alexander's office. "I'm ready," he said loud enough for Selma to hear.

Selma Jones whispered, "Good luck," as he passed by her and entered the doorway.

"Thank you Selma, I appreciate it."

Kwame walked into an office that was brightly lit from the sun shining through floor to ceiling windows. He was struck by the expansive view of Central Park. It was an office fitting of a corporate president. Its interior was the modern-design he expected. And just like in the hallway, Alexander's office furnishings were all modern designed leather sofas and chairs. On the walls throughout the office were numerous photos of Alexander with top movie stars, Hollywood producers, performing artists, professional athletes, politicians, and dignitaries. In all of these photos, Donald Alexander was the real star. His magnetism was undeniable.

Donald was seated at his desk. He looked just like the guy that Kwame had seen in press clippings, close-cropped black hair, dark brown skin, clean-shaven face, flawless white teeth, chiseled facial features, about six foot two tall, with a lean muscular physique. When he stood up to greet him, he did so with the smooth grace of an athlete.

He spoke first and with a masculine, clear voice that completed his very commanding presence. He reached out his hand to Kwame for a handshake.

"Mr. Kwame Mills, where have you been all my life?"

Kwame was star-struck. Being in the presence of celebrities was usually a non-issue for him. Donald Alexander, however, was different.

He lost his cool for a second. He couldn't help himself and it was reflected in his awkward answer, "Uh, Chicago?"

"I'm sorry," Donald chuckled lightly, recognizing the awkwardness of the question. "Welcome Kwame, relax please and have a seat."

He pointed to a large leather chair opposite his desk. As Kwame sat down, Donald continued, "Let me just say, it's a pleasure to meet you and that I'm very happy for you and your success at NewsInc."

Kwame was taken aback again. He thought, how could this guy, the most successful black man in the history of the media industry, be impressed with him? He must be kidding. Kwame knew that he had to be sharp and calm, so he accepted the compliment and returned it with an even stronger one.

THE PUBLISHER'S DILEMMA

"Mr. Alexander," he started.

"Call me Don or Donald," Alexander interrupted.

"Okay, Donald. Thank you for the compliment, but let's get things right here. Your success is the stuff of legends, and I am very proud of what you've accomplished. If there's any pleasure in this meeting today, it is in me having the chance to meet you."

"And by the way," Kwame quipped, he had relaxed enough to summon up the composure that he needed to be impressive, "I love this office and view. It is amazing."

"Thank you, Kwame. I love this view too. It's one of the best perquisites of this role. I get to look out there every day."

Kwame Mills and Donald Alexander hit it off. They talked for two hours. They discussed sales strategy and business development. Kwame shared with him success stories for the large Conoy computer account and Waba, the new Japanese car account that he had steered into NewsInc. He also shared the go-to-market strategy that he successfully used to introduce NewsInc to the Midwest advertising market.

Finally, at 11:15, and after they had talked about everything from the advertising business to current events, music, wine, sports, and Church, Kwame Mills stopped talking about other stuff and asked Donald Alexander for the job.

"I want this job, Donald. I want to be the next Head of Sales for World Media."

These were the words Donald wanted to hear. "Kwame, you just passed the acid test by asking for the order. I want you to have this job, but before you accept it, I want to give you a reason or two to think about why you might choose not to accept."

DARIUS MYERS

Donald continued, "For starters, over the last five years, we've had four Heads of Sales at World Media. That means this is a very tough job, and you have to be a superstar to cut it. The publisher, Wynne Shields, is very demanding and intolerant of mistakes and incompetence. We know that this gig won't be easy. Yet if you can be successful, you will have a very successful career at World and, eventually, open the door for other opportunities for yourself at Harris Simmons."

"Donald, I appreciate you being so honest and sharing this as a downside for consideration," Kwame responded. "However, I know all about the recent history at World, and I know Wynne Shields is tough, but I think I can handle him. I want the opportunity to prove it."

The Harris Simmons President stood up from behind his desk. He was impressed with Kwame's credentials and confidence. He had the right attitude, but he was hopeful that he could keep it because Wynne Shields would try to break him.

He extended his hand to Kwame and said, "Congratulations, you won't have to interview with Wynne. I have full responsibility for completing this search, and I like you for this role. You've got the job."

Kwame was surprised and shocked. He expected this process to be a marathon with a series of interviews. He didn't think it would be just one meeting. He broke into a big smile.

"This is fantastic," he said and continued to smile broadly. Kwame felt, his glee was a bit unprofessional and apologized. "Sorry for smiling so, but this is great. I am thrilled and excited about this opportunity."

"Please, Kwame, don't apologize, this is a big moment for all of us. I'm glad that we're going to be able to bring on a special talent like you to our great company."

After they shook hands, Alexander turned the discussion to

THE PUBLISHER'S DILEMMA

compensation.

"So, how much are we going to have to pay for your services?"

Kwame was still smiling uncontrollably and unprepared to respond to this request. His mind was scrambling to come up with a value for his services. Typically, the company made the first move. He had heard that Head of Sales roles at the top Harris Simmons publications brought down salaries of $250,000 to 300,000, with bonuses of 100%.

"Just kidding Kwame. I know that question may have caught you off guard. How's this? We are prepared to offer you a $300,000 salary, and if your property meets its annual goal, you will receive a year-end bonus equaling 100% of your salary. We also are prepared to offer this in a three-year contract that would include an annualized 10% salary increase. You'll also get 25% of your salary in a company profit-sharing plan, provided of course that we make a profit. Does that work for you?"

Kwame's research said that Donald Alexander was not shortchanging him. He would be getting paid par value with other top Heads of Sales at Harris Simmons. He was also excited that he would now be making more than double the $300,000 he made at NewsInc, and the offer would include a three-year contract. He needed to review the deal but was confident that in a worst-case scenario that it would provide him some protection against Wynne Shields' potential turbulence.

All of this was happening so fast. Kwame needed to gain his composure. When he did, he looked at Alexander and said, "The compensation is fine. I would like to have a day or two to have my lawyer review the contract. Those conditions aside, I think this is a very generous offer, and I accept it."

"Great, then welcome to Harris Simmons. We'll get you that contract in the next day. Now, if you are free, let's grab lunch at our executive dining room."

"That sounds great Donald."

Donald and Kwame spent the next two hours having lunch in the Harris Simmons executive dining room. They talked about benefits, goals for the property, and other perks, including a country club membership at the golf and country club of his choice. They also agreed on a start date of three weeks from the upcoming Monday.

At the end of lunch, Alexander said, "I think it would be a good idea for you to meet with Wynne Shields. Let's go back to my office, and I will call him, introduce you, and you can stop by for a meeting."

When they got back to Alexander's office, he called Wynne Shields. His secretary answered the call.

"Wynne Shields's office, Sandi Williams speaking," she said.

"Good afternoon Sandi, this is Donald Alexander, is he available?"

"Hello, Mr. Alexander. Wynne is out of the office this afternoon. Can I help you with anything?"

"No, just tell him to give me a call as soon as he returns."

"Well, I don't expect him back today."

"Oh really, Sandi, when will he be back?"

Donald realized as she's talking that he should have gotten Wynne's schedule and committed him to be around today.

"He'll be out until Monday."

Donald scratched his head and murmured loudly, "Crap."

"Excuse me," Sandi Williams said.

"Oh, nothing. No worries. Let Wynne know that I called." He then hung up the phone

THE PUBLISHER'S DILEMMA

As he ended the call, Donald wondered if Wynne's sudden absence had anything to do with his Gill beat down. He thought that Wynne was probably somewhere licking his wounds. What a sight that would be after all the havoc that he's wreaked.

Donald then turned his attention back to Kwame.

"Listen, Wynne Shields is out for the rest of the week. I would like for you guys to meet before you start. As I said earlier, he's a demanding boss, and it would help to meet with him and break the ice."

"I agree," Kwame said. "I can come back next week, but I need to get back to Chicago today." He opened up his calendar on his phone as he talked and saw an opening. "I can come back next Wednesday."

"That is fine. I will call you on Monday to confirm Wynne's attendance."

After discussing a few more matters, Kwame finally departed from the Harris Simmons building. It was 3:30, and he was ecstatic. Kwame had a new job, with great pay at his dream company. He was happy.

Donald Alexander was happy also. He said to himself, "I like Kwame Mills, he is a good guy, an excellent media advertising salesman, smart and tough. He is just the guy to have opposite Wynne Shields."

As the day wore down, Donald contemplated all of this and felt very satisfied with himself. Most importantly, he had finally made a difference. He wanted to tell Ron Cherry, he called his office, but Cherry was unavailable.

"It'll have to wait until Saturday," he said to himself. "And that's okay." With his burden lifted a bit, he was now really looking forward to going to Ron Cherry's party.

DARIUS MYERS

Chapter Nine

Donald Alexander arrived at Ron Cherry's at 6:20. The Cherrys lived in The Dominico, a posh West Side apartment building that was even more exclusive than The Sanchez Palace. Ron and Marcia moved into The Dominico ten years ago and bought both apartments on the top floor. They also purchased the penthouse roof. The Dominico, is located at 77th Street and Central Park West, and as the owners of the top floor and penthouse roof, the Cherry's had to themselves unobstructed 360-degree views that spanned east to Central Park, south Midtown, west to the Hudson River, and north to Harlem.

All of the guests were outside on the penthouse roof. The first-person Donald saw was Miki Nomura, the owner of Satoru's Joints, a very successful high-end restaurant chain that was known for its eclectic French, Japanese, and Chinese menu.

Nomura was formerly an officer in the Japanese military and educated in the states. He had an MBA from The Kelibre School at Sheraton University. After business school, Nomura returned to Japan, took early retirement, and joined forces with friends from Kelibre to start Satoru's

THE PUBLISHER'S DILEMMA

Joints. They now have 12 restaurants nationally in the top 12 U.S. cities. Miki was standing near the door when Donald arrived, and from the aroma in the apartment, Donald could tell that Miki had catered tonight's party.

Donald has known Miki for two years. They met through Cherry, whose firm has been handling the investment banking for Satoru's Joints, including an upcoming IPO.

"Miki, my man, how are you?"

"I'm fine, Donald. How are you? How'd I do?" Miki Nomura said slowly with a thick Japanese accent.

"Oh, no, no. Come on now Miki. You are supposed to say, it's all good, or everything's cool, Brother. Is that all you got Miki? Really?"

"How about this, my Main Man?" Miki exaggerated my Main Man for emphasis, his accent now gone.

He then said in hipster's slang, "What's up, cool brother man Donald? How you living, My Dude?"

"Okay Miki. You had me there for a second. You know I'm fully invested in teaching you how to be cool in an American way."

"Don't worry about me, Donald, I'm okay and very cool."

"I know, and you're pretty funny too, Miki. Let's go upstairs and check out what's going on."

Miki and Donald walked up to the Penthouse deck to join the rest of the party's guests. It's crowded, and they start to make their way to the penthouse bar when Miki grabbed Donald's arm.

"Hey Donald, look, look. Check her out, now that's a beautiful woman," Miki pointed to a stunning black woman at the bar.

As Donald looked to see the subject of Miki's attention, he was awed.

DARIUS MYERS

"You are right, Miki, she's a knockout. Wow."

Standing at the bar was a tall, light-skin black woman with long brown hair that hung loosely down and into the middle of her back. She wore a sleeveless black dress that tugged close to her perfectly shaped body.

"That dress certainly fits her well. Could a woman possibly be more beautiful, Miki?"

"I don't think so, Brother Donald. That woman is a knockout, for sure."

"No question about that Miki, you're right, she is a knockout."

"Donald, let me work on my English with you, my Brother."

"What do you mean, Miki? You speak perfect English?"

"I know Donald, humor me for a second Brother Man. I need to get warmed up before I speak to her. I'm going to describe her to you, so I make sure I have all my words right. I don't want to get tongue-tied."

"Okay, Miki," Donald said and laughed, "do your thing. Let me have it, what you got?"

"Great, now look at her Brother. Her face is a perfect oval. She has a light-skin complexion that is flawless. She has big brown eyes, high cheekbones, and a perfect white smile that completes a most pleasing set of physical features. Donald, she is probably a supermodel. How'd I do?"

"You might be right, Miki, she definitely could be a supermodel. You described her well."

He looked at Miki, who was now popping a breath mint in his mouth.

"Wish me luck, Brother Man. I'm going to give her the Power Move."

Donald chuckled and said, "Don't do that, Miki. You know women can't resist your power moves."

"Don't hate Donald. Just watch and learn, my friend. Watch and learn,"

THE PUBLISHER'S DILEMMA

he then walked off to use his Power Moves.

Donald laughed as he watched Miki begin his self-proclaimed Power Moves conversation, which typically started with, "I'm Japanese, and I can't speak English too well."

Miki was very successful with Power Moves as a pickup tactic. He had movie-star looks, was smart, funny, and spoke six languages. Miki would never tell Donald his job in the Japanese Military, but Donald suspected it had to be spy work.

It looked like the Power Moves were working today, because in seconds he had successfully engaged her in conversation. After watching Miki for a while, and with more than a bit of envy, Donald looked at his watch. It was now past 7:00, and the Titans game had begun. He wanted to find Ron Cherry and check out as much of the game as possible before dinner.

First, however, he had to work the room. Tonight's party was a gathering of many of New York's business and political elite. Huddled in the northwest corner, having a spirited conversation was Lincoln Andrews, the senior partner at Britton, Gault, and Kreston, a blue-chip law firm. He was talking to David Winston, the former Mayor of New York City. Winston was now the U.S. ambassador to South Africa. Donald considered breaking up their conversation, but they appeared to be talking about something a bit heavier than their golf games, so he chose to pass.

Standing just 15 feet away on the same side of the room was Gail Fischer and her husband, Miles. They spotted Donald and waved for him to come over. Gail was the owner of the Doolittle Company, a book publishing company that specialized in books for the younger children market, ages 3 to 10. Miles was a real estate developer, who for years was the lead developer for The Dunk Group, one of Manhattan's premier real estate development companies. He recently started his own development company, Mile High Developers, and had been getting a lot of press for landing some significant projects. When Donald reached them, he kissed Gail on the cheek.

"It's good to see you, Ms. Fischer."

"Thank you, Donald, it's great to see you too."

As Donald looked at Gail, he could sense her mind racing. He knew she was going to come up with something funny or smart-alecky. But before she could say anything, he turned to Miles.

"Way to go, Miles, I've been reading nothing but good things about you of late."

"I'm just trying to be like you Donald. Congratulations, but my news pales in comparison to your frequent mentions in the New York society pages."

"Oh, stop with that Miles, you know that's just gossip."

Then Gail said, "Donald, when are you going to take this business off of my hands? It's killing me."

Whenever they would see each other at these cocktail and dinner parties, Gail would always kid with Donald that she was at her wit's end, and he could buy her company at a steal. Donald would indulge her, jokingly, of course, because Harris Simmons had no interest in book publishing.

"You know Gail, Gill just approached me a couple of days ago and asked me if I knew of a younger children's book company that might be right for an acquisition. I couldn't come up with one. Maybe you could offer a suggestion or two?"

Gail Fischer punched him playfully in the arm. "That's why I love you, Donald. You're always thinking about your friends."

THE PUBLISHER'S DILEMMA

Suddenly, Donald hears Ron Cherry's voice.

"Donald, where have you been?"

He turns around and sees Cherry walking towards him and the Fischers with a drink in his hand.

"Man, I'm glad you didn't blow us off, Marcia would have killed me," before asking him again. "Now, where have you have been?"

"Ron, I've been here for a few minutes. I've just been working the room a little bit with Miki."

He looked over to the bar. Miki and the woman whom they had been ogling just minutes ago were both gone. He was hoping that she was the woman Marcia had intended for him to meet.

"Well, I promised you that we would watch some of the game. I have it on in the family room. Let's go downstairs and catch up."

Donald excused himself from the Fischers, who were by now in a conversation with another couple. Donald turned back to Ron Cherry and headed to the staircase and the family room. As they headed downstairs, Ron is summoned.

"Ron, Ron, where are you, honey?".

"That's Marcia. You go on. I've got to report to the boss for a second. Go ahead. I'll catch up with you in a few minutes."

"Cool, I'll see you there."

Donald headed to the family room, and as promised, the game was on. The room is also empty, which meant that when Ron returned, they could talk a little bit about the activities of a few days earlier. Donald took a seat on the sofa opposite the 70-foot screen. It was a spectacular room and more of a home theater than a family room. The crowd noise from the state of the art audio system was so dramatic that Donald felt like he was at Titan stadium. A couple of minutes later, Cherry rejoined him.

"Sorry Bro, Marcia wanted me to taste some appetizers. What's the score?"

"We are in the second inning, and it's still zero to zero," Donald answered.

He still hadn't had a drink. Ron offered to make him one, "Let me get you a drink," He said as he walked to the bar. "What would you like?"

"How about a Vodka and tonic?"

"Coming right up."

As Ron walked to the bar, he brought up their last phone call.

"Hey Donald, have you given any more thought to the discussion we had a couple of weeks back?"

"Well, yes, I have Ron. I took your advice and did something about it."

Ron turned to him with a look of surprise on his face.

"Really, what did you do?"

"Yeah, Man, after our conversation, I realized that you were right. I have the power and position to make changes like this happen, and if I don't do anything to change matters, it's my fault."

Ron walked back over to the sofa and handed him his vodka and tonic. He had also refreshed his glass of bourbon drink.

"Cheers, my main Man, it's good to see you."

"Cheers, back at you, Brother."

They clanked glasses and took a sip of their drinks. Donald placed his glass on the table in front of him and continued with the story. Ron sat on the other end of the sofa. He looked at Donald and asked.

"So, what happened, what did you do?"

THE PUBLISHER'S DILEMMA

"Well, I started by putting together a list of quality prospects, people that could fill senior-level jobs, and I found out what jobs were open."

"Good move, nice start."

Ron took a sip from his glass and looked at the ceiling, not at the television screen. He was listening intently and concentrating on what Donald had to say.

"Then I had a meeting with Gill and told him that we were losing focus of our marketplace, that our decision makers were no longer solely white males, and that we had to keep pace with cultural change."

"What did he say to that?"

"He agreed. He also said that this is the kind of leadership that he expects from me and that I made him proud. He said that whatever I decided to do, he would support me."

"That's great. I don't know Gill very well, but he sounds like a good guy."

"He is. He's phenomenal. I'm thrilled to be working for him."

"So, what's next, what are you going to do?"

"Well, I told Gill that we had a Head of Sales position open at World, and I thought that would be a good place to start."

"Okay, And?"

Donald could tell that Ron was excited and anxious to know about the next steps.

"Gill told me to go ahead and make the full hiring decision and to not worry about Wynne Shields, the publisher of World. He would take care of him."

"Wynne Shields, isn't he the guy old man Cornwall was touting to be president before you?"

Ron took a swig of his bourbon. A look of concern crossed his face.

"Yep, the same guy Ron."

"Well, is he dangerous? Have you considered what this could mean."

"Very much so. Wynne is an asshole, without question, the nastiest and most arrogant person at our company."

Ron put his drink on the table next to him. He turned to face him and then looked at Donald.

"Well, what do you think?"

"What do you mean? What am I going to do with Shields?"

"Yes, Don. Will this be a problem for the guy you're going to bring on? And maybe for you too?"

"Well, maybe. But I think I found a guy strong enough to handle him. And as for me, don't worry, I'm not afraid of him."

Donald continued, he knew that Ron would want to know why he felt his candidate could stand up to Wynne.

"As far as my candidate is concerned. He's quite experienced, well-educated, and has a strong track record of success. I think he's going to be a star. We checked him out pretty thoroughly."

"Sounds like someone else of less stature would get eaten alive by this Wynne Shields guy."

"You're right. But Gill told him that he better make sure this guy succeeds. We can't afford another Val Tolliver situation. Between you and me, we ended up having to pay her $4 million to avoid all of the wrongful termination lawsuits after Wynne had her escorted from the building. We had to fulfill the remaining two years on her employment contract plus give her some goodwill money."

"Damn Donald. That was expensive."

"I know. Gill's Uncle, Cornwall, loves the guy, and I just don't get it. The guy is a cancer. He deserves an old-fashioned Goon Squad beat down and banishment from our company."

Ron smiled and then congratulated Donald and this accomplishment.

"Great job, Donald. I'm proud of you. That's great work. You deserve a nice reward for your service to the community work."

"Now on to more fun topics, I must say that I think Marcia might have outdone herself this time. You'll like this one."

Donald's thoughts raced to the woman that Miki sought out for a Power Moves chat. He was curious about her, and as he began to ask a waiter walked into the Den, "Mr. Cherry, your wife has asked me to gather everyone in the dining room for dinner."

"Oh okay. We'll be right there," Cherry rose up from his chair. "Let's not keep Marcia waiting." Both their glasses were empty, and Ron looked at Donald and said, "We'll freshen up our drinks in the dining room."

As they walked to the dining room, Donald was happy that he had shared his story with his close friend. Now he was intrigued about the mystery woman that Marcia wanted him to meet, especially after Ron gave her the thumbs up.

"So, who is this woman that I'm supposed to meet?" He was still hopeful that it was the woman Miki went after earlier and that he would steal Miki's thunder.

"Oh, I'll save that for Marcia. I have nothing to do with matchmaking. That's her specialty."

"Ah man." He knew then that Ron was messing with him.

DARIUS MYERS

They got to the dining room early. The Fischers had already arrived. They were talking to Lincoln Andrews and his wife, Andrea. Missing was David Winston and his wife, Gloria, Marcia, Miki, and the mystery bombshell.

Moments later, everyone else arrived, except for the mystery woman. She wasn't missed for long as another woman was now in the room and she was just as beautiful. This woman was tall and lean, with a stunning light brown face and elegantly dressed in a strapless chartreuse dress that fit snuggly and hung to her mid-thigh. Her hair was curly and long and ran to her shoulders. She was equally breathtaking. Miki was now talking to her and putting on his charm.

Ron Cherry noticed that this new woman had snared Donald's attention and tapped him on the shoulder.

"Good luck, my friend. She could be your date for the evening."

"Wow, now this could be worth missing a ballgame. Very nice, very nice. Marcia's done well Ron."

Marcia then tapped a water glass with a butter knife to get everyone's attention. Once the room got quiet, she asked everyone to take their seats, but first made a big deal about the seating arrangements.

"Thank you all for joining us tonight. This evening, we have special seating arrangements at the table, and I would like everyone to sit at the seat with their names."

Donald was excited as he knew he would be seated next to Marcia's blind date prospect for the evening, but before they sat down, Miki approached him.

"Would you like to switch seats with me?"

"Not a chance, my Brother. You wouldn't want to upset the host, would you? Besides, I have to work on my Power Moves."

THE PUBLISHER'S DILEMMA

Miki sighed, mocked a little anger, and protested, "I have no luck, and by the way, Power Moves don't work. If you need any help Donald, I'll be at the other end of the table."

Donald rubbed it in with Miki as he walked away. "I'll be okay Miki, see you in a couple of hours."

He stopped, turned around, and then snarled before saying, "You've got all the luck, my brother."

As Miki walked away, Donald thought to ask Miki about the woman from earlier, but this thought was interrupted as Marcia began walking towards his seat with her friend.

Marcia spoke first, "Good evening, Donald."

"Good evening, Marcia, you look great as always."

Marcia was looking beautiful with a dazzling summer yellow dress. Her hair was pulled back and in a long mane that ran across the back of her neck. Before marrying Ron, she was a garment and cosmetic industry executive. She was and remained extremely attractive. Tonight, she had all the touches of her glamour industry background working and looked terrific. After Donald kissed her on the cheek, Marcia introduced him to his dinner mate, the beautiful woman who, to Miki's disdain, would become his Power Moves subject.

"Donald, let me introduce you to Carrie Sinclair."

He turned to Carrie, smiled and bowed as if she was a royal princess. "It's a pleasure to meet you, Carrie Sinclair." She smiled in response to his bow.

Marcia continued the introduction, "Carrie, this is Donald Alexander, he's gorgeous and rich."

"I'm expecting you guys to have a spectacular time together. I'll be keeping an eye on you both." Marcia said as she walked away. Carrie looked embarrassed at her friend's statement.

Donald then pulled Carrie's chair for her to sit. "Would you like to sit down?"

"Thank you, Donald," Carrie said as she sat down.

As Donald stood at the back of Carrie's chair, he took special note of the glow of her skin, and the smell of her perfume. She smelled great. When he sat down, he complimented Carrie on her dress.

"I hope this is not too forward, but I must compliment you. That's a stunning dress, and you look amazing in it."

"Thank you, Donald, how very kind of you. Marcia speaks highly of you. She did tell me that you are a gentleman. I see that she was right. Now tell me, how do you know Ron and Marcia again?"

"They are the investment bank for the publishing company I work for, but over the years, we've also become friends."

"What company is that?"

Carrie then reached for a water glass in front of her. She seemed to be a little nervous, but Donald Alexander didn't notice as he was a bit nervous as well.

Donald's answers to her questions were blunt and bland, and it took him a couple of seconds to realize his curt answers might even be rude.

He answered her second question very matter of factly, "My company is Harris Simmons, the media company."

It wasn't until her third question that they finally broke the ice.

"And what do you do, Donald at Harris Simmons?"

"What is this? 10,000 questions, Carrie?"

THE PUBLISHER'S DILEMMA

"I'm sorry, Donald. I suppose you already know that Marcia has briefed me. I'm just making a little small talk."

She was right, and Donald knew so. They were starting badly. He apologized and then steered the conversation to make it more comfortable.

"Carrie, it's not your fault. I know Marcia, and I know her style. She's always trying to set me up. I just figured she'd already given you my full story. However, I don't know anything about you because they wouldn't tell me anything about you."

"Okay, that's cool Donald. How about we start over?"

"Great, let me start by saying Carrie, you are the most beautiful woman in this room. You look amazing, and I'm thrilled to spend this evening getting to know you."

Carrie blushed uncontrollably and said, "That's the second time you've complimented me, and even though a girl is not supposed to admit it, I liked it the first time and even more the second time. You're smooth, Donald Alexander. Very smooth, good comeback."

"Well, thank you Carrie."

For most of the dinner, Carrie spoke. She told Donald about her education, her rise through The Minnion Company, and she talked very enthusiastically about her new career as a photojournalist.

As she talked, Donald, from time to time, caught Miki's envious glare. They were getting along fabulously, and Miki could tell. What Carrie didn't mention to Donald was that she was once married.

When dinner ended, Ron and Marcia had their guests participate in a Bid Whist card tournament. Donald and Carrie partnered. Although he was not much of a card player, they held their own, winning most of the hands at the table for an hour.

DARIUS MYERS

At midnight, Carrie announced to Donald that she had to leave to prepare for a trip to London the next day.

"I've got this trip to London tomorrow, so I have to get ready to leave."

Donald knew from this evening that he liked Carrie Sinclair and wanted to see her again.

"When will you return?"

Carrie answered, sassily, "Why do you want to know?"

By now, they were getting along very well, and all of the tension from earlier was gone.

"Because I want to see you again."

He looked at her, reached over to her with his right hand, and grabbed her left hand and just held it.

He then said, "Your hands are soft Carrie and warm, and they fit in mine like a glove. I would like to see you again and hold your hands some more."

She was overcome by Donald's charm. It sent a warm jolt up her arm that made her quiver in a way that she had never experienced. It melted all her sassiness from a moment ago.

"I'll be back this Thursday," she blurted out and blushed.

Then she said, "Damn that wasn't very hard to get, was it?"

Donald smiled. He was interested in Carrie Sinclair, and with that response just learned that she was as well. He made his living closing deals, and he knew that he couldn't just let her leave this party without knowing when he would see her again.

He then leaned close to her and whispered in her ear, "Would you like to come out to my beach house next weekend? I just bought a summer house, and I would love for you to come out."

Carrie still shook from the hand-holding gesture took a step back as if he was moving too fast.

"Oh, I'm sorry Carrie. That sounds a little forward, I guess. I'm having a large party 100 or so people, Ron and Marcia will be there. I'd love for you to be there."

Carrie giggled and smiled, but she still hadn't responded to his invitation.

Donald was now off-guard and confused. He said, "What's so funny?"

"That look you gave me a few minutes earlier when you held my hand, and I just melted. I don't like being so obvious, and you're so smooth. It's nice to see that you can be unnerved too."

She then said, "your request was not too forward. I'd love to come."

Embarrassed but undaunted and encouraged, Donald responded, "Great, I have eight bedrooms in the place. Why don't you stay for the weekend? We can play tennis or some more Bid Whist or something on Sunday?"

"What's or something?" Carrie answered flirtatiously.

Donald didn't have an answer. He was still on edge, so he thought for a second and said the same thing, "I don't know, or something. Just come, we'll have some fun. I'll even send a car for you."

"Okay, I'll be there. When shall I come, is it Saturday?"

"Yes. Let's talk when you return, okay?"

"Sounds like a plan," Carrie said. They then exchanged phone numbers before she kissed him on the cheek and then excused herself for the evening. But before leaving, she found Marcia and talked for a few minutes.

DARIUS MYERS

After Carrie left, Marcia walked over to Donald and teased him, "Oh, you'll send a car for her."

Donald was surprisingly smitten, and more than he expected. He felt that jolt of electricity that Carrie felt when he grabbed her hand too. He was playing it cool and offered a longwinded thank you to Marcia for this introduction, "Yeah, I said that. She's nice, smart, fun and beautiful and I must give you props for this one. I am interested, so what would you have me do, make her walk?"

"In all of that, did you just say thank you?"

"Thank you, Marcia. She's very nice. And when I leave, you can call her and tell her I said it."

"Oh, you know I will, Buddy, you know I will."

She then said to Ron, who was walking in on their conversation, "Ron, he likes her. I knew he would."

Ron said, "You called that one honey and good for you, Donald. Carrie's a knockout. Glad you like her. Mission accomplished honey, looks like you done hooked up New York's most eligible bachelor."

They all laughed, and with his date on her way home for the evening, Donald Alexander, smitten and feeling pretty excited, decided it was time for him to leave as well.

As he headed home, Donald realized he never did get to ask Miki about the mystery woman. Later on, in the summer, he would meet her again. Had Donald pressed Miki, he would have learned that the mystery woman was at the party for one reason, to learn more about Donald Alexander.

Chapter Ten

"Hi, I am Miki Nomura, what is your name?"

"Hi, my name is Samantha Rivers. It's nice to meet you Miki."

"You are quite beautiful Samantha, I must say. Are you here with a date tonight? Or might I be lucky enough to sit next to you during dinner."

Samantha looked at Miki, "Well, you are direct, aren't you, Miki?"

"It's what I call Power Moves."

"Actually," Samantha continued, "I am waiting to meet a friend, and I don't think I am staying for dinner. I just intended to meet her for drinks here."

"Power Moves, tell me about how that works?" Samantha said as she took a drink from the glass of wine she was holding.

"Oh, it's more about me being direct with a beautiful or pretty woman I meet. No one wants to waste time talking with someone. So, I've come up with a foolproof system of making each meeting work."

"Really. I'm curious, tell me more. Is this a pickup line, or are these moves that work for women equally as they do for you or men?"

"Can I be honest Samantha, I don't know if they even work for men, but I'll let you in on a secret."

DARIUS MYERS

"Please, I want to know," Samantha said, her attention now entirely on Miki.

"The secret is in just being sincere with my interest in introducing myself. Not being rude or disrespectful, just highly curious about the people I meet."

"So that's it? Is there more to it? Come on. There has to be?"

"No, not really. You ask the most direct question, respectfully, of course, and see where it goes."

"Okay, can I do a trial run past you?"

"Of course, happy to do that, let's go."

"Okay, I know you were talking to Donald Alexander over there, I've never met him before. Tell me everything you know about him?"

Miki turned around to look across the room at Donald, who was oblivious to being the topic of discussion.

"What do you mean? Like is he a lady's man or a good guy?"

"No, I am only interested in his character. I hear that he is a great person and is in line to be the next CEO of his company and everybody loves him. I saw you guys over there chatting and laughing, so I guess you know him."

"Yes, I do. We're friends, and he's always giving me tips on how to be cool and more hip in an American way."

"That's funny," Samantha said flirtatiously, "I guess it's working because you seem pretty hip to me."

"Hey, are you flirting with me, Samantha?"

"It was a power move, Miki," Samantha said and smiled. "I am learning your game. Now tell me more about Donald?"

THE PUBLISHER'S DILEMMA

"Oh yeah, Donald. He's okay, but I'm more handsome than him. Wouldn't you agree Samantha?"

She looked at Miki and chuckled, "You certainly are persistent Miki, and yes, you are adorable. Now stop flirting for a second and tell me more about Donald, and then we'll flirt some more."

That comment caused Miki to share all he knew about Alexander. "Let's see we're both connected to Ron Cherry, Ron is my investment banker as well as Don's at Harris Simmons. I've gotten to know him over the last few years and admire and respect him an awful lot. He's got a big job over there and is just hitting the cover off the ball."

"Nice," Samantha said, and then her cellphone began to ring.

"Excuse me a second. I need to take this call." She then walked towards the living room and the front entrance.

Miki was enjoying his conversation and looking forward to flirting more until he saw the front door open, and Samantha walked out. She had left and not bothered to say goodbye.

"Power moves suck," Miki said to himself. He then rejoined the rest of the party.

Chapter Eleven

A week after getting his job offer Kwame Mills returned to New York to meet Wynne Shields.

Donald called him to arrange a breakfast beforehand, "Kwame, let's have breakfast before your meeting with Wynne. I want to coach you a little more and prepare you for the difficulties you'll likely face with Wynne. Meet me at 7:30 am at the Colleague Club."

Kwame arrived early at the Colleague Club at 7:15 am. He was excited as the Colleague Club is the most exclusive member club in the city. He flew into New York the night before and stayed at the Sherrod, a boutique hotel, right next to Harris Simmons, and a short walk to the Colleague Club. He arrived five minutes before Donald. The host seated him at a corner table in the main dining room.

"This is Mr. Alexander's table," the host said. Donald's table was next to a large window that looked over Central Park. To Kwame, it was the best seat in this impressive dining room.

While he waited, he thought how this setting fit Donald's stature in New York, "here I am in a room filled with a who's who of business executives having a power breakfast. Donald Alexander, my new boss, is as accomplished as any of these guys. And he has a personal interest in my career. God has ordered my steps. I am divinely blessed."

When Donald entered the room, he did with the majesty of a crowned prince. It took him a couple of minutes to make it across the room as numerous people stopped and engaged him. Kwame was awed as he watched him gracefully make his way through a sea of admirers.

Finally, he made it to the table and said, "Good Morning, so glad to see you, apologies for taking a few minutes to say hello to people. That's what it's like at this place."

"Donald, please no apologies are necessary. I've always heard about the Colleague Club, and I'm excited to be here. There are a lot of movers and shakers here today," Kwame said and gazed upon the room filled with the city's top executives having confidential business conversations.

"Yes, it is Kwame. This club is great for business, and this is in one of New York's most renowned power breakfast rooms. I come here for two reasons. One because it is very exclusive, which means top-level clients always want to come and two because it is a great place to see and be seen."

Donald then looked up and smiled. Kwame noticed that he was responding to the frantic wave of a beautiful middle-aged white woman seated at a table on the other side of the room.

He said to Kwame, "That woman waving is Marianne Michaels. Marianne is President of Michaels, Partridge, & Cluess Consulting. She's a maverick, started the firm 12 years ago, and is one of the most powerful women in this town. She's also been trying to get us under contract for years. Watch out for her. I'm sure she'll be over before we leave."

Donald then took Kwame through a light inventory of the room, pointing out the numerous investment bankers, consultants, lawyers, and media bigwigs.

Shawn, a waiter came to their table. Before he could speak, Donald ordered, "Good morning Shawn, good to see you. I'll have fresh fruit, coffee, and wheat toast with jam."

He then said, "Let me introduce you to Kwame Mills, he's new to our company, and you'll be seeing him a bunch around here."

"Good morning and welcome, Kwame," Shawn said, "I look forward to being of service. Enjoy the club. You'll enjoy this place. Now, what can I put on your order for breakfast?"

Like his first meeting with Donald Alexander, Kwame felt a bit of unease with Donald's graceful style but composed himself.

"Thanks Shawn, for those kind words, I look forward to seeing you again. I'll have coffee, wheat toast and an egg white omelet with spinach."

After he took their orders, Kwame looked up to see Marianne Michaels working her way across the room and to their table. Donald also noticed and whispered to Kwame, "Get ready, here she comes."

Shawn, who was filling their coffee cups, smiled, and said, "Good luck. She's something else, but you can handle her, follow Donald, I mean Mr. Alexander's lead."

Donald smiled after Shawn's kind comment. He then said to Kwame, "Marianne Michaels didn't build a world-class consulting firm by being shy and demure. She is one of management consulting's most dynamic and energetic leaders. As you can see, she is a tall, elegant brunette, and she's got a killer smile. Most people, especially men, are so taken by her looks that they become marks for the dazzling sales pitch for her firm's strategic consulting services. She is, however, more than an attractive package. She is a real workhorse, a superb salesperson, and an excellent consultant. She's also New York street tough. I've seen her drink four bourbon shots straight and punch a punk's lights out. Seriously, she punched out a guy two inches taller and 30 pounds heavier for touching her ass. Besides being barroom tough, Marianne is legendary for getting the ears of a guy smitten by her looks and using her brains to get a project. She then takes that little contract and turns them into a satisfied, long-term customer. "

"Kwame was impressed with how buttoned-up Donald was about Marianne Michaels, but then he thought, its why he's so successful. He is diligent and pays attention to details."

"Donald, my dear," Marianne Michaels said as she reached the table.

"Good morning, Marianne," Alexander rose from his seat to greet her. Kwame stood up as well.

Marianne started into her pitch, "Why haven't you returned my phone calls? You know one good business person always returns another's call."

Donald smiled. He knew he had a little cleaning up to do. "Yes, I do, Marianne. I owe you an apology. I've been so busy, but you were on the top of my list for…."

She cut him off, Marianne Michaels was not interested in his answer. She knew that she would get a meeting with Donald, but now she chose to show how deep her contacts and access ran. The word was out about Kwame Mills, and that he was an African-American. She put two and two together and decided to force an introduction. "Is this your new Head of Sales for World, the very talented Kwame Mills?"

"Yes, he is. Michaels, you don't miss a beat," Donald said.

Kwame was caught off guard. He had been enjoying the genteel banter between his boss and this powerful businesswoman, but his heart skipped a beat when she mentioned his name. Marianne Michaels, stuck her hand across the table for a handshake.

"Kwame Mills, I am Marianne Michaels. As for your new boss, he sometimes has bad manners. Get used to it."

Startled, but recovering quickly, Kwame reached out his hand to return the greeting.

"Nice to meet you, Ms. Michaels. I've heard great things about you."

"From Donald, I hope." She then sat down at the empty seat opposite Donald and next to Kwame and smiled broadly.

DARIUS MYERS

Donald smiled back as he and Kwame sat down. Not returning Michaels's calls meant that he could be in for some heavy hazing, so to hold her off, he decided to strike first.

"Marianne, can you tell me again your line of work? Are you a private detective or a management consultant?"

"Hey Man, what's the difference?" Michaels said in the rough and tumble way that Donald just referenced. "I know about your business, don't I? Isn't that what you guys pay people like me to know?"

"Okay, okay, you are right. Call me later this afternoon, and we'll schedule a time late next week."

Satisfied that she had done enough and not wanting to overstay her welcome, Marianne Michaels flashed her perfect smile again, "Fair enough. I'll be calling you later."

As she rose from the table, Kwame and Donald stood up. She then looked at Kwame with the most alluring hypnotic look, winked, and said, "Nice to meet you, best of luck. World is a great magazine."

Donald smiled and said as she walked away, "I saw that. She gave you the look."

Kwame shook his head, not quite knowing what to make of it, "Yes, I'm glad you saw it, what was that? She's smart and disarming. That's a pretty lethal combination to get people to pay attention to you."

"I'm telling you Kwame, Michaels is the best. I like her a lot, and we'll be doing business with her. She's like us, a master seller. I always have to tell her that game knows game to get her to stop selling so hard."

Michaels was already across the room, working another table.

Donald and Kwame and watched in admiration. Finally, Kwame said, "Man, she's something else."

THE PUBLISHER'S DILEMMA

Donald seconded Kwame's comment and nodded before saying, "Sure is."

"Now, I want to go over how I want you to manage this situation."

"Kwame, as we discussed last week, Wynne Shields has had numerous Heads of Sales over the last couple of years. They've not worked out mainly because he gets them on their heels with a lot of intolerable behavior. He is a very extremely difficult person. You should not expect him to treat you any differently."

"This is the plan I want you to follow. When you meet, tell Wynne that you will spend your first three weeks to a month on the road visiting the sales offices for World, and afterward, you will report to him on the status of each. You'll get an opportunity to evaluate our talent and also some time for him to relax a bit and distance himself over your selection."

"Fine," Kwame said as he pulled out a note pad from his suit jacket and wrote down Donald's orders.

"When you return, I want you to send me a copy of the report you make to him, and then let's see where we are. All I want you to do is stay out of his way for the first month or so. Is that understood?"

"Loud and clear. Just stay clear for a month."

Donald's plan was simple and easy enough. Unless there were some major incident, the first month or so would go by without a wrinkle.

Now with the primary purpose of their breakfast meeting behind them, Donald switched gears to another reason for having breakfast at the Colleague Club.

"Now, what do you think about this club?"

"It's quite impressive and since walking in I've thought about the deals I could do here."

"That's good because we have a corporate membership here, and as of today, you are a member. I want you to use it. Bring your clients, your staff members, your girlfriend, or your wife. Are you married?"

"I'm single with a girlfriend."

"So, bring your girlfriend, be sure to use it. I want you to be seen and for the people in this town to know that you are a significant player at Harris Simmons."

"Thank you, and I will," he said to Donald. He then thought, "this is big time and a great perk. These guys sure know how to make an impression."

Shawn then returned with their breakfasts. While they ate, Donald outlined an itinerary for Kwame to follow.

"Go to Detroit first. We get big business from the big three car companies. Next, get out to Chicago, then Los Angeles and San Francisco. Get those guys to take you out on sales calls."

After he finished the overview, Kwame turned to Donald Alexander and asked, "What else should I know?"

"Let them know that you're the boss Kwame. I want all of your staff to know it."

Donald then began to rise from the table.

"Excuse me for a second. I'm going to the men's room, when I return, let's get to the office and get this over with."

While he was away, Kwame continued to take in the room and the exclusive access it would afford him.

When Donald returned, he waived for Shawn, who was on the other side of the room. When they made eye contact, Donald held his hand up and made a scribble motion into his palm. Within seconds, Shawn was at their table with a check. As Donald signed the check, Kwame looked across the room once more, and he became even more excited about getting to work for Harris Simmons.

As they exited, Marianne Michaels caught their attention once more with a big wave and said, "I'm going to call you."

"Okay Marianne, looking forward to it."

Donald and Kwame rode to Harris Simmons in Donald's chauffeured car. Once in the car, Donald made and returned several phone calls. Kwame gazed out of the window, watching the busyness of Manhattan in rush hour. When Donald finished the last phone call, he turned to Kwame and asked, "What are you doing this weekend?"

"I'll be in Chicago, spending some time with my girlfriend."

Kwame was still on a cloud and ecstatic about his job offer with World Media, but he was troubled with how it would affect his relationship with Michelle Nubani. They had been dating for six months and getting along fabulously. Being with her had become the best part of his time in Chicago. She was away the previous weekend, and he had not celebrated his excellent news yet.

"If it's possible, I would like for you and her to come out to my house in the Hamptons for the weekend. I'm having a party, and it promises to be a great time. Do you think she can make it?"

He thought about Donald's request before responding, "Do you think she can make it?" That sounded more like a demand as opposed to a request. Kwame wanted to make sure things got started right.

"I'll have to see Donald. She has a hectic schedule, but we'll work something out."

"I hear you, Kwame. I know it's short notice, but can I count on you at least being there?"

DARIUS MYERS

He sensed again that his new bosses' request was a command performance and answered appropriately.

"What can I bring?"

"Good, good. Just yourself and, hopefully, your lady as well."

They arrived at the Harris Simmons building at 8:45, just 15 minutes before his meeting with Wynne Shields. As they exited the car and entered the building, Donald reminded him that the job was already his.

"Don't worry, remember what I told you. You manage Wynne, don't let him bully you."

"Thanks Donald, I will. I'll make you proud."

"I know you will. After the meeting, give my office a call, and I'll get you the details for this weekend. We'll talk about today's meeting this weekend, okay?"

"Great, I'm looking forward to it, Donald."

Kwame's introduction to Wynne was just as he supposed it would be, cold and indifferent. Wynne was clear in letting Kwame know that he felt no obligation to be pleasant.

The meeting began with Wynne's secretary, Sandi Williams, leading Kwame into his office at 9:20. It was a lengthy wait, considering Kwame's early arrival.

Wynne was seated behind his desk and appeared to be busily peering through a file of papers. He did not rise to greet Kwame. Instead, he waived, condescendingly, motioning him to sit down at one of the two chairs opposite his desk.

To occupy himself, Kwame began to visually peruse the room, hoping to find an item of mutual interest and a potential subject of conversation. On the walls were pictures of Wynne with many celebrities and personalities, many of whom were the subjects of editorial stories in past issues of World Media.

Finally, without a greeting, a hello or a good morning, Wynne put down the papers and looked across his desk.

"Look, let's get one thing straight. You're not my guy."

Whew, Kwame thought to himself, "This guy really is an asshole."

The comment, however, steeled Kwame in his resolve not to be unnerved. He accepted it as a challenge to demonstrate his poise. With that, he stiffened in his seat, returned Wynne's eye stare, and said blandly, "I understand."

"Do you?" Wynne asked with enough anger to let Kwame know that he wanted this meeting to be uneasy.

"Yes, I do. I know that I'm not your guy, so that means we're a long way from where I want to be," Kwame answered again in a bland voice

"And where is that Kwame?"

Kwame then remembered the counsel that Donald Alexander gave him just a couple of hours earlier and stayed on the plan.

He turned to him and said, "Wynne, you need a trusted aide and a formidable one-two team for this property. I want to win over your trust and help you make this property what you want it to be."

"And how do you think that will come about?" Consternation was still heavy in Wynne Shields' voice.

Kwame grew nervous but thought again about Donald and his counsel. He leaned forward and said, "it means I do what I was hired to do, which is to make money for this property and you. To do that, I need to be here to help you, not get in your way or to hurt you."

Wynne knew that Kwame was saying the right things, but he wasn't interested in liking him. He had to make it clear that he wasn't his guy, so for effect, he emphasized his position as boss.

"You better believe that the only way you'll survive here is that you do just that. And trust me, I'm not concerned about you hurting me. I've handled more formidable foes."

Kwame realized he was not going to win Wynne Shields over, at least not today. So, he turned to the plan Donald Alexander laid out during breakfast.

"Look Wynne, I'm going to make a suggestion, and you tell me if you think this is a good way for us to transition into this."

Wynne was now looking at the window. He didn't want to dignify Kwame with eye contact. Kwame looked at him, but Wynne wouldn't look back. As he studied his aristocratic profile, all of a sudden, Wynne didn't look so stern anymore. He seemed to be pouting, and at that moment, a wave of compassion overcame Kwame.

"He's in terrible shape. What a pathetic, sad guy," Kwame thought. "Something is deeply wrong with him. I must remember not to pass judgment, I will pray for him."

Wynne, unaware of Kwame's compassion, snapped, "Go ahead, tell me what you are thinking."

Kwame cleared his throat. "Here's my suggestion," he said in a robust, affirmative tone. "I'll spend the first three weeks on the road and do meetings with the sales offices and managers. Once I complete the tour, I'll report back to you, and we can take it from there."

Wynne looked to the window again and seemed to be contemplating his suggestion, but he was slow to respond. Kwame wondered why he was deliberating. This was a great idea and would keep them out of each other's way. Wynne had to see it that way, or could he be that stubborn? If he said no, Kwame didn't have a solid Plan B. His mind began to race for what he might offer as a Plan B.

Wynne then spoke, after what in reality was only 30 seconds of contemplation, but it seemed ten times as long, he said curtly, "Fair enough. Now when will you start?"

"In two and a half weeks," Kwame said right back. He was relieved and ready for this meeting to be over.

"Fine. Talk to Sandi on your way out. She'll get your office together."

Wynne then turned back to reading his papers and without looking to him, dismissively said, "Goodbye Kwame. Have a good day."

"Thank you, Wynne," Kwame said as he stood up from his seat. "I look forward to seeing you when I start in two weeks."

Wynne Shields predictably did not respond.

Chapter Twelve

Wynne's secretary, Sandi Williams, was seated at her desk. She smiled at Kwame as he walked out of Wynne's office. He looked at her and his first thought was, "how does this woman deal with this crazy man?"

Kwame was bruised but not broken. He hadn't even started yet and Wynne made it a bad day at the office. He learned that he was going to have to put a plan together that included more than running around the country on airplanes and avoiding Wynne. She might have some tips and he was going to have to get to know her better.

DARIUS MYERS

Before he could speak, Sandi said, "Kwame, let me escort you to your office and introduce you to your secretary."

"Thank you Sandi. What's her name?"

"Sheila Duncan. She's the best. I'm sure you'll like her."

"I'm sure I will." He was hoping Sandi was right because he just entered into a war zone. Wynne was going to make it hard on him.

"Walk with me, Kwame. Your office is a bit away from here. I'll tell you more about Sheila as we walk."

As they walked and talked, Sandi impressed Kwame. Her pleasant demeanor was helping him to calm down. He looked forward to picking her brain for suggestions to win over Wynne. For now, she was giving him a quick rundown of his assistant.

"Sheila is great. She's intelligent and trustworthy. She knows her way around this building as well as anyone. You should know that Donald Alexander personally selected her as your assistant."

"I did not know that, but it's great to hear Sandi. She sounds like a star."

"She is. Sheila's as good as they come around here. I have a lot of respect for her."

The walk was long. So long that when they arrived Kwame realized that they were on the opposite side of the floor. It was as physically far away from Wynne Shields' office as possible. He wondered if this was Wynne's doing or Donald's. When they arrived, Sheila Duncan was waiting for them. She was a curvy figured African-American woman, attractive and a bit older. Kwame guessed her to be in her early 50's. She had a warm smile that glowed brightly.

"Hello Mr. Mills, it's nice to meet you."

She stuck her hand out for a handshake. Kwame reciprocated and found her hands soft and warm, her voice comforting. He instantly liked her warmth and took it as a good signal. She seemed like an aunt or an older sister.

"No, Mr. Stuff, please don't do that Sheila, it's Kwame. It's nice to meet you too."

Sandi Williams interrupted their introduction to say that she had to get back to her desk.

"Now that I've introduced you two, I've got to get back to my side of the floor. Sheila, I'll talk to you later."

"Thank you Sandi for escorting me. I appreciate you taking the time."

Kwame's mind began to race. He thought again that he needed to stay close to Sandi and get advice on how to best work with Wynne. He'd do that after he returned from the road trip to visit the sales offices.

She smiled warmly and said, "It was my pleasure Kwame, welcome to the company, and I wish you all the luck."

"I'll ring you later Sandi," Sheila said as Sandi walked back to her side of the building. She then turned her attention to her new boss.

"Follow me Kwame," Sheila said as she opened the door to a large office. "Let me give you a tour of your office. As you can see, it's a big space. So that you know the dimensions are 11 x 14, and this is the standard size office for all of our sales heads. It's also filled with furnishings from your predecessor."

The contents were a Cherry wood wall unit, a large-screen television, and stereo. In the center of the room was a large Cherry desk. A ten-foot-long burgundy leather sofa completed the furnishings of this space.

Kwame was impressed. As he looked things over, he felt that they were quite suitable, if not a bit extravagant. But then, he remembered that he was now at Harris Simmons, and this was the big time.

"You have a budget, Kwame for office furnishings. If this furniture is not to your liking, we can outfit this office any way you'd like."

DARIUS MYERS

"Is that right? That's a bit excessive, isn't it Sheila?"

"That's how we do things around here Kwame. The company is doing great, and we pamper our top executives. We can outfit this office any way that you'd like."

Kwame began to daydream and compare Harris Simmons to NewsInc. At Harris Simmons, he had an office furnishing budget and a large office, at NewsInc he had a desk in an open floor.

The NewsInc people were told that open flooring seating where no one had privacy is the 21st century workplace, Kwame wasn't a buyer. He knew that there were countless hours lost to all the distractions in a loud workplace. He knew his production was tied to a quiet office and relieved that he didn't have to reserve a conference room anymore to have some quiet time during his day.

He then examined the furnishings and what else he might like. He walked over to the leather sofa, sat down, looked once more over the room, and with a nod of approval, said, "Sheila, I like all this just fine. But I would add just one piece."

"What is that Kwame? Anything you want, remember you have a budget."

"I want a small circular conference table and chairs that would accommodate four people. When I have meetings in my office, I like to sit around people as opposed to across from them."

"I'll order it today. Can I help you with anything else?"

"Well Sheila. It's my understanding that you were picked to be my right hand."

"That's correct, Kwame."

"Why do you think that this is so?"

The directness of his comment seemed to catch Sheila off guard.

Sheila was standing in the doorway of Kwame's office. She stepped

120

inside and shut the door.

"I'm here because I can help you maneuver through this monolith. Harris Simmons is a very bureaucratic organization, and you need someone who knows their way around. Otherwise, you'll never get anything done."

"I'm sure I'll need your help with that. Is there any other reason?"

"Well, then there's Wynne. I can help you run a buffer between him. I want you to be a success. That's why I think I was selected."

Sheila Duncan did not tell Kwame everything. She had a deep resentment for Wynne Shields and hated his sense of entitlement. She didn't share that with Kwame, but she wanted to be in his corner and help in a fight she knew was inevitable.

After the office tour and chat, Kwame realized that he needed to call Michelle Nubani. He needed to see if she could fly to New York for the weekend party at Donald Alexander's Southampton house. He interrupted Sheila, who had now started giving him the rundown on the sales staffers at World Media.

"Oh, excuse me. I'm sorry, I've got to make a phone call. Can you excuse me for a few minutes?"

"No problem. I'll be outside at my desk when you need me."
She quickly gathered her files and left the room. Kwame felt good vibes from Sheila and was confident that they would build a trusting relationship and work well together.

He sat behind his new desk and called Michelle at her office. She picked up the phone on its second ring.

"Professor Michelle Nubani, how can I help you?"

Hearing her voice made him smile, "Hi sweetheart, it's Kwame."

He could hear her voice rise with excitement, "Hi Baby. How are you? How'd it go?"

"Great, really great. Donald Alexander is a fantastic guy, and I think

I'll be able to handle Wynne." He decided not to share with her just how difficult their meeting was.

"That's good. When are you coming home? I miss you. We still have to celebrate."

"Well, I don't know. I'm calling to see if you can come to New York for the weekend."

"New York, this weekend? What's up? Is this a romantic interlude?"

"Well, not exactly. But that's a great idea. We can certainly make it one."

"You know I'm all for romance Kwame and spending time with you Baby, but I suspect that's not what this is. What do you have in mind?"

"Well, honey, Donald Alexander is having this big party at his home in the Hamptons this weekend, and he invited us out."

Kwame knew from his research on Donald Alexander that he recently bought the estate belonging to the late oil tycoon, Clarke Dryden.

"It's a must-do thing for me, and he would like for you to come out as well. We will stay there for the weekend."

"Well," Michelle began, "I've got a lot of work due. I don't know. Is this important to you?"

"Yes, but listen," he didn't want to force her to attend, "if you're under the gun, I understand."

She interrupted him, "No, I'll be there. I know this is important for you, and I want to be with my man. I can't have you out there by yourself. Some fancy Hampton chick might try to steal you from me."

"That ain't happening Michelle, not a chance. I'm smitten."

"You're so sweet Kwame, and I'm smitten too," she said. The decision made her curious about the party. "So, baby, is this going to be one of those beautiful people Hampton parties?"

"I don't know but probably so. Don Alexander is pretty cool, and he is rich, so I'd be shocked if it wasn't. I promised Donald that I would do my best to make it."

"Fine baby, it's not a problem. I'll rearrange a few things and make it work. I know this will be fun. You know, I've never been to the Hamptons, and I'm going with you. I'm excited now."

"Well, this party will be a fantastic first visit. Thank you so much Michelle."

They spent the next couple of minutes making plans. Kwame would return to Chicago that evening, and they would fly into New York together on Saturday morning and drive out to the Hamptons together.

When he hung up the phone, he couldn't help but be excited. Everything seemed to be going his way. Donald Alexander was a great guy. He got through his first meeting with Wynne Shields with a few body blows but otherwise reasonably unscathed. Sheila, his new secretary, was great, and the new love of his life, Michelle Nubani, was making accommodations for him. He thought a moment about his ex-wife, Carrie Sinclair, at the end of their marriage, accommodating was something she rarely, if ever, was.

"Things are all right," he said out loud. "Life ain't that bad."

Chapter Thirteen

Kwame and Michelle's early morning plane ride from Chicago was enjoyable. The plane was nearly empty on their Saturday morning, 7:00 am flight. They landed at 10:00 am, and Kwame rented a convertible. It was fancy enough to fit in with the pretentious Hamptons crowd.

The weather was perfect. It was a warm and sunny day, and riding out east for two hours in a convertible with the sun and breeze in their faces got them in the mood for the weekend. On the ride, Michelle found an article in Design & Style Magazine about Donald Alexander's Hampton's Home.

"Kwame, this place is amazing. I have to read this paragraph to you. It says, 'The Dryden Estate is an incredible piece of architecture. It is set on three acres of land, on the Hamptons exclusive North Fork. A ten-foot brick wall surrounds the compound. The main gate opens up to a massive front yard of manicured lawns and gardens that also features an eclectic collection of statues and yard ornaments, the most impressive being a bronze-colored family crest embedded into the lawn as the centerpiece of the front lawn and gardens. The house is equally impressive. It is a restyled 10,000-square-foot center hall Colonial mansion.'"

"Well, all right then. I guess Donald Alexander is showing us why he's the big baller and shot caller."

"Indeed, I'm even more excited now. I can't wait to see this place," Michelle said and smiled. She then reached over and squeezed his arm and said, "My baby is taking me to a party with the big ballers and shot callers. Hamptons, here we come." They both laughed and enjoyed the remainder of the drive out.

The traffic was light, and they made the usual two-hour trek from the airport in just a little more than an hour and a half.

As they pulled into the Dryden Compound, Kwame's and Michelle's jaws dropped.

"Wow. Come on now. This place is something else," Kwame said. "I thought the article was over the top, but it did not do it justice."

"I agree," Michelle said. "This place is amazing."

Kwame drove the car slowly as they did an inventory of all the notable statues and yard ornaments featured in the article.

"It's like a museum Kwame," Michelle said in awe.

THE PUBLISHER'S DILEMMA

"A museum for the uber-rich, I'd say, Michelle."

They pulled up to a reception area in the huge circular driveway. As soon as Kwame put the vehicle in park, a valet appeared.

"I'll take your belongings and park your car," said a young blond-haired man dressed in a white shirt, blue bow tie, and brown khakis. He then pointed to the houses main entrance and said, "You can walk to the front of the house and ZyZy will take care of you."

"Okay, nice touch, first-class valet service," Kwame said as he handed over the keys. "Our bags are in the trunk."

He looked over to Michelle, who smiled and said, "I could like this life."

They then walked 30 yards across the lawn from the car to the front entrance. "So, this is what you can do selling advertising? Look Kwame," Michelle said as she admired the busy sea of workers, "the valet bit was very cool, but look at all these people working at this party. Donald Alexander has got servants."

She was right the cadre of attendants, waiters, and waitresses on the grounds was impressive. They were all beautiful, hip, fit, young, and busily serving the guests.

At the entrance, a tall, dark, modelesque African-American woman greeted them. She was wearing a white tight-fitting linen dress and holding a clipboard. "Good afternoon, thank you for joining us. Can I get your name, please?"

"Good afternoon. I'm Kwame Mills, and I'm with Michelle Nubani."

"Welcome to the Dryden Compound, Mr. Mills and Ms. Nubani," the woman said. "We should be calling it the Alexander Estate, but Mr. Alexander does not seem to care about such details. My name is ZyZy, and I will be helping you with any of your needs for this weekend."

"Thank you ZyZy, we are excited to be here."

DARIUS MYERS

He looked at Michelle. She was now gawking at the interior of this gigantic house. She could see that it was lively and festive and filled with happy party attendees.

ZyZy then explained the activities and the layout of the home. "Mr. Mills, most of the guests have arrived for brunch and are now enjoying cocktails and conversation. If you walk straight through, you'll get to the rear of the house. There you'll find the backyard grounds and garden, and also an Olympic size swimming pool. Beyond the pool, the grounds open up to a private beach. It is a fantastic property."

"Indeed, it is ZyZy," Kwame said. The house had massive floor to ceiling windows in the rear that made it easy for Kwame and Michelle to look through all the way to the private beach.

They could see that some of the guests had already donned their bathing suits. He was excited about the energy, glamour and ready to join the fun. "These people seem to be having a good time," he said to ZyZy and Michelle.

"Yes, they are," ZyZy said. "We have a bedroom for you two for the weekend, so you are all set. Now you two go join the fun."

Kwame grabbed Michelle, who still appeared to be a bit overwhelmed by her hand, "Good idea. Come on honey."

For the next couple of minutes, they walked around the house, taking in the art and other interior furnishings. A young male waiter came by with drinks, and they helped themselves to glasses of red wine from a local winery. As they tipped their glasses in a toast, Kwame heard his name.

"Kwame, Kwame," the voice was coming from the top of the circular stairway, it was Donald Alexander.

He looked up to see Donald smiling and decked out in white linen slacks and a blue linen shirt. He rushed down the stairs and gave Kwame a hearty handshake.

THE PUBLISHER'S DILEMMA

"Good to see you Kwame. I'm so glad that you could make it. What a great day for a party, huh?"

"Oh man Donald, do you know how to pick them. It is a great day for a party at such a wonderful place. I have to tell you I am awestruck. What a house."

"Awestruck, that's a proper term for this place, I admit to being awestruck by it too. It makes me pinch myself. It's a long way from my days as a kid in Cleveland."

"You're doing Cleveland and the rest of us proud Donald," Kwame said.

Michelle was standing behind Kwame. She nudged him, and then she stepped forward to stand by his side. Donald saw her, smiled, and said, "Is this lovely lady your girlfriend, Kwame?"

Kwame put his arm around Michelle and pulled her close, and said, "Yes, Donald, this is Michelle Nubani, my lovely girlfriend."

Michelle then said, "Hi Donald, it's a real pleasure to meet you. Kwame says nothing but great things about you. Thank you for having us here this weekend. This place is beautiful."

"That's a high compliment coming from Kwame, I'm a big fan of his and thrilled that he's coming on board with us at Harris Simmons. And it's nice to meet you too, Michelle. Thank you for coming out. I am delighted to have you both here this weekend."

Donald then snapped his fingers as he remembered something important. "Hold on. I want to introduce you both to my date for the weekend." He turned around and scanned the room "Oh, there she is. Let me introduce you guys. Carrie." Donald yelled across the room.

Kwame's heart sunk upon hearing this name, and when Carrie turned around and saw her ex-husband, so did hers. Kwame almost dropped his drink. Michelle Nubani, who knew enough about her boyfriend's ex-wife and he had seen photographs of her, did drop her drink. Her glass of red wine splattered all over Donald's white linen pants.

"Oh my God, oh my God," Michelle yelled. "I am so sorry. I am such a klutz. I've ruined those gorgeous pants."

Amongst the chaos of a dropped glass of red wine, a room full of people, Michelle Nubani seeing Carrie Sinclair for the first-time, Kwame's first thought was, "This world is too damn small."

Donald Alexander, now with his pants soiled, sensed an immediate tension and wondered too if this was just an overreaction or something more sordid. He chose to let the moment pass and to find out later. Besides, his pants were soiled and ruined by the red wine from Michelle Nubani's dropped glass.

A waiter quickly moved in to clean up the mess and Michelle, still stunned, continued to beg for forgiveness. "Donald, I apologize. I can't believe I did that and my goodness, look at your pants."

She was overcome with embarrassment and grabbed Kwame and held on to him tightly. Then hoping to help out, she snatched a napkin from the waiter, knelt down, grabbed Donald's pants leg, and began dabbing at the wine stains.

"Here, let me try and get this stain out, maybe if we can dab some of the wine out, we can save these pants." She then asks the waiter, cleaning up the mess, "Do you think you can get me some club soda? That might help."

Donald, Kwame, and Carrie, who had now entered their space, smiled nervously. Donald was not yet in on the secret.

"Michelle, Michelle?" Donald said as she kept dabbing at the stained pants.

Kwame tapped on her shoulder, "Michelle, Michelle stop, honey, stand up, please?"

THE PUBLISHER'S DILEMMA

Finally, she stopped and stood up, flustered, and still embarrassed.

"I'm so sorry Donald. Those were such a nice pair of pants. Send me the bill for them please, I doubt if the stains will ever come out."

"Please Michelle, if this is the worst thing that ever happens to me, I'll have lived a grand life. Besides, I hated these pants anyhow. They fit kind of funny. I was going to throw them away."

Donald attempted to make light out of this embarrassing moment. He was more concerned about his new Head of Sales and making him happy. So, what if he had a $500-custom pair of linen slacks destroyed.

Carrie Sinclair then walked up to her ex-husband and kissed him on the cheek. She looked him in the eye and said, "Hi Kwame."

Donald was startled by this gesture and thought to himself, "Now, how do they know each other?"

"Hello Carrie," Kwame said. He reached for Michelle's hand. It was now his turn to be flustered. Michelle grabbed his hand and sidled up close to him. Having her close at this moment relieved him.

As he calmed down, he introduced them, "Michelle, this is Carrie Sinclair, my ex-wife."

A stunned Donald Alexander then dropped his glass of red wine. The waiter who had just finished cleaning up the first mess was walking away. Upon hearing the crash of another wine glass, he sighed and turned around.

Donald, with a sheepish, embarrassed look on his face, turned to Michelle and said, "Now you're truly forgiven."

Part Two

Chapter Fourteen

"What a beautiful morning, look at those clear skies, this is a picture-perfect summer day," Kwame said to himself as he walked to work on July 9th.

"Business is great, and there are a lot of smiles at Harris Simmons nowadays. I couldn't have picked a better time to join, even with crazy-ass Wynne Shields as my boss."

Kwame was right. Under the leadership of Gill Harris and Donald Alexander, Harris Simmons's recent success had been nothing short of spectacular. Everybody was happy, except for his boss.

"We've got 15 world-class digital media brands and all but one, mine, are extremely profitable and successful. And editorially, we're killing it too."

While the properties were cash cows, breaking records for revenue generation, he was also referring to the editorial hot streak. Last year Harris Simmons titles won six Grand Reporter Prizes for outstanding editorial.

Kwame began to think about Gill Harris, Donald Alexander, and Wynne Shields. This morning they were holding their bi-annual managers meeting with the Publisher's and CFO's of their 15 properties.

He wasn't invited to the meeting as he wasn't high enough on the food chain. Only the Publishers and CFOs attended these meetings, he was the number four business executive behind the general manager and not invited. Wynne's potential performance, however, concerned him. He talked about it the night before with Michelle Nubani.

DARIUS MYERS

"I hope Wynne doesn't act out. He needs to be more respectful and work through the tension he's having with Don and Gill. Otherwise, he will regret ever stepping into that Conference room."

"We're not making any money, and every other property is killing it. At these meetings, all Gill and Donald want to hear is good news. You can get chopped up bad if you come in with excuses."

"He's a grown man Kwame, and he needs to start acting like one," Michelle said. "You know I'm not a fan. My only concern is you."

"You're right honey. Steve Ryan shared with me how these meetings go down. It's pretty intense. He said the executives always arrived early in an attempt to grab a seat on the side of the room facing Central Park. These are the room's best seats. Except for the two seats reserved at the head of the table for Gill and Donald, seating is first-come, first-serve. If you show up right before the meeting starts, all the good seats are gone. It's also a sign that you are one of the last to arrive. You'd better have an outstanding report if you are one of the last to arrive."

"That does sound like an intimidating setting, Kwame."

"I know Michelle, and it's even intense to Donald. During my interview, he talked about how Gill uses the view for head games."

"He said when Gill Harris is in a sour mood, that he closes the blinds, and turns the bright and dramatic visual landscape into a dark and intimidating den of doom. Donald said he is a master of head games."

Kwame's instincts about today were right. Only one Publisher needed to be concerned with Gill, and it was his boss, Wynne Shields. As the senior executives entered the 39th-floor conference room, they saw that the blinds were open. The room was brightly lit with reflections from the sun jumping off the mahogany-paneled walls. Each executive breathed a sigh of relief when they entered the room and saw the pulled-back shades.

Gill Harris and Donald Alexander were thrilled. Donald Alexander started the meeting by reading the highlights of the first half performance to the executives.

"Good morning, ladies and gentlemen. Thank you all for joining us here this morning and getting here on time. Our performance has been great for the first half of the year. Let me share some highlights and give some props to a couple of our star performers and their properties. There are two in particular, and they are Tennis Week and Gourmet Life. These properties are reporting 35% increases in revenue. The fabulous Deirdre Francis leads Tennis Week and the equally amazing Sheri McCready runs Gourmet Life, our Home Cooking magazine. They are also our only two female Publishers at Harris Simmons."

Donald Alexander continued to heap praise on his female publishers and their performance, "I want to single you ladies out and give you some love and a well-deserved moment. I want you both to know that you continue as Gill and my personal favorites. We are so proud of you both, and thank you for your outstanding leadership here at HS."

Alexander then asked everyone in the room to stand up and give them a round of applause. This request received tepid approval. Francis and McCready were competition to the 13 male executives and they all knew it.

"Please stand up everybody and join me in a standing ovation for our rock-star ladies."

As Gill and Donald stood up and applauded their success, their peers rose reluctantly and clapped in feigned approval. McCready and Francis smiled graciously.

Gill didn't like the feigned approval. He used the opportunity to deliver a challenge to the remaining Publishers, criticizing them as slackers and threatening some drastic changes if they could not catch up to the performance of his superstar women.

DARIUS MYERS

"Look guys, let me make one thing clear. Francis and McCready are raising the bar here. They've been complaining that there is too much testosterone around this company. Donald and I happen to agree with them, so all I will say is that some of you guys better start looking over your shoulders, because they've got friends lining up at the door. So, step up and be on the lookout, identify and start hiring the next McCready and Francis for your team. We're always on the lookout for great talent, and so we must do better than hiring guys from your fraternity or country club."

The 13 men squirmed in their seats uneasily and scribbled notes to identify new female staffers. Gill and Donald could expect to see some new female senior talent at the Old Boys Club of Harris Simmons soon. These comments were one of two tense moments during the meeting.

There was no real bad news. All of the Presidents and CFO's, except for Wynne Shields, forecasted second half of the year results that would make this the best year ever for Harris Simmons.

Wynne Shields was 42 years old, four years older than Donald Alexander, and 12 years younger than Gill.

He kept a perpetual tan that, on this day, was glowing and showing off his long wavy, sun-bleached blonde hair that was brushed back off his forehead. He sat on the far end of the conference room table, in the last seat, on the wrong side of the room. The side of the room that faced the wall and indicated that he was the last executive to arrive.

"Look at him. Look at how he's dressed," Gill whispered to Donald. "See how he's seated. His back straight, chin erect, with the regal Mayflower descendant look. He's got the look all right, dark blue Saville Row double-breasted suit accented by a white shirt and red silk tie. The white handkerchief neatly folded into his suit jacket's top pocket."

"Yeah, he's got that corporate uniform stuff down for sure," Donald whispered back.

THE PUBLISHER'S DILEMMA

"But, he's the last to arrive, as always. I bet you he just got to the office."

Gill was right. Wynne arrived just moments before the meeting's start. He had only made it to the main lobby of Harris Simmons at 8:00 am. To get the meeting on time, he took the private elevator, which was off-limits to everyone except Gill, Donald, and the support staff of the 39th floor. But that was Wynne Shields. He lived by his own set of rules.

When it was time for him to make his report, he slowly stood up, buttoned his suit jacket, brushed with his hands his blonde locks backward, and cleared his throat.

"I am expecting World's second-half performance to remain flat from the year before. My first-half performance was also flat, but I am confident that we will not lose money for the year."

He then cited his usual reasons for poor performance. "As a newsweekly, World Media is in a tough category with a legendary set of competitors including the Daily News Weekly, The National News Report, and The Weekly News Review. Gill and Donald, you know that we are flat because of this stiff competition."

He then sat down and looked away from Donald and Gill and leaned back in his chair. His posture projected a confidence and certainty that his report or its veracity would not be questioned. Today it was not so.

After Wynne presented his lousy news, Gill decided to flog him publicly. He ignored Wynne's flat performance report and focused instead on Kwame Mills.

"How's Kwame Mills doing?" and before waiting for a response added, "The word on the street is that he's a stud, and he's going to help you get your property back on track. It's time we start seeing some profits. What has it been two years now that you haven't made any money?"

He then looked at Wynne with an intense, penetrating stare. This was not going to go well and he knew it. He expected a smack down because of his poor performance. He hadn't forgotten the beat down of a few months back when Gill told him that Donald Alexander would hire his new head of sales that turned out to be Kwame Mills. He also hoped that with all the other good news he'd be spared Gill's wrath. Today was not that day.

Nervously, Wynne sat down and began to shuffle his papers and squirm in his seat. He then looked through a stack of neatly piled folders in front of him as if the answer was in a file. He knew Gill Harris was right.

Gill turned to Donald Alexander and said, "Isn't that right, Donald? Wynne has built a record of failure around here."

Donald didn't comment. He just nodded affirmatively to the question. The room was silent; the other executives had their heads down and were scribbling away once again. They didn't want to be in harm's way as it was gut-wrenching and humiliating to be flogged publicly by Gill Harris. Even Francis and McCready had their heads down. He was now ripping Wynne Shields a new butt hole in front of everyone.

Wynne's expression was blank, but his response was what Gill and Donald expected from the wounded, but always arrogant and defiant tyrant. He had to respond, and he did so by instinct. He straightened up in his chair and spoke, his voice and his words loud and clear.

"I'm still breaking in Kwame Mills, and it will probably take a couple of more months. Mills is taking a little longer to catch on than initially thought."

After this response, Gill Harris looked hard at him again with that same penetrating stare.

"Wynne, that is not the answer I expect. Have we not gone through this already? In case you've forgotten, let me reiterate my demand of you. I expect Kwame Mills to succeed, and you better start making some money around here. Your playtime with my money is over."

THE PUBLISHER'S DILEMMA

He then looked away from Wynne, he wanted to end this dismissively and to send a message that would be both humiliating and clear. He said loudly, "I'm done with this guy, who's next to report?"

It was a stinging rebuke and wounded Wynne in front of his peers. It was a public beating that was a long time coming and for company morale needed to happen. Everyone knew that Wynne got away with bad performance and behavior. The executives were all pleased to witness him get smacked hard by Gill.

When the next executive, Clark Winchester, stood up and prepared to speak, Gill leaned back in his chair and closed his eyes. A grim scowl crossed his face. He leaned back further, looked to the ceiling, and started rubbing his temples. And then he said loud enough for everyone to hear, "God help that fool."

It was a final comment that summarized his frustration with Wynne Shields.

Gill then scribbled a note and passed it on to Donald. "We better keep an eye on Kwame, he may open a can of whup-ass on Wynne."

Donald wrote back, "I don't know if he could do better than you just did, but if he does, it might be good for morale."

Gill Harris laughed out loud, he was at his wits end with Wynne Shields, and the laugh eased his anger and frustration. This laughter interrupted the presentation of Clark Winchester, the Publisher of Celebrity Profiles, Harris Simmons's weekly gossip media property.

Covering his smile, Gill excused himself to Winchester. "Sorry, Clark." Winchester was in the middle of a long, boring monologue about the evolution of the gossip category. Neither Gill nor Donald wanted to hear it. All they wanted to know today was the numbers.

Gill interrupted him, "Clark, Clark, Clark. We get it, Man. We know you are on top of your business. Today is a beautiful day. Look outside and tell me it isn't beautiful out there. It's gorgeous out there, isn't it Clark?"

"Best day this summer, not one day better Gill," Winchester answered.

"Then tell me some good news that makes this beautiful day even better. You got any good news for me? Make me happy, my man, make me happy, my friend."

Winchester smiled back. He didn't want to do a boring presentation either. He closed the book, threw his shoulders back, and flashed a big smile. Gill and Donald looked at each other and smiled. They knew Winchester was such a tight ass that they enjoyed his happy face.

Gill said, "Well, let's have it Champ. What you got?"

Winchester began, "Gill and Donald, we're up 25% over the first half of last year, and our contracts are real solid for the second half of the year. I am confident we are going to finish this year up 25%. Frankly, Sirs, we are kicking ass. My team is on fire, and I couldn't be prouder of them."

Gill nodded his head and gave him big thumbs up. "Nice work Winchester. Way to go."

The meeting continued with more bragging from the executives who, like Clark Winchester, felt compelled to use these sessions as opportunities to boast and suck up to Gill and Donald. They smiled, applauded and cheered through the remainder of the meeting.

After the last report, Gill Harris addressed the group.

"Ladies and gentlemen, let me say I am ecstatic with the success of the first half and strong projections for the remainder of the year. As you all know, it has been five years since I took over from my Uncle Cornwall. You guys are all doing fantastic work and have made these five years the best years in the company's history. I thank you for your great work and look forward to many more great years ahead."

Cornwall Harris retired at the company's mandatory retirement age of

THE PUBLISHER'S DILEMMA

65. Harris Simmons was a family-owned, private company, and Cornwall Harris wasn't bound by any legal or corporate governance statutes to retire. He could have fought the company bylaws and not retired.

However, Cornwall's older brother and predecessor as CEO, Gill's father, Oliver Harris, Jr., both felt Gill was ready to assume control. When it came time for Oliver, Jr. to make way for Cornwall, he did so with hesitation. To keep the family peace, Cornwall Harris stepped down.

Before concluding the meeting, Gill provided a company financial report to the executives.

"Again, thanks to your great work, we have a AAA credit rating and cash in reserve of $50 million. We keep this amount kept liquid for operations and emergencies. Organizationally we now have a bit more than 2000 employees, which represents a 10% growth over the last year. Harris Simmons is a great place to work, and we want it to continue to be so. We need you guys to continue doing what you do and making this an awesome workplace."

To keep the peace in the family, Gill had to make sure that Harris Simmons performed well enough to meet the annual projected revenue number necessary to pay off his Father and Uncle, the two primary shareholders of the company. As both were former CEO's, they knew that the company was a cash cow and had grown accustomed to the astronomical amounts of cash that the company generated annually.

He once complained to Donald Alexander about his Dad's and Uncle's expectations for their annual payouts.

"These guys are filthy rich, they have more money than they'll ever need but are just unrelenting when it came to their end-of-the-year shareholders payoffs. The good news is that they don't interfere, except for when it's time to get their money. I tell my Dad all the time that you and my Uncle are like old-school pimps. All you say at partnership payoff time is where is my money? No excuses, just where is my money?"

"But you have done well by them," Donald said. "They have to be happy with you. They have nothing to complain about."

"Yes Donald, I have done well by them, with a lot of help from you, and I should not complain. My role now is more comparable to that of an investment manager for the Harris clan. My success as the leader of the family company provides them with the necessary cash that they could use for their pet projects."

"Well aside from their demands, it's a pretty good job to have Gill. Your family has built a great company, and these guys are pretty harmless. They leave us alone to run this thing."

"Thank you for saying so Donald. Again, I should never complain. I guess in the heat of the moment, these people and their pet projects can be a bit much. And as you know, some of these things don't make any sense. Like Fruit Fly migration. Who even cares about such things?"

Oliver Harris, Jr., pledged a scientist $5 million over five years for a study to follow the journey of fruit flies from Alaska to the continental United States. It became Gill's job to make sure the research was supported.

Gill and Donald laughed hard the day he told him about the fruit fly research.

"Let me tell you what you are working for now. Fruit flies, freaking Alaskan fruit flies. Wouldn't a fruit fly die in the artic? Is this crap even real? My Dad has lost his blasted mind. Please shoot me if I ever start to think like that. Free me from my agony."

If Gill made his number, everyone was happy. If he did poorly, there was hell to pay. The retired Harris people never used their private accounts to support their ventures, their civic and social investments were always funded from their annual company payouts. Gill Harris lived under an immense amount of pressure to keep the family happy. While the last five years had been great, over the previous two years, Harris Simmons had been making record numbers, as it recorded net profits of 145% of its forecasted corporate goal. For now, Gill had no problems with the family.

For Donald Alexander, who for the last three years, ran the day-to-day operations of the company, this performance made him a star. The Harris family loved him, and he had grown in admiration by his subordinates at Harris Simmons. The business press also adored him. Even though Harris Simmons was a private company, Wall Street media analysts, competitive media companies, and the business press had watched Donald Alexander closely since he became the number two at Harris Simmons.

As the African-American president of a high-profile company that generated nearly $800 million in net revenues annually, his notoriety had grown to the point that whenever there was a CEO search for a leading company, his name began to show up on the shortlist of top candidates. His success was undeniable inside the halls of Harris Simmons and to the outside business world. Donald Alexander made Gill Harris and his family a lot of money, and in turn, they made him rich, famous, and a hot commodity.

Gill Harris was also the last of the family leaders of Harris Simmons. There were no other Harris descendants in line to lead Harris Simmons. Upon his retirement, Gill faced the unenviable challenge of naming the first non-Harris family member, CEO of Harris Simmons.

That decision had already been made for some time now. Gill knew that Donald Alexander was his likely replacement, and he reminded him of this fact three months earlier during the Kwame Mills hiring. Alexander was now putting his stamp on the company, and Gill was firmly in his corner.

"You've made me proud, and I look forward to you being the first non-Harris CEO of this company."

All the talk of the succession plan to have an African-American become the CEO of the world's largest Media company was years away as Gill was only 54, and the retirement age at Harris Simmons was 65. For Donald Alexander, this was fine. He was in no rush. He was just 38 and enjoyed having Gill around. They got along exceptionally well, and he was still was learning a lot from Gill Harris.

Chapter Fifteen

For the Celebrity Hack Patrol, July 9th started as a light news day. Luke McFlemming was whining and complaining. He was also talking to himself because the other reporters weren't interested in listening to him complain.

"Man, it looks as if all I am going to get this day is a caffeine buzz from bad coffee and a few dollars of winnings from this afternoon's game of poker."

The Celebrity Hack Patrol typically hung out in the parking lot of City Hospital on most days waiting for a celebrity admittance, drug overdose, or some newsworthy gossip story. Today had been very quiet until the police radio went bonkers.

Luke McFlemming, the star reporter from the News, kept a police radio in his car, as did his key competition, Mike Desanctis of the City Post. They were bitter rivals. Each always battled for front-page dominance and star reporter distinction in New York press circles. They both heard over their police radios, "Gunshot victim being brought in to City Hospital is an

THE PUBLISHER'S DILEMMA

executive at Harris Simmons Publications. He is critically wounded."

McFlemming and Desanctis didn't know how big this story would be, but it beat an otherwise empty day. Neither had any significant story set for deadline, which was just four hours away.

When the tall and gangly McFlemming and the stocky, barrel-chested Desanctis ran to the emergency room entrance, their colleagues knew something was up. Like an Army troop, the others snapped quickly into formation. The card games ended, and coffee cups got tossed to the ground. A chaotic rush ensued by the remaining New York Press to the emergency room entrance.

Minutes later the ambulance arrived and the victim is unloaded to the flashing lights and the flicking sounds of cellphones and digital cameras by the Celebrity Hack patrol. McFlemming, Desanctis, and the other press are yelling questions as the paramedics moved the victim.

"Who is this guy?" McFlemming hollered.

"What happened, is he going to live?" Desanctis yelled.

The other press Hacks from the smaller papers joined in, screaming questions. Paramedics Johnson and Lucas and the half-dozen hospital police had now come to form a protective wall around the ER entrance. Johnson and Lucas did not respond to their calls.

The barrier was so thick that the media was unable to get a clean look at the victim.

"Who was on that stretcher Luke?" Jennifer Kung of the Ledger asked McFlemming. "You had the best position to see the victim. Did you recognize him or her? I couldn't see anything."

Kung was a stunning Asian beauty in her mid-30s. She stood at five feet six with a flawless complexion, a thin athletic build, a radiant smile, and large brown eyes. The press hacks loved Kung because she was one of the guys, despite being a knockout beauty with a dynamite personality. She drank bourbon, talked trash, and was smart as a whip. Kung graduated Magna Cum Laude from Harlowe, had a black belt in Jiu-Jitsu, and didn't take any crap from anyone. They also envied her because she got a lot of stories because she was so gorgeous, and it opened doors for her with both men and women.

"All I could see was that he was an African-American male, TV."

McFlemming started calling Kung by the nickname of TV because he felt she should be a TV personality with her movie-star looks. Kung, on the other hand, liked the rough-and-tumble world and the notoriety of being part of the Celebrity Hack patrol.

"Do you know where they came from?" she asked.

"Harris Simmons Publications, I think. All I caught on my radio was that there was a shooting at the Harris Simmons executive offices."

"My God. Isn't Donald Alexander, the president of Harris Simmons, African-American? Guys, he's on the list me and my girls keep of Top-10 hot New York Celebrity Crushes. Donald Alexander is Number 2 on my list. Number 1 on my list is the actor JoJo Littlejohn."

"Wait, hold up, aren't both of these guys black?" Desanctis asked.

"Yeah, so what? They are hot, that's all that matters."

McFlemming ignored the Top 10 list talk. He focused instead on the shooting, "If he is indeed the victim, we have a huge story."

"I met him a couple of months back at a charity event. He's a great guy, and oh my God. He is gorgeous and sexy," Kung said.

"I wouldn't know about the, 'Oh my God, he's gorgeous, and he's sexy stuff.'" McFlemming said. "But I do know that everyone says that he is a cool guy. Let's hope that's not him because if it's so, that might be the lead for his obituary tomorrow."

McFlemming continued, "Well, not in my paper. I could see your paper running with that crappy headline. 'Great Guy and Oh My God, He Is

THE PUBLISHER'S DILEMMA

Gorgeous and Sexy.' We're a serious newspaper. We don't roll like that."

Kung smirked at McFlemming and said, "Shut up stupid. And you really shouldn't talk. You guys probably would write, 'Boy Pulls Girls Hair,' because most of your readers are third-graders anyhow."

"Ouch, ouch. Is that your best shot TV? I bet you were a mean girl in high school."

"Whatever Luke, I bet you were a punk. I probably would have taken your lunch money."

"Shut up TV."

"No, you, shut up, Luke."

Suddenly their trash talking was interrupted. A black chauffeured car pulls up to the emergency room entrance. A well-dressed, handsome, and distraught-looking black man slipped out and walked briskly with his head down into the emergency room. Luke McFlemming, Mike Desanctis, Jennifer Kung, and the rest of the Celebrity Hack patrol tried to get his attention.

Kung yelled, "Hey, who are you? Stop? Sir, stop please."

McFlemming attempted as well, "Hey Man, can you stop and tell us what is going on? Was somebody shot?"

Desanctis chimed in, "Do you work at Harris Simmons? What happened there?"

Ignoring them all, he heads inside. Seconds later, a police cruiser pulls up behind the chauffeured sedan, and two male police officers get out and hurriedly head into the Emergency Room. McFlemming and Desanctis were able to take a couple of shots of the African-American man with their pro-quality digital cameras. Kung didn't have her camera with her. She snapped a photo with her phone, but it was second-grade compared to the high-quality cameras of her peers. If this was a big story, she knew this would be a problem.

"Who was he?" Kung asked McFlemming as they all looked into the frames of Desanctis's digital camera. "I don't recognize him at all."

Jennifer Kung smiled in appreciation of the clean-cut and handsome appearance of the African-American man. "Guys, he's hot too. Maybe I should get a job over at Harris Simmons. The eye candy is much better than hanging out with you two bums."

McFlemming and Desanctis both smirked at Kung, "Did she just call us ugly?"

She smiled at her Hack Partners and continued with the smack-talking, "That's what I said. What are you going to do about it?"

Mike Desanctis just turned to Jennifer Kung, "You meant to bring your camera this morning, right?"

"Ah man, Mike you wouldn't? Come on guys, don't do that."

On most days, they looked out for each other. If the story was small enough, they shared photos and additional information. This story was already shaping up to be significant. Kung's fascination with hot-looking black men and jokes about her not-so-hot colleagues had eliminated any chance she had for shared photos this day. But that didn't stop her from begging.

"Come on, guys, hook a girlfriend up?"

"Sorry Sista," Desanctis said in an awkward Brotha man tone.

"Ain't happening, so sorry hottie," McFlemming added in an equally unhip attempt at slang.

"Okay, I'm sorry fellas, I apologize," she said as they headed for the emergency room entrance. "Maybe we can get in there now and see what's going on."

McFlemming said as they walked, "We probably can't get a good look at things, but I'm going to hang around for a while."

"Yeah, me too," Desanctis said. "You hanging out TV?"

"I'm hanging Mike, you know I can't let you suckers beat me on the story. I'm not going anywhere."

"Okay, follow me. I got a top-secret way to get in without getting kicked out by the hospital police," McFlemming said.

As they entered the hospital through a side door, 20 feet away from the central ER room entrance, Desanctis and Kung looked at each other and shook their head in dismay. "This genius thinks this is a secret entrance," Desanctis said.

"I know top-secret for dummies," Kung said, shaking her head.

Inside the emergency room, there was a flurry of activity as the ER team worked furiously to keep Donald Alexander alive. Paramedic Johnson updated Nurse Dulany on the patient's condition.

"He has suffered a single gunshot wound to the abdomen. He's lost a lot of blood and consciousness once during the ride, we were able to revive him. He is looking quite bad."

As the Emergency Room team worked on Alexander, Dr. Ewell, the lead ER doctor, yelled, "We have to get him Type O blood now, make that two pints of O fast. Hurry, please, or we can lose this guy."

Nurse Dulany ends her chat with Paramedic Johnson to get the blood. Anna Dulany is five feet four, fit, and attractive Irish woman with auburn-colored hair. She has led the ER crew of nurses at City Hospital for over a decade. She's a hardened, battle-tested ER veteran who, over the years, had been through many dramatic trauma sessions that included high-profile celebrities and personalities. Donald Alexander had New York's best ER professionals working on him.

"I'm back, is the IV ready?" Dulany yelled as she returned with the blood.

"It's ready," the other attending ER Nurse answered.

"Good, then I'll hook him up." Dulany said and moved to the head of the patient stall and hooked the blood bags into the IV tube.

DARIUS MYERS

The other attending nurse, Simone Williams, had been busy recording his heart rate and blood pressure. She then yelled to Dr. Ewell, "His blood pressure is still dropping."

Williams and Dulany had worked together for the last five years, they were a great team, and Dr. Ewell had a lot of confidence working with them.

"Simone, I'm certain we have some internal blood vessels that are going to be a problem. We need a coagulant. Let's also see if we can stabilize his blood pressure with a line of Zrod."

"Okay, Dr. Ewell, I'm right on it."

Outside of the trauma stall, the paramedics are now talking to Kwame. He had been directed to the trauma stall as Dr. Ewell wanted him close by until they stabilized Donald. Kwame is seated on a bench and staring ahead with a stunned, blank look. His blue suit jacket, suit pants, white dress shirt, tie, and shoes are blood-splattered, as are his hands. His white handkerchief is now beet red. He had used the handkerchief to wipe the blood from his hands and his clothes.

"Are you okay Sir?" Paramedic Johnson asks as he observes Kwame's catatonic look. "I know this is a pretty traumatic event, but the Doctor is going to need to chat with you in a second. The police are going to be here in a minute and will also want to talk with you. We'll shield you from them for a while, but make sure you take a minute to get composed before speaking with them."

Kwame said nothing in response to Paramedic Johnson.

While the nurses continued to treat Mr. Alexander, Dr. Ewell rushes out to consult with the paramedics and Kwame Mills.

"What happened here Johnson?".

"Dr. Ewell, we picked him up at the Harris Simmons headquarters. He was barely conscious when we arrived and bleeding from the gunshot wound. Mr. Mills, who's sitting here, was there when we arrived. We

THE PUBLISHER'S DILEMMA

stabilized Mr. Alexander somewhat and rushed here."

"Great work Johnson, you guys did great."

Dr. Ewell then leans over and calmly begins to talk to Mills.

"Are you okay?"

Kwame nods his head up and down and mutters. He was barely audible, "Yes, I am. I'm pretty shaken up, but okay."

"Do you know what happened?"

"No, I have no idea," Mills said as he nervously wrung his bloodied handkerchief in his hands.

Now the two New York City police officers that followed Mills into the hospital are standing on the periphery of this interview. They are eyeing Mills suspiciously as if he was a suspect.

"Donald called me in my office and asked me to come upstairs, when I got there, he was standing facing his window, he was holding his stomach. He turned and fell on his sofa. When he fell, blood was streaming everywhere."

In his head, Kwame was furiously trying to make sense out of all the night's events. "Three months earlier, I am in Chicago, running the advertising sales office for NewsInc., making a good living and dating a phenomenal woman. Then one day, I get this phone call from Harris Simmons, and a great new job, a job that was supposed to be the opportunity that would make my career. Now I am sitting here in the emergency room with blood-drenched clothes."

He snapped out of these thoughts as he recognized that two uniformed police officers were now standing in front of him. The shorter one, his nametag read McClellan reaches out his hand to greet him.

"Mr. Mills, I am Mac McClellan from the 105, I heard what you said to the Doctor. Can you tell us about the other body?"

"What? Another body? I don't know about another body." Kwame nervously started ringing the dry, blood-soaked handkerchief again.

"There was another body found down the hallway from Donald Alexander's office. Do you know Gill Harris?"

"Yes, he's our Chairman and CEO."

"Not anymore, he was pronounced dead at the scene," said the second officer, his badge read W. Trombetta. He was burly and baldheaded, with a full mustache, and a muscular physique. He had a tight-fitting police uniform that showed off his immensely thick and defined arms and a tattoo on his forearm, which read Tough Enough. If he weren't a cop, Trombetta would be a dead ringer for a tough ass biker or Manhattan nightclub bouncer.

"Oh my God, no, not Gill."

"Guys give him a second. Let me talk to him please," Dr. Ewell said. The police officers backed up as the Doctor requested. Dr. Ewell then sat down and spoke calmly to Kwame.

"Listen, the first 24 to 48 hours of the crime scene is when it is the hottest. It's a time when the memories of the witnesses are freshest, and recollections are clearest. It is a critical time for information collection. It's why these officers are trying to get information that would be most helpful, but they are out of their league. They are not detectives and lack the savvy interviewing skills for a distraught witness under duress. That's why I asked them to back off for a second."

"Thank you, Doctor," Kwame muttered.

The Doctor then turned to the cops and shouted, "they are also preventing me from doing my job."

Mac McClellan and the other officer had just knowingly interrupted Dr. Ewell. They had a bunch of questions and are determined to not lose this moment. Kwame Mills is feeling woozy from all the excitement. His head begins to spin, and his mouth is dry.

THE PUBLISHER'S DILEMMA

"Can I get a glass of water? I am thirsty." Kwame's request and discomfort is of no concern to the uniformed police officers who, despite Dr. Ewell's presence, callously push back into Kwame's space with questions.

"What time did Donald Alexander call you? Have you ever shot a gun?" Mac McClellan asked in a rapid-fire barrage, leaning forward and to within inches of Kwame's face.

Dr. Ewell snapped at McClellan, "Hey you. Is this necessary right now?"

"Just a couple of more questions, Doc," McClellan said, and he raised his hands to signal Dr. Ewell to back off. It was a gesture that irritated the head ER Doctor.

"Hey. I said no more questions. I'm trying to save a man's life. Now get out of the way."

Kwame answered the first part of the last question, "About 7:00 or thereabouts, I think." And then he asked again for water, "I'm thirsty, my head is spinning, can I get some water?"

"What did he say? Did he say anything about ever shooting a gun?" snapped the other officer against Dr. Ewell's orders.

These guys had no care about Mills's request for water and the Doctor's demand that they cease with the questions. Meanwhile, Kwame's mouth and throat were so dry that his tongue was now nearly pasted to the roof of his mouth.

"Stop it right now!" Dr. Ewell stood up and yelled loudly at the two cops, and moves in between McClellan and Trombetta. He physically pushed them both back and away from Kwame Mills.

"Hey, don't touch, don't touch," Trombetta said and glared at Dr. Ewell.

While all this is going on, Kwame Mills's discomfort is growing. His head has begun to ache, and the head-spins have turned to nausea. He has no clue about what is going on with Dr. Ewell and the cops and how hot their argument had become.

Paramedic Johnson then sat next to Kwame, "Don't worry, Dr. Ewell will make everything okay, and if they don't watch it, he will kick both of their asses."

"Those guys don't know, Dr. Ewell is no soft touch. He was an All-American defensive back 15 years ago in college and also a former national karate champion. He carries himself with the refinement and disposition of a lead ER doctor. I'd put my money on him being tougher than Trombetta and with his karate pedigree, definitely a better fighter. He demands and always gets respect from the police in his Emergency Room."

"Thanks, I appreciate you saying that Johnson. I don't think he likes this Trombetta guy. He is way out of line."

Dr. Ewell took his glasses off and turned chin-to-chin to face Trombetta and said in a calm but intimidating tone, "Get out of here right now, before I have to give you a reason to stay."

Trombetta glared back with a menacing stare. Just as it seemed fists were going to fly, the standoff between Dr. Ewell and Trombetta is interrupted by a woman yelling, "I told you that you couldn't go down there, you must stay here in the reception area."

"Sorry lady, but I can go down there, and I will." It was a familiar voice to Kwame. Everyone looked to see the person causing all the commotion. Rambling down the hall, at six feet five and 270 pounds and fire in his eyes is Charlie Humphrey, the head of security at Harris Simmons. Silence envelopes the area as everyone turned their attention to the large man walking towards them. He sees Kwame and heads towards the trauma area where Donald Alexander is fighting for his life, and Trombetta and Dr. Ewell are ready to come to blows.

Humphrey recognized the two uniformed officers who are surrounding

THE PUBLISHER'S DILEMMA

Mills and exploded in rage.

"What the hell is going on here?" He then eyeballed McClellan, whom he knew from his work with the NYPD.

"Just doing our job, Hump. Just doing our job," answered McClellan, with a look of irritation. He knew that Charlie Humphrey was not going to let this interrogation go any further. Their moment was lost.

"Job my ass. We have a murder here. Where are the homicide guys? Murders are for Teddy Walker's team. Not you, you bunch of stupid morons."

"Easy now," says McClellan as he puts his hand on his nightstick. Trombetta still itching for some action now turned toward Humphrey.

"We just want to make sure he didn't get in the wind," McClellan continued.

Humphrey sensed Trombetta's challenge and being overly agitated himself invites him to battle. "Come on you Goon."

Now Trombetta's fisticuff face-off of a few minutes earlier had a new foe in Charlie Humphrey. It was a switch that offered Trombetta no better odds as Charlie Humphrey was three inches taller and 50 pounds heavier than Dr. Ewell.

"Let's go. I'll break you in half," Humphrey barked.

McClellan, realizing they had lost their chance for an interview, and the hell they would have to pay if they got into a fight in a hospital pulled his partner to the side.

"Look Trombetta, you know I never liked Charlie Humphrey, and while I would love for you to kick his ass, we can't do this. With all these witnesses, we'd both be facing some serious questions tomorrow morning, maybe even an assault charge."

Trombetta angrily contemplated his partner's assessment. He agreed to stand down but not before he turned to Humphrey and said, "Another time buddy, you and me."

"Why not right now? Now is as good a time as there ever will be," a still angry Humphrey said.

McClellan grabbed Trombetta by the forearm, stopping his hot-headed partner. "Okay Trombetta, let it go, let it go." Shut out twice now for a brawl, Trombetta reluctantly turned away.

Charlie Humphrey, however, wasn't ready to stop the berating of the uniformed cops. He was hot. "Well, I guess you can see that he's not in the wind. He's not going anywhere. He's a witness, you damn idiots."

Trombetta turned back and yelled, "You've got a real big badass mouth."

McClellan adds, "Come on now, Hump, that's not necessary. You know better than that Man."

Mac McClellan then turns to Kwame and gives him a cold stare and said, "Don't go anywhere. We got eyes on you."

Kwame Mills is oblivious and doesn't recognize the look or statement.

Nurse Anna Dulany with two glasses of water in her hands, arrived as McClellan and Trombetta walk away. She gave him the first glass. He took it and drunk it down with three gulps.

"Thank you so much. I was thirsty."

The water felt cool going down and sent a jolt to his insides, Kwame realized then just how dehydrated he was. He took the other glass and smiled weakly in appreciation at Nurse Dulany.

Humphrey, still incensed, barks again to the departing police officers. "Do your job by getting Teddy Walker down here."

Charles Humphrey was a former Navy Officer and Seal, who upon the resignation of his commission, spent 20 years with the Department of Alcohol, Tobacco, and Firearms. For the last five years, he had been the Director of Security at Harris Simmons. Humphrey had an intense, no-

nonsense style. He considered himself to be far superior to a regular, uniformed New York City police officer. This attitude earned him no friends with the City Police. Humphrey also had a law degree from Graytown, which meant that he knew the law. When he worked with the uniformed cops in the NYPD, he didn't hesitate to pull out the rules and conduct investigations by the letter of the law. Humphrey did this because he liked to get under their skin. Tonight, was one of those times, the uniformed guys knew his manner and reputation and didn't like it or him.

After departing the ER, McClellan called his contact on Teddy Walker's team, Walt Bigelow. He was Teddy Walker's second in command and friendly with McClellan. Bigelow recognized his number and answered the call.

"Hey Mac, how are you buddy? What's up?"

"Walt, we are leaving City Hospital. Trombetta and I followed Kwame Mills down here. Charlie Humphrey kicked us out and demanded we get someone from your team down here."

"Oh Damn, Hump hates uniformed cops Mac, everyone knows that."

"Don't we know that, we had to get out of there. Trombetta wanted a piece of him. He was showing off and embarrassed us pretty badly. Anyhow he wants Teddy down here."

"Okay Mac, I'm glad you guys kept your composure. Thanks for the heads-up."

"No problem, Walt. We're just doing our job. That's what we tried to tell Humphrey."

"I know you are Mac. I'll let Teddy know that Hump dressed you guys down. Just keep your head up. We've got you on our list for detectives. Stay patient and don't let Humphrey jam you up."

"Thanks Walt, I appreciate you saying that. This beat stuff sucks, and so does the money."

"We got you Mac, both you and Trombetta. But you got to tell him that he can't be beating up guys in hospitals or anywhere. That's not detective grade policing."

"I will Walt. I'll let him know. Thanks so much."

After McClellan and Trombetta leave, Humphrey turned his attention to Kwame Mills. His manner and voice became warm and friendly.

"Are you okay, Kwame? These guys would arrest their mother if they thought it would bring them some acclaim."

Humphrey sat down next to Kwame. "Unfortunately, this is a customary part of any murder or attempted murder investigation. So, you will have to answer some questions."

"I'm okay Charlie," Kwame said. "I just drank two glasses of water and I'm feeling better."

"But you won't have to answer questions from those two buzzards. McClellan and Trombetta are idiots, so don't answer any of their questions under any circumstance." His voice rose in anger as he thought about McClellan and Trombetta.

The Harris Simmons Security head was a real pro and helpful to Kwame. While he wasn't a young man anymore, he still worked out regularly and physically was in great shape. Kwame was comforted by the shield of Humphrey and impressed with how he handled the two uniformed police officers.

"Thanks a lot. Those guys were bearing down on me."

"This is already a high-profile case, and you'd better believe that everyone and their mother will want to get involved. Numbskulls like those two morons, see it as a career opportunity."

Humphrey then said, "Let's get out of here. There's too much chaos. You'll have to hang around here for a bit to speak to the real homicide guys, so let's go to the cafeteria and get a change of scenery."

Humphrey and Kwame began to walk towards the cafeteria. They see

THE PUBLISHER'S DILEMMA

Carrie Sinclair, Alexander's younger brother Rick, and the Reverend Joseph Frank Hall of the Free Will Baptist Church. They had just entered the Emergency Room reception area.

"Charlie, that's Rick Alexander, Donald's brother and Carrie Sinclair, his girlfriend and Rev. Hall. I know Carrie really well. We should greet them."

Humphrey agrees, "let's do that Kwame, I want to make sure Rick and Carrie are up on what we know, as well."

Kwame met Rick Alexander at his Donald's Hampton party. He had never met Rev. Hall but knew about him and the Free Will Baptist Church. It was a legendary church and had the largest congregation of any church in New York City.

He knows that this must be tough on his ex-wife and Donald's current girlfriend. He embraced her, and she squeezed him even more tightly. He could feel the tears on her still wet face.

"We're going to get through this, Carrie, don't fret. God is in charge." He said to her during the embrace. She smiled, and it was a look Kwame knew too well. She was putting on a brave face.

He then greets Rick with a hug. Rick introduces him to Rev. Hall.

"Rev. Hall, this is Kwame Mills, he is a friend of Carrie's and Donald's. He works with Donald at Harris Simmons."

Humphrey then introduced himself to the group. "Hi, I'm Charlie Humphrey, Director of Security at Harris Simmons. I know you guys want to see Donald. However, he's off-limits for now as they work to stabilize him. Let's go to the cafeteria and talk."

"Okay, that sounds like a great idea," Rick said, as Carrie and Rev. Hall nodded in agreement.

Kwame was comforted by seeing familiar faces, even if one of those faces included Carrie Sinclair.

Humphrey led them all to the hospital cafeteria. They sat at a table in the center of the room. Humphrey's back is to the door, and Kwame is next to him. Rev. Hall, Carrie, and Rick Alexander sat next to each other, across from Humphrey and Kwame.

Humphrey then said, "The press guys will be all over you for the next couple of days, especially you, Kwame."

Kwame starts to think again about how he got in this dilemma when Humphrey interrupted his thoughts. "Kwame, you are going to have reporters calling, and this will be 24 hours a day. They are relentless, expect them to bother, you, your parents, and your friends."

This statement unnerved him, and he began to daydream about his re-entry plans to New York. "I guess a quiet return is not going to happen," he thought to himself.

"Kwame," Humphrey's loud voice snapped Kwame back to the moment. He then continues to provide instructions on how to proceed. "Please be careful and tell the press that you have no comment. These shootings and the murder investigation are going to be a big and sensational story. Any leaks of the news could impede the investigation. Also, we have a special problem in that our CEO is dead, and second-in-charge is critically wounded. The press will be headline-grabbing, so no story, especially salacious ones will be off-limits. They will be pushing for answers on corporate control. Between us here at this table, the Harris family will likely convene in the morning and come to a determination. At this point, we don't have any answers. We'll have the PR department at Harris Simmons deal with that."

With all that Humphrey said, it was the phrase "murder investigation" that unnerved Kwame. The words sent a chill up his spine.

He once again got lost in his thoughts. While he sat there in the cafeteria of the emergency room listening to Charlie Humphrey give directions on how to handle the press, he began to feel guilty for thoughts of

THE PUBLISHER'S DILEMMA

his own welfare.

"Gill is dead, and Donald Alexander is fighting for his life, and here I am, worrying about being bothered by the press. How could I be so selfish?"

He then turned his full attention to Charlie Humphrey, who had not stopped talking and issuing instructions. Kwame thought once more about how fortunate he was with Charlie Humphrey there taking control.

Humphrey's final instruction was, "Have any press contact me directly. I will direct them to the PR department at Harris Simmons. Here's my business card with my private phone number." They all understood Humphrey's instructions. He then shared with them what he knew about the shooting.

"Here are also some details that I can share. Please keep all this confidential for now. I arrived at the office after the shooting. Gill was pronounced dead at the scene from one gunshot wound right through the heart. Another group of paramedics and a team of murder detectives are at the Harris Simmons headquarters on the 39th floor, which is now a crime scene."

After Humphrey finished talking, Carrie Sinclair looked at him and said, "Thanks for having your assistant call to let me know about the shooting."

"Of course, Carrie. You're welcome."

She then turned to her ex-husband. "What can you tell us about what happened?"

Kwame looked back at her. Her eyes were red and puffy, and her face tense as if she was expecting to hear the worst. Nevertheless, even under this kind of duress, she was still stunning.

"At about 7:00, Donald called me and asked me to come to his office immediately. I went right upstairs, found him, and called security. They called an ambulance, and I stayed with him until the paramedics arrived. I took a car down here right after the ambulance left the building. He's in the emergency room now. I understand he's lost a lot of blood."

Rev. Hall then grabbed Kwame's hand, "Jesus will see him through." Carrie began to cry, and Rick Alexander moved closer to her. He embraced her and held her close and whispered, "Don't cry Carrie, Donald is tough. He is going to be fine. I know my brother, and he is going to make it through."

Rev. Hall then stood up and began to talk, "Folks, we are in a moment of great despair, and I know a God that never fails. God loves his servants, and Donald Alexander, I know loves God. I believe that he still has a lot of work to do on this earth. I believe the Lord agrees with me, so I think it's time for prayer. Will you join me in prayer? Stand up, please and let's join hands," Rev. Hall then motioned with his hands for them to stand up. The group stood up, held hands, and formed a circle. He started to pray.

"Dear God, Father of us all, we come to you humbly the only way we know how, asking you to intercede Father Jesus. Our brother, Donald needs you now, Father. Put your arm of protection and healing on him right now, Father Jesus. Heal him completely, dear God. Carry him through this ordeal."

The prayer became emotional, as Rev. Hall's cadence grew louder and stronger. For Kwame, it was profoundly moving. He felt the spirit of God comforting him, and it was what he needed. Finally, with a cry of "In your name, Father, in your name," Rev. Hall brought the prayer to a close, as he said, "Amen."

Kwame suddenly felt his legs grow weak, he stumbled, and Charlie Humphrey grabbed him to break his fall. He became dizzy, and then he went blank.

Nurse Anna Dulany was in the cafeteria for a coffee break, but she also was keeping an eye on Kwame.

"Let's admit him. I've been watching him for a few minutes now. I think this man is in shock."

Seated behind Charlie and Kwame Mills were Luke McFlemming, Jennifer Kung, and Michael Desanctis. They had covertly wandered in and sat down long enough to hear Kwame Mills's account of the incident. They too were in shock. McFlemming and Desanctis looked at each other and then looked at Jennifer Kung and smiled deviously. They had their front-page story and a photo of Kwame Mills.

After everyone left, the press hacks now sat in an empty cafeteria contemplating what they just heard, and Luke McFlemming broke the silence. "Sorry TV." He knew she was going to ask for the photo again, "Today, you're the competition. There's no way you're getting this photo."

She looked at Desanctis, and before she could ask, he said, "Don't even think about it."

"You both suck. You really do. I've got to get my story in for the morning, so I'm out," Kung said and got up from the table and ran to her car in the parking lot.

Chapter Sixteen

Kwame woke up groggy. The sedative he had received the night prior hadn't yet worked its way through his system.

Yet, through his grogginess, he knows that he's not in his bed. The twin-sized soft hospital bed mattress is much smaller and softer than the firm, king-sized bed in his home.

He also noticed two men in the corner of the room whispering. Kwame strains to make out the cloudy figures, he's nearsighted, and the drugs are not helping either, but he still recognizes the big one. It's Charlie Humphrey.

"Oh man," Kwame moaned. "Charlie, what are you doing here? What am I doing here, and where are my eyeglasses?"

Charlie Humphrey was listening attentively to the other man as Kwame woke up. His body language suggested that he was not pleased. Through Kwame's blurriness, he could tell that they were engaged in an intense quarrel, so fiery that neither noticed Kwame waking up and taking account of the room. Upon hearing Kwame's voice, Charlie immediately put up his hand as a signal to stop talking.

"Enough, for now, we'll get back to this later." Humphrey wanted the conversation to end anyhow as he was getting ripped by the Man, for berating the uniformed police officers the night before.

Humphrey dashed over to the medical tray that doubled as a nightstand with all of Kwame Mills's belongings. He retrieves Kwame's eyeglasses and hands them to him.

As he put his glasses on, Humphrey leaned close to him, "Kwame, do you know where you are?"

Kwame sat up in the bed, and as his vision cleared, so did his understanding of his whereabouts.

"Oh my God, this was not a dream. Charlie, please tell me this was a dream?"

"I'm afraid not. Last night was a nightmare, unfortunately for us all, but it was not a dream".

Kwame's heart began to race with anxiousness and concern as to the condition of his boss and sadness for Gill.

"Where's Donald? What's up with Donald? Is he okay?"

THE PUBLISHER'S DILEMMA

"He's lost a lot of blood, and we almost lost him twice last night. The doctors performed six hours of surgery. The gunshot severed a kidney. Quite frankly, he's lucky to be alive. We don't know if he's going to make it, the next 48 hours, according to the Doctors, will be very critical."

Kwame slumped down into the bed and stared at the ceiling, his gaze locked in a trance. He said nothing more.

He remained in this catatonic state for about 30 seconds. For Charlie Humphrey, it seemed like a half-hour. He continued that way until Humphrey gently prodded and roused him out of his trance.

"Kwame? Kwame?" Charlie asked gently, consolingly, "Are you okay?"

He could hear Humphrey speaking, but he couldn't respond. He wanted to, but his mind kept racing back to the 39th floor last night at Harris Simmons. He was thinking about Donald Alexander's phone call and running up the stairs and finding him in his office.

"Are you okay? Are you okay?" Charlie continued to ask.

Kwame knew that he needed to respond. He looked at Charlie and said, "Oh yes, I'm fine. I guess I'm just a little drugged up still. It's just that I can't believe it. Two people were shot, with one dead, and I am involved somehow, even if just as a witness."

"I know, I know Kwame. It was a bit much for you. Nurse Dulany thought you were in shock. She wanted you to calm down and get a good night's sleep, so they pumped you up pretty good."

He then waived for the man he was arguing with to come closer to the bed. Once he arrived, Charlie introduced him, "Kwame, this is Teddy Walker, he's the homicide chief for the New York City Police Department. Teddy has a few questions for you, do you feel up to talking with him now?"

Before thinking about the answer, Kwame responded just as he did last night.

"Sure, anything I can do to help."

The head of security for Harris Simmons then turned to the Chief of Homicide for New York City.

"Be easy Teddy, he's still groggy and last night was rough on him."

He had now moved to the side of the bed and sat in a metal chair.

Teddy Walker was a lot like Charlie Humphrey. He wasn't a Navy Seal, but he was a Navy fighter pilot. He was 50 years old, African-American, and although he never talked about it, was admitted to Mensa and recorded a 185 IQ when he was 14.

After he resigned his commission from the Navy, Walker attended law school at Harlowe and upon graduation with his J.D., did a 20-year stint with the CIA. Walker's primary area of responsibility with the CIA was cracking rogue international espionage and intelligence rings.

Homicides rarely went unsolved with Teddy Walker on the case. He was a brilliant cop and highly regarded in national and international circles. The Gill Harris murder and Donald Alexander attempted murder had one of the best cops in the world on the case.

He leaned closer to Kwame and whispered, "I'm Ted Walker, Chief of Detectives for the New York Police Department. Sorry to have to meet under these circumstances."

Walker reached over the bed and patted Kwame softly on the back of the hand.

Kwame looked at him. He was nervous as he was still processing the events of last night himself. He knew he had to speak to the police and he wanted to be of help. He then returned Walker's greeting, "Good Morning Ted, I'm Kwame Mills." He reflexively waved his hand as a hello to Teddy

THE PUBLISHER'S DILEMMA

Walker.

Walker smiled. It was a warm, consoling smile that eased Kwame a bit. He pulled out a note pad before he continued. "Kwame, I know you are tired, and I really don't want to bother you, so I'll make this brief."

At that time, Nurse Anna Dulany entered the room and stood in a protective stance at the door. She said nothing, but her determined look and body language were clear messages that she was not going to let this meeting get out of line.

When Kwame saw her enter, he smiled. Seeing her further eased his anxiety. Teddy Walker and Charlie Humphrey nodded in recognition of her entrance. Walker said, "I know you are in charge. I have a few questions."

"Thank you. I'll give you two minutes, be careful," Nurse Dulany said.

Walker turned back to Kwame, "Is there anything you can tell me about last night?"

Charlie Humphrey interrupted, "Teddy, getting the big picture is all we have time for this morning."

Humphrey knew with Nurse Dulany hovering, the full interview would have to come at another time. He was reminding Walker of such. "I know you don't appreciate my interjection, but my first job is to make sure Kwame Mills is okay."

Ted Walker glared at Humphrey. He then turned his attention back to Kwame, "We'll get to the minor details later Kwame, but it is important to get as much information as we can early on, while your memory is fresh. Can you give me as much of the big picture stuff from last night as you can?"

Kwame then looked at Nurse Anna Dulany, and she nodded that it was okay to continue.

DARIUS MYERS

He straightened up in his bed and concentrated on recalling what he remembered. "Last night about 7:00 or so, I got a call from Donald, he asked me to come over to his office immediately. When I got there, he was facing the window, and he seemed to be holding or wrapping himself with his hands and arms over his midsection."

Walker stood up to imitate the position that would show how Donald Alexander was holding himself. "Is this how you found him?"

"Yes, that is it, exactly, except his back was to me. His office was dark, and the lights were not on. He had his suit jacket on, so I didn't see the blood until he turned around. His entire front was red from blood. It looked to me as if he was holding himself together. Then he fell down on the sofa. But he never passed out. He actually sat up once he fell on the sofa."

This thought made Kwame's voice quake. Sensing his unsettling, Nurse Dulany moved in and took charge.

"Okay, that's enough for now, you guys need to come back later."

Nurse Dulany's intrusion was premature. Kwame was okay. He just became a little emotional as he recalled seeing Donald Alexander bloodied. He raised his hand to let her know that he was okay to continue.

"Everything's cool, I'm fine to go forward."

"Nope, you'll have to do this later Kwame."

She moved from the door to the other side of the bed from Charlie Humphrey and Teddy Walker and stared at them menacingly.

Kwame said again, "I'm fine. If it's okay with you, I'd prefer to get this over with."

Nurse Anna Dulany realized Kwame was right and relented.

"Okay, I know you guys will continue to come around until he speaks with you, so let's get this done, but fast. Next time, it's my way and no discussion. It's over."

Teddy Walker knew from her look not to push her too hard. He had one, maybe two questions left. "Just another minute, and I'll be done."

After Anna Dulany backed off, Teddy Walker looked at Kwame and reassuringly said, "You're doing good, and I know this is hard. Now, did Donald Alexander say anything to you in his office?"

"He said, I need your help, I'm hurt, and it's bad. He moved to the sofa and kept talking. It was like he didn't want to stop talking, so he sat there on the sofa and was yapping. I could sense the fear in his voice."

"What did you do then?"

"I then turned on the lights, and it was then that I realized how much blood he lost. I called security and told them to call 911 and that Donald had been shot and to get an ambulance. I then got some towels out of his office's bathroom and tried to get him to release his grip on his midsection so that I could put more pressure on the wound. He was still very alert and strong. But finally, I was able to get him to lighten up enough to apply the towels."

"What was he talking about during all this?"

Kwame grew silent. Walker was patient as he waited for an answer. He knew Kwame was recollecting his thoughts.

"You know, he was pretty calm. He was telling me where his contact list for next of kin was, and we prayed. He was praying and in the Holy Spirit almost the entire time."

"Did he say anything else?"

Kwame's eyes lit up as if he remembered something important. Then he looked at Charlie Humphrey and Teddy Walker as if he might have an important clue.

DARIUS MYERS

"I don't know what this means, because he didn't say anything else before blacking out. But right before he lost consciousness, he said, I can't believe he would do this."

Anna Dulany decided that was enough for now and sternly interrupted.

"Okay gentlemen, that's enough. He'll be much better this afternoon when the sedatives wear off. Now let him get some rest."

Walker then kindly said, "Kwame thanks so much for your time. Feel better, and get some rest, we need your help. I want to come back and go over the details more thoroughly this afternoon when you feel better. Is that okay?"

Kwame Mills looked at Teddy Walker and nodded his okay for a follow-up meeting. "Sure, anything I can do to help."

He then reached over the bed and tapped him on the hand again. "Thank you, Kwame. You've been helpful."

Teddy Walker then stood up to leave. Charlie Humphrey did as well. He didn't say thanks or goodbye to Kwame. Instead, he gave him a thumbs-up sign followed by a wink.

Kwame returned Charlie Humphrey's acknowledgments with a thumbs-up sign of his own, followed by a weak smile. Humphrey's non-verbal gestures assured Kwame that he did an excellent job with the first interview and that everything was okay.

As Humphrey and Walker walked out of the room, they spotted Rev. Hall, who had returned to the hospital.

"Ah, that's Rev. Hall from Freewill Baptist Church, he's probably here for morning Prayer with Donald Alexander," he said to Walker.

Rev. Hall was standing in the hallway. In his hand were two

THE PUBLISHER'S DILEMMA

newspapers. When he saw Charlie Humphrey, his eyes lit up, "Good morning, praise God, Brother Charlie."

Before Humphrey could respond, Rev. Hall handed him the two newspapers. "Have you seen the morning papers yet? The story is all over the press."

Humphrey grabbed the newspapers and looked at the covers. When he did, his stomach turned.

Rev. Hall said. "The Post and News have front cover stories about the shootings, and the stories had photographs of Kwame Mills."

Humphrey read the captions from both and turned to the first paragraph of both stories.

"This is everything we talked about at the table last night Rev. Hall. How in the...?"

Humphrey started to swear before catching himself and immediately apologized to Rev. Hall.

"Sorry, Rev. I don't know how these guys get their information. This story is a serious blow."

"God bless you Brother Charlie," Rev. Hall said and smiled. "I appreciate the apology, and I'll add you to my prayer list."

Rev. Hall also knew based on their conversation and Humphrey's warnings for secrecy that this story could seriously affect the police investigation. "Charlie, how do you think these guys got this story? They couldn't have made this up," he asked.

Humphrey's mind was racing. How did this happen? He stood in the hallway in disbelief while Teddy Walker and Rev. Hall looked at him. They were waiting for an answer and also for an introduction. Humphrey then recognizing his second misstep, apologized, and introduced Teddy Walker to

DARIUS MYERS

Rev. Hall.

"Oh, I'm sorry Reverend Hall, this is Detective Ted Walker, Chief of Detectives for the NYPD. Teddy, this is Rev. Joseph Frank Hall of The Free Will Baptist Church. Rev. Hall is Donald Alexander's pastor. We spent some time together here last night together praying for Donald and talking about protocol and how important it is to steer clear of the press. That steering clear of the press part didn't work out so well."

"It's a pleasure to meet you Rev. Hall," Teddy Walker said first. He was excited to meet Rev. Hall.

Rev. Hall also was eager to meet Teddy Walker, too. Rev. Hall knew about Ted Walker, as did most New Yorkers who followed the NYPD. As a senior-level crime fighter and leader in the overly bureaucratic New York City Police Department, Teddy Walker was a highly publicized hire in the New York City press and political circles because of his blue-chip pedigree and also because he was a man of color. He offered hope as a potential healer of the tense divide between the NYPD and the black and brown communities. Rev. Hall's notoriety as an advocate for social justice and a fighter against racial injustice put him on the front line often against the police department. He was relieved to meet someone who looked like him the next time he needed to talk to the NYPD.

"God Bless you, Chief Walker. Your reputation proceeds you, I'm delighted to meet you, and I hope once we get beyond this tragedy, that we can become friends."

Teddy Walker knew of Rev. Hall as well. Everyone in New York City knew Rev. Joseph Frank Hall. Teddy Walker smiled in appreciation of Rev. Hall's greeting and kind words.

"Thank you, Rev. Hall. I guess we are mutual admirers. It's terrible to meet under these circumstances, but I look forward to getting to know you

THE PUBLISHER'S DILEMMA

as well."

As Rev. Hall and Teddy Walker were talking, Humphrey stared at the front covers. Suddenly, the realization of how the story leaked hit him like a ton of bricks.

"Oh my God Rev. This was my fault. It was my stupid mistake."

Rev. Hall looked at Humphrey. This statement didn't make sense. "I'm sorry, what do you mean Charlie? I don't understand?"

"Last night, I had gotten so overwhelmed by the prayer that I let my guard down and I didn't clear the cafeteria. After our talk, I knew that you, Kwame, Carrie, or Rick Alexander wouldn't speak to the press. Besides, these stories were too detailed."

Teddy Walker looked at Humphrey and then shook his head in recognition of the mistake.

"I had my back to the door when we were talking in the cafeteria."

"So. what does that mean? I still don't understand Charlie."

"Room and environment control Rev. Hall," Walker said.

Humphrey then explained, "Rev, Teddy is right. It's what we call in the business, room, and environment control. The only way this makes sense is because I forgot to clear out the cafeteria. I sat with my back to the door, and I didn't see who had entered once we sat down and began to talk. That had to be how they got the scoop. It was a rookie mistake, and I have to take the blame. I would torture my staffers at the ATF over something some so basic."

Rev. Hall nodded his head as it made sense. Humphrey continued to share the gravity of this mistake.

"You always control your environment. It's a golden rule to security and prevention. You never know what people are likely to do in a public place. If they happened to be shooters and they wanted to take Kwame out, we gave them the green light. That's why you always control your environment. You do your best to know who everyone is in the room, the entrances, and the exits."

"You're giving me a Masters Class in how to be a super cop Charlie. I am impressed," Rev. Hall said.

"Well, I'm pissed," Humphrey said. "We've got one guy murdered and a second person is fighting for his life. All these press guys are concerned with is grabbing a headline. I may as well as have written the story myself. By not clearing the room, I gave them the scoop on a silver platter."

Humphrey continued, "Rev. Hall, do you remember seeing anyone else in the cafeteria with us last night?"

"Let me think, I don't know," he stared into space as he tried to recollect the events of last night.

Before Rev. Hall could recall, Humphrey's memory clicked in. "Dammit, I remember now." He then smacked himself in the forehead. "Sorry again, Rev. I have a bad tongue. I'm just pissed, I know now. They were seated right behind us."

"Yes, you're right Charlie. Three people came into the cafeteria after us, as I recall. There was a tall blond-haired, Irish-looking guy and a dark-haired Italian fellow and a striking Asian woman."

"That's the Celebrity Hack patrol," Walker said. "They're always snooping for stories about celebrities. We don't need them in this thing. It's going to go public really quick now."

Walker continued, "You don't need a story like this one played out in the press. We have no early clues, and we don't need the bad guys or the press to know everything we know. Desanctis, McFlemming, and Kung will let the whole world know that we have nothing. No eyewitness, no leads, just a distraught witness. Now we have our work cut out."

Teddy Walker, Charlie Humphrey, and Rev. Joseph Frank Hall stood for a minute in stunned silence with this realization. The press had dealt them a severe blow, and they needed to get them under control. Walker closed his eyes, he nodded his head back and forth as if he was seeking his own approval for what he was thinking, and then he blurted out, "I got an idea."

"What you got Teddy?" Humphrey asked.

"I've got an idea to get these guys in check and even get them working for us," Walker said and began to smile. It wasn't a happy smile, it was more a devilish grin. "Charlie, how about a Scuttle Story? I'm going to plant some scuttle stories and get them working for us."

"Hell yes, Teddy, yes. That's an outstanding idea." Humphrey exclaimed and grinned and it was the same devilish grin Walker flashed. "We'll teach those bastards a lesson." Humphrey was so pissed he didn't even bother to apologize to Rev. Hall.

Rev. Hall didn't wait or ask for an apology either. He was intrigued by these super cops and wanted to know more about how they worked. "What's a scuttle story, gentleman?"

Teddy Walker and Charlie Humphrey looked at each other. "You tell him Teddy," Humphrey said.

"It's how we fool the bad guys, Rev. Hall. A scuttle news story is when the police department holds a news conference or lets loose to the press a slightly fabricated account of an investigation to keep the bad guys unnerved. The objective is to get the bad guys to follow the local press accounts for information as to what kind of clues the police have on a case. A Scuttle Story, in this case, would engage the press and get them to tell the story to our advantage".

Rev. Hall shook his head in disbelief, "You guys do this? It's

DARIUS MYERS

underhanded, isn't it?"

"We deal with bad guys Rev., not good guys," Walker answered.

"Yeah, these dudes are not good at all," Humphrey added. "Bad guys are often brilliant. So, we got to do what we got to do."

Teddy Walker then began to conceive a plan for the scuttle story, "We're going to focus on McFlemming and Desanctis. We'll leave Jennifer Kung alone for now, just in case we need to use her later."

Scuttle stories and misinformation were the kind of covert activity that Teddy Walker enjoyed.

Rev. Hall smiled as he watched these super cops conceive their plan to dupe the Celebrity Hack Patrol, "You guys are good. Remind me to never get on your bad side."

"Don't worry," Charlie Humphrey said, "you're a man of God. We're not looking to get a one-way ticket to Hell. You're safe with us."

"That's right," Teddy Walker said. "Now, let me get with my team and finish putting this plan together."

174

Chapter Seventeen

After surgery Donald Alexander had slipped into a coma. The reports of the shooting by the Celebrity Hack Patrol quickly made it the most fantastic murder story and shooting since the Yancey Stuart murders and they were hungry for more. The parking lot where the press hung out had tripled in size with reporters and television teams waiting for any breaking news. To keep the news hacks at bay the next morning Dr. Ewell held a press conference in the Hospital Chapel.

The Celebrity Hack Patrol were jockeying each other and the other news teams and reporters for a position close to the podium and Dr. Ewell.

"Tell us, is he going to live?" Luke McFlemming yelled as Dr. Ewell walked to the podium. He was followed by two other surgeons on his team, but he would do all the talking. Dr. Ewell ignored the calls of McFlemming and the rest of the press. He stepped behind the podium and reached for the microphone.

He turned on the microphone and as he did Jennifer Kung shouted, "We know he's lost a lot of blood. Is he okay?"

As a veteran ER and Trauma pro, Dr. Ewell knew how to handle the press. He looked to McFlemming and Kung, "We'll take a few questions after we give a report."

He then said to the larger group, "Okay everyone, this will be brief, so please pay attention."

The press continued to push to get closer to the podium and Dr. Ewell. He then spoke from a prepared statement.

"Donald Alexander, the President of Harris Simmons, was admitted as a shooting victim last evening at about 8 pm. He suffered a blockage of oxygen to the brain after the shooting. We were able to stabilize him and then conduct emergency surgery. Before we operated, an MRI revealed frontal lobe swelling. It is too early for us to know if there will be any brain damage. This is a common aftereffect of oxygen loss and severe body trauma. He is now in a coma."

The coma announcement drew a loud gasp from the crowd of more than 30 news crews and photographers.

Jennifer Kung was standing next to Mike Desanctis as Dr. Ewell finished the statement, whispered to him, "Coma wow, this is bad. We may have a double homicide here."

"Jesus, this is getting crazier by the moment. The doctors look spent," Desanctis whispered back.

After the loud gasps following the coma announcement, Dr. Ewell continued to read from the prepared statement.

"If he comes out of the coma, we don't know what the effects will be on his brain. This type of brain trauma frequently leads to short-term and long-term memory loss. It means that if Alexander makes a full physical recovery, he may not recall any of the events that led up to the incident. He is in God's hands now. We ask that you pray for him."

Donald Alexander was the only eyewitness to the event. His recovery was crucial for Gill Harris's homicide and the attempt on his life. Teddy Walker had two uniformed officers posted full-time outside his hospital room in the event there was a second attempt. His critical state also made Kwame Mills's recollection of the crime scene even more important to Walker's team.

Chapter Eighteen

Carrie had not left Donald's bedside all night, and she looked it. Puffy and fully bloodshot red eyes marked her usually flawless face. Her linen pantsuit was crumpled. Her long hair back was tied in a neat ponytail. But even under this duress, she was still strikingly beautiful.

Ron Cherry, Donald's brother Rick and Ron's wife, Marcia, also spent the night at the hospital. They, along with Carrie, met with Dr. Ewell after the surgery.

"I ask you to stand on your faith and pray for he is in God's hands now. We have done all that we can do. It's time to lean on prayer now. The next 48 hours will be critical."

They all huddled in prayer, as Dr. Ewell suggested. He even prayed with them. Once Donald slipped into a coma, they feared for the worst.

At daybreak, Ron and Marcia Cherry, who managed about an hour's sleep aboard some plastic chairs in the lobby of the emergency room, made their way to Donald Alexander's recovery room. Carrie was seated in the armchair at the head of the bed. She was staring into space and holding Donald's hand.

"There's Carrie," Ron said. He tapped lightly on the window of Donald's room to get her attention. Carrie looked up and smiled at the familiar face of friends. She walked out and hugged them.

"How are you Honey?" Marcia asked, "Did you get any sleep at all?"

"No Marcia, the constant stream of attendees to Donald by the team of doctors and nurses kept my adrenaline going. I haven't thought about sleep, and now that it is daybreak, I'm sure there will be little time to catch a nap in this room. But I'm okay."

"Let me call a car for you," Ron offered, "why don't you go home and catch a quick nap and come back after you rest a little?"

"That's okay. I'm fine Ron, but thanks so much for the offer."

Carrie then changed the subject to them. "How are you guys doing? I know you have been here all night also. Where were you? In the lobby? I meant to come out and find you, but I didn't want to leave him."

"Oh, we're just fine Honey," Marcia answered. "We found a couple of chairs in the ER room lobby. It was pretty quiet in there. We got a couple of seats and prayed a lot."

"Thank you guys, you don't know how much that means to me, and I know Donald will appreciate it too when he recovers."

"That's right Carrie. He's going to have a full recovery." Marcia said as she moved closer to Carrie. She grabbed her hand and stroked it slowly.

Carrie smiled. Marcia was always like a big sister to her. She was appreciative of her positive words and loving gesture.

Her thoughts then turned to Donald's brother, "Where's Rick? I know he volunteered to donate blood. They both share O positive blood types, and since Don lost so much blood, Dr. Ewell thought it was a good idea for him to donate. Did he go home?"

"No, Rick is down the hall in room E-4," Ron Cherry said. "They admitted him afterward. He's fine and has been on the phone all night with his parents. Their mother is coming in from Ohio and will be here later this morning. The father is in Europe. He's on a plane from Amsterdam and will be in later today."

"What can we do, Sweetie?" Marcia asked Carrie.

"Pray Marcia. The doctors don't like this brain swelling, and neither do the detectives. They're afraid it may affect his memory. If," and with this word, Carrie Sinclair began to shake and shudder, "he recovers, he may never remember what happened."

Marcia reached for Carrie to console her as she broke down and began to cry.

Nurse Anna Dulany saw them standing in the hallway talking. She approached the trio and offered what she thought was a bit of advice.

"Good morning everyone, Donald's resting and you all are exhausted. Can I suggest that you go home and try to get some rest? Of course, we'll call you if there is any news."

"I'm not going anywhere," Carrie snapped with a degree of irritation. Her response made it clear to Nurse Dulany that she was not going to leave.

Ron Cherry chimed in, "We offered a car to take her home. She's here for the long haul."

"Oh, I'm sorry," Nurse Dulany knew immediately that her suggestion was off base. "You're right, I do this for a living, but trust me if my Man was here, I wouldn't leave either."

"Thanks for understanding Anna, and sorry for snapping at you just now. I know that you are just doing your job."

Carrie then turned to Marcia and said, "I told Anna that Kwame is my ex-husband, and Donald is my current boyfriend. Anna then told me that even though I was having a bad day, she liked the way I roll."

"You do know how to pick them," Marcia said. "Donald is amazing, and Kwame ain't chopped liver."

Anna Dulany and Marcia smiled big, and Carrie let out a big laugh. It seemed to lessen her stress. "I guess I do pick well, huh. I'm a pretty lucky gal."

"That's why I'm saying Girl. You're a boss," Anna Dulany said.

Even Ron Cherry had to agree, "Marcia will tell you that normally I stay out of girl talk, but Nurse Dulany, you got it right. Carrie Sinclair, you are a big, bad boss."

Carrie took a deep breath and exhaled. The laughter and the company made her feel better, "Thank you guys for being so kind, I needed to hear that. I am indeed a lucky gal."

Nurse Anna Dulany then came up with a solution for Carrie to get some rest.

"I have a solution Carrie. There is an empty bed behind the curtain in Donald's room. Why don't we set it up, and you can rest there until he wakes up? When he does, you'll be right here."

"That's a great idea," said Ron Cherry.

"Can you do that?" Carrie asked.

"Sure," Dulany said as she walked in the room to the curtain and slid it to the wall, revealing the empty bed. "This is a recovery room, not an operating room or emergency room. Plus, I'm in charge. No one is going to say anything. You won't be in the way, so yes, we can do this."

"I'll go to your apartment and get you some fresh clothes," Marcia Cherry said.

"Oh, that would be great. Thank you so much, Marcia."

"Then let's get this set up and Carrie, you can stay as long as you want," Nurse Dulany said.

As Nurse Dulany set up Carrie in Donald's room, down the hall, in Room E-4, Rick Alexander woke up to find a copy of the Post, a note, two bottles of water, and a container of orange juice on the nightstand next to his bed.

He read the note aloud, "Mr. Alexander, please drink the orange juice and water as you awake. You need to hydrate."

Rick Alexander sat upright in his bed and drank down the orange juice. He said to himself, "Man, this OJ taste good and even better running through my body. I had no idea that I could get so dehydrated giving blood. I already feel much better."

Rick then picked up the newspaper and read aloud the headlines of that day's Post. His stomach began to turn as he said the words "Murder and

THE PUBLISHER'S DILEMMA

Mayhem at Harris Simmons: Family Scion Killed, Second In Charge In Critical Condition."

"Oh, I can't read anymore," Rick said. The headline upset his stomach. He put the newspaper down and vomited up the orange juice.

A few doors away in room E-8, Charlie Humphrey sat at the foot of Kwame Mills's bed, reading the same headline. He had been re-reading it for hours, and every time he did, he got hotter under the collar.

"Those Damn Hacks."

Rev. Hall was long gone, so he could curse and swear all he wanted. "I'm going to make those bastards pay for this one."

Kwame Mills was asleep again. Anna Dulany had given him another sedative following his interrogation by Teddy Walker.

Humphrey turned to page 3, where there was a photo inset of three people. The first photo was that of Gill Harris with a caption that read "Deceased."

The second photo was of Donald Alexander with a caption that read "Wounded."

The third photo was of Wynne Shields and the caption that read, "New Successor???"

Humphrey decided not to read anymore. He put the newspaper down and wondered if this was what Alexander meant when he said, "I can't believe he would do this. Was Wynne Shields so desperate for the job that he would go to these extremes?"

As he looked at the headlines, Humphrey began to think about Teddy Walker and their conversation about the scuttle story.

In his office at Police Headquarters, Teddy Walker was thinking about the scuttle story as well. The press appeared to be their best ally. He picked up the phone and called Charlie Humphrey's cell phone. Humphrey picked up the call as he recognized Walker's number

DARIUS MYERS

"Humphrey here, hey Teddy."

"Hey Charlie, getting back to you on the scuttle story. I'm feeling better and better about a scuttle story as the Celebrity News Hacks might help us solve the case."

"Me too, Teddy. You still going to use McFlemming and Desanctis and leave Kung out?"

"Yeah, I think they make sense. I'm going to call my second in command, Asst. Chief of Detectives, Walt Bigelow, and get this going. I'll keep you in the loop."

"Thanks Teddy, please do and let me know if I can be of help."

Walker hung up the phone, and as he dialed Bigelow's extension, his other line rang. It was a call from Walt Bigelow.

He picked up the line, "Hey Walt, I was just calling you."

"Well, I got you first," Bigelow said. "I'm a faster dialer."

"Walt, tell me what do you know about these press guys that call themselves the Celebrity Press Patrol?"

"You mean the Celebrity Hacks Teddy? I was looking at today's headlines and wondering how we could use these guys. They put these stories out today, and as this is a big story, I'm sure they're looking for a follow-up," Bigelow said.

"Walt this morning, I was with Charlie Humphrey, the director of security at Harris Simmons, and we thought it might be a good time for a Scuttle Story."

"That's why I'm calling Teddy."

Chapter Nineteen

Teddy Walker knew the Celebrity Hack Patrol was pretty smart, and they had to move with stealth precision to successfully execute this Scuttle Story.

He shared his strategy with Bigelow. "Walt, let's get together with the two Hacks who wield the most power. Tell them they will get an exclusive on the Harris Simmons murders for a limited time, just 24 hours. Following the 24 hours of silence, we'll hold a press conference that will be open to all of the media."

"Which two, Teddy?"

"McFlemming of The News and Desanctis of The Post."

"Perfect, that's who I was thinking of as well."

"Great. Okay, now Walt, if they ask if we are talking to the other newspapers and media sources, we say we are not. We'll let them think they've got and exclusive."

"Okay Teddy, but what about Jennifer Kung? You know she's going to be salty for being left out."

"I thought about that. Kung is too friendly with both McFlemming and Desanctis. She might leak her scoop with either of them, so let's not deal her in, at least for now. We'll take care of her another time."

Bigelow shook his head in agreement. "I agree. McFlemming and Desanctis definitely won't share. Especially McFlemming, he is too selfish. He's a headline hunter, and I'm going to enjoy embarrassing him."

"We got any files on them?" Walker asked.

"Yes, we do."

"Okay, give me a read."

Bigelow began to read from the McFlemming file first.

DARIUS MYERS

"Luke McFlemming from The News has been training to be a Hack all of his life. He grew up in Hell's kitchen. As a city kid's life goes, his was the ordinary dime version. He went to public school, was an altar boy at St. Agnes on 54th Street and 10th Avenue, played high school baseball, football, and basketball with no major notoriety. He worked after school for pocket money and got in just enough trouble to stay out of jail."

"He was a good kid, and coming from Hell's Kitchen knew a lot of bad guys, some bonafide Irish gangsters or Westies as they are also called. He liked to pretend, depending upon who was listening, that he had connections to that kind of life. It also helped that his daddy was a teamster, and his brother, Tim, was a former contending prizefighter. Tim now owns the legendary Irish bar, Fitz's, in their old neighborhood. The boys shared a pet bulldog when they were kids. They named the bar after the dog. He's a good journalist, and his ego makes him perfect for our con."

Walker shook his head side to side as he thought about McFlemming's ego.

"Walt, he does have a pretty big opinion of himself. This shooting is a big story, so I'm sure we won't have a problem getting him on board."

"Oh, trust me Teddy," Bigelow continued, "he'll bite for sure. He won't be able to help himself."

"Great, tell me about Desanctis?" Walker asked. "They hate each other, right?"

"They are rivals for sure, but you know they spend so much time with each other as part of the Celebrity Hack Patrol that I am not a buyer on if this hate is for real. I do know that Desanctis is the opposite of McFlemming. He is the son of an Italian accountant. He grew up in Scarsdale and went to college at the highly regarded Romar College in New Hampshire. His file says he wanted to be a playwright, but he doesn't have the life experience and imagination. In the world of writers, this is a combination of skill and talent,

THE PUBLISHER'S DILEMMA

often referred to as content."

"Desanctis is a good writer, but deliberate, cautious, meticulous, and precise. Not bad skills for a newspaperman, but he doesn't have the coolness, hipness, and the personality to make him a legendary talent. Desanctis is safe and competent and would never get sued for printing anything out of context. His bosses at the News love him for that."

"They do sound like opposites and real rivals," Walker said.

"Very much so, and their rivalry will make this Scuttle Story fun to watch."

"Well, Walt," Walker said as he flashed his devilish smile again, "We're now making the biggest, most dramatic murder mystery of the year a contest for these guys. It's a story that could make both of their careers. I hate to say that this will be fun, because we've got a dead guy and another guy fighting for his life, but this is the kind of covert stuff I like."

"I hear you, Teddy, reminds you of your old spy espionage days, huh?"

"Exactly, Walt, exactly. So how do you want to split this up?"

"I know Luke McFlemming through his Brother, so unless you want him, I'll take him. Plus, he's such a blowhard that you might punch him in the nose," Bigelow said.

"That's funny Walt, and you're probably right. I met Desanctis at a Police Athletic League Fundraiser. We sat at the same table and had a good conversation."

"So, I'll work on McFlemming, and you'll take Desanctis," Bigelow said.

"Perfect Walt. Let's go make chumps out of these Hacks."

Chapter Twenty

Kwame felt better after a full day in the hospital. Aside from his brief interview with Walker and Humphrey, he spent the entire day strongly sedated and asleep.

He woke up surprised to see his best buddy, Tom Wilson, Tom's lady Danielle Jackson, and his girlfriend, Michelle Nubani, who had flown in from Chicago. They were all seated in the corner of his room. They looked stressed out and stunned. No one still knew what to make of everything.

Kwame straightened himself up in the bed and reached for his eyeglasses. He heard Danielle say, "he's waking up."

Michelle was reading a newspaper. She put it down and rushed to his bedside. "What was she doing here?" Kwame thought. He was surprised and glad to see her, Tom and Danielle. Anyone besides the policemen asking questions. Michelle grabbed his hand, bent over the bed, and kissed him on the cheek.

"How are you, baby?"

Michelle's touch was comforting. He felt warmth and concern from her kiss and how she held onto his hand. He squeezed her hand back and did not let it go. Tom and Danielle joined her at the side of the bed. They all looked nervous. Their concern was noticeable, even for laid back Tom Wilson.

"I'm okay Michelle, but they drugged me up pretty good."

As his eyes cleared, he noticed there was no longer the glare of the sunlight. It was dark outside.

"What time is it?"

Michelle, Tom, and Danielle all looked at their watches and responded in unison, "It's 8:15."

THE PUBLISHER'S DILEMMA

"Wow, I guess I slept through the whole day."

"Yes, you did," Tom said. "Nurse Dulany said they loaded you up pretty good. The only way they could keep all the police officers out of here was to fill you up with sedatives and put you to sleep."

"What did they give me?"

"I don't know. The nurse will be back in a few. Why? Did you like it?" Tom asked, smiling, and attempting some humor. "Maybe we can get you some more for later."

"Not at all. Those drugs are scary. My body feels limp."

Michelle chimed in, "Yeah, she said, you'll be fine in the morning, but they plan on keeping you here again tonight."

Kwame shakes his head in acknowledgment, "These drugs are so strong that I wouldn't be able to get down the hall much less home. It's probably a good idea to spend another night here."

He then turned Tom Wilson's girlfriend, "Hello there, Danielle. Thanks for coming. I guess you and Michelle have met?"

"Yes Kwame. We picked her up at the airport, we've been here since early afternoon. We're best friends by now. Right, Michelle?"

"Oh yeah," Michelle said as she reached with her free hand to Danielle. When she did, Danielle reached back. They connected like they knew each other for years and cared for each other. It was a look that warmed Kwame.

As Kwame looked at his gorgeous girlfriend, he noticed that while Danielle was beautiful, she didn't have anything on Michelle Nubani. He felt fortunate to have her in his life. He knew for some time that he was in love, and the sweetness she showed at that moment was a big reason why.

Tom interrupted his thoughts. "Your parents are here. They went downstairs to get some coffee and tea."

"Oh man. My Mom must be going crazy?"

"Well, your Dad finally got her to relax. We did have prayer about four times, though."

"Yeah, Tom as you know, my Mom is a worrier. I know she is going to be a bundle of nerves until she sees me, alert and clearheaded."

"Your Dad figured it was best to get her out of here for a while. The nurses told her that you were going to be fine. She did come in with her prayer oil, though."

Kwame touched his forehead and felt an oily spot. He smiled and said, "Thank God for her. Anyone else come with them?"

"No, just them, I called your sisters and brother. I told them that the Doctors said you were not injured, that you were just a witness, and are going to be fine."

"I hope she didn't find out about this in the newspaper?"

"No, the security guy, Charles Humphrey, called her and then your parents called me. I spoke with your secretary, Sheila Duncan. She had already called Michelle. I then called Michelle, and when she said she was going to come in, we picked her up from the airport."

Kwame looked up at Michelle again and smiled.

"Thanks Tom, I appreciate you, my Brother."

He was glad his best friend was there for him and took care of what needed to be done, especially keeping an eye on Michelle. He felt so lucky to have all these loving people around him, especially his new girlfriend. Then he thought about his new secretary and the day she must've had.

"Is Sheila okay, Tom?"

"She's fine. She did say that it was like a Zoo at the office. The press, clients, and associates have been calling her all day. The press is trying to find out about you. And your friends have been calling from all over to find out if you're okay."

"Thank God for Sheila."

Kwame drifted off again his thoughts as he began to think about what kind of circus the office must have been.

Through his daze, he heard Danielle say, "Did you tell him that Sheila was here earlier?"

"Oh Man, I almost forgot," Tom said, "Sheila also came by at about 6:00 this evening. She wants you to know that everything is okay at work. She said that Cornwall Harris, Gill's uncle, came to Harris Simmons this morning and convened everyone in the company cafeteria along with a guy named Wynne Shields."

"Wynne's my boss," Kwame said.

"Oh, that guy, right. How could I forget? Captain Asshole."

Tom then rolled his eyes. Kwame told him about Wynne and the details of their dreadful first meeting.

"Well," he continued, "they let everyone know that there was a police investigation, and while there are no leads, the police are working with the Harris Simmons security team. They also set up a bereavement center."

"I'm sure everyone is devastated," Kwame said, "those folks at Harris Simmons loved Gill Harris."

"Yes indeed, Kwame, that's what Sheila said. She said the staffers were emotionally wrecked."

"Gill was a good guy Tom. I didn't get to know him that well. Met him a couple times, with Donald. He was always happy and upbeat."

Kwame's thoughts then turned to Donald. He grew quiet and deep in thought as he recalled the day before. His silence didn't last very long as it was interrupted by the voice of his Mom, Jean. He turned to see her standing at the door of his room and smiling broadly. Kwame's Dad was standing behind her.

"Thank you, Jesus," she said as she stood at the door. She then made a beeline towards his bed. "How's my son doing?"

Kwame straightened up. He didn't want her to worry. She gave him a hug, touched his forehead to check his temperature and looked at his eyes to see if he was alert. Jean Mills was a worrier and she needed to do her own check-up despite the doctors saying that he was just dehydrated from the day before. She then said, "Okay Kwame, I know they've been giving you drugs. I don't like the way your eyes look but otherwise, you seem okay."

"I'm doing great, Mom. You know me, I'm Louis Mills's boy. I'm fine. Besides it's nothing that a little prayer and good drugs wouldn't cure. I heard you had Church up in here."

Tom started laughing real loud and said, "Bro, you sold me out."

She looked at Tom, scowled, and said, "Jesus going to get you yet, Thomas."

Jean Mills always called Tom by his full name. She liked Tom and treated him like he was her Son.

Tom looked back at her and said defensively, his voice rising, "What did I do? All I said was that we had prayer, four, five, six times, and that you came in here wielding some prayer oil."

His joke made everyone laugh, even Kwame and his Mom.

Kwame turned to his Mom, "So, I guess you know everyone now. You've met Michelle and Danielle."

Jean looked at her son, "Yes, I did. She's a very nice young lady and really, quite pretty, and so is Danielle."

Michelle and Danielle blushed after this comment. Michelle had now moved to the doorway to make space for Jean to sit at the chair at Kwame's bedside. Louis, Kwame's Father, looked at his son, gave him a thumbs-up sign, smiled, and said, "So when is the date Son?"

Kwame turned to his Dad, "Come on Dad, How about how are you doing Son?"

Louis looked at his Son and said, "Come on Kwame, we've been through that already. We checked it out with the doctors nine, ten times already, we know you're going to be fine. Your Mother was worried, so you know how she is, she got her answers from the Doctors, the Nurses, the other doctors, the security guards, the janitor. Everybody in this place." Louis Mills rolled his eyes in exasperation "We talked to any and everybody, we know that you are fine."

He then asked his son again, "Now, when is the date?"

Michelle Nubani blushed again, Kwame signed and said, "Ah, come on now, Dad, you need to stop Man."

Tom couldn't help but laugh at this Father and Son hazing, but he shouldn't have as Louis got after him as well.

"That goes for you too Tom. I'm looking at two beautiful and successful women. Both of you guys can't do any better."

Louis then winked at Michelle and Danielle, "Not you two anyhow. You knuckleheads better get hitched to these women before they find out what kind of dirty rotten scoundrels you really are."

Jean Mills looked at her husband with a stern look on her face and said, "Louis, you know better. You need to mind your business."

Louis ignored his wife, his son, and Tom's plea. "All I'm saying is that these women are a serious upgrade from any of those you guys ever introduced us too. Right Jean?"

That statement was enough to get his wife in on the hazing.

"Now that's true, and they're both God-fearing. You know I checked Kwame and Tom," Jean said and nodded at Michelle and Danielle. "You guys need women like these two to keep you close to the Cross."

Both Kwame and Tom looked at each other. Kwame slunk down in his bed and covered his head and ears with his pillow.

"You guys are terrible," Tom said to Kwame's parents.

Suddenly, Anna Dulany appeared. Kwame was relieved to see her. She seemed never to leave the hospital. The hazing stopped when she walked into the room.

"Thank God Nurse Dulany. It's good to see you. These people are disturbing me. You might want to ask them to go get some coffee or something."

"Well now, you seem to be coming along well," Nurse Dulany said with a smile.

"Parental harassment will do that. I've had to endure this for a lot of years from these two." He said, with a deadpanned expression aimed at his parents.

"Oh, I see. Well, you only get one set of parents, and they seem like good people, so I'm not dealing with this at all."

"Ah man," Kwame and Tom raised their hands in exasperation.

Chapter Twenty-One

The next morning Kwame woke to find the effects of the sedatives completely purged from his system.

Nurse Dulany came to his room at 8:30. "Good morning Kwame, let me take your vitals."

She then took his blood pressure and his heart rate. She checked his charts, smiled and said, "You are doing great young man. I'm going to release you. I'll put in some paperwork, and you'll be free to go in about an hour."

"Thank you Jesus, and you too Nurse Dulany. You are the best."

THE PUBLISHER'S DILEMMA

"The pleasure has been all mine Kwame. I want you to know that it has been an honor to help you. I wish you the best. Everybody here does. We all know how crazy this story is. We haven't had a dramatic shooting and murder story in this hospital since Madame Hot Temper, Dawn Davis Stuart, shot and killed her husband Yancey five years ago."

Kwame thought for a second, "Madame Hot Temper. I remember that story. What a big tabloid drama that was."

"Indeed, it was Kwame, we only get these big celebrities and VIP emergency room admittances every now and again. So just be careful, we know that the press can be tough and we want you to be okay. Lay low for a while if you can and away from any drama. We don't want you back here."

"Thanks Nurse Dulany, I appreciate it."

After she left the room, Kwame grabbed his mobile phone and called his secretary, Sheila Duncan. She picked up the phone on the first ring, "Good Morning, Sheila Duncan here."

"Hi Sheila, this is Kwame, how are you?"

"Hi Kwame, how are you?" Her voice rose with excitement. "It is so good to hear from you. Are you feeling better? Oh, thank you Jesus. Thank you, Lord."

Her glee made Kwame smile, "Thank you so much Sheila, it's good to hear from you too. I've got some good news. They are releasing me this morning. I'm hoping you can get me a car down here in an hour or so."

"Absolutely. Are you going to come into the office or going home?"

"I'm going to go to my apartment and continue to rest. The Nurse here suggested I take it slow for a while and avoid the drama that's going to follow this shooting. I'll probably hang out there for the next couple of days but be reachable by phone."

"That's probably best as it has been pretty crazy around here. We can talk once you get home as you need."

DARIUS MYERS

Sheila Duncan arranged to have a car service pick Kwame up at 11:00 am. He then called Tom as he wanted him to stop by his place and pick up a fresh change of clothes. When he called Tom's, Danielle answered the phone.

"Hello," Danielle said. Kwame recognized her voice.

"Hey there, Danielle, this is Kwame. How are you this morning?"

"Hi there Kwame, great to hear from you. I'm well. Oh boy, we had a crazy night here. The press called most of the night. Tom eventually had to turn the phone off."

"Oh wow, I'm so sorry about that Danielle. That's terrible."

"Please. You don't have to apologize at all. The big question is, how are you doing?"

"I'm feeling much better, back to normal, I guess. I hope you guys got some sleep?"

"No worries, we're fine. Your Boy just got out of the shower. Hold on, let me get him, okay?"

"Sure, no problem Danielle."

As he waited, Kwame thought about the peskiness of the press and how crazy his life would be for the unforeseeable future.

When Tom picked up the phone, Kwame could hear him say to Danielle, "Thank you, baby."

He then said, "Hey Kwame, how are you this morning, Brother? Did you sleep well last night?"

"I did. But I heard from Danielle that you guys had a pretty eventful night."

"Oh, it wasn't that bad. I kept getting calls from The News and The Post, a Luke McFlemming, and Michael Desanctis. They are the guys who did the front-page stories. They're now looking for anything they can find out about you. How they put us together so fast, I'll never know."

THE PUBLISHER'S DILEMMA

"My goodness, these guys don't let up. I'm sorry about that."

"Not a problem at all Kwame. I got your back through this, you know that, my friend. You can count on me for whatever you need. I'm taking a few days off from work to be there for you."

"Thank you so much Tom, but you don't have to do that."

"This is what friends do Kwame, so no worries. I was going to call and ask if I could bring you a change of clothes or anything. I also figured you'll probably need someone to run interference for you from home. I can only imagine that your home phone and cell phone have been ringing like crazy."

"Thanks buddy, I don't know what I'd do without you. I was calling to see if you could pick up some fresh clothes, but on second thought, with all the drama, why don't you take a taxi down here. I've ordered a car to pick me up. I'll wear what I have here and change when I get home."

"Sounds like a plan, Kwame. I'll be out of here in 20-30 minutes and at the hospital in an hour."

"Great Tom, see you then buddy."

"Okay," Tom said and hung up the phone.

After he ended his call with Tom, Kwame began to think about Donald. He realized he should have gotten an update from Anna Dulany. He would check on him before he left the hospital.

He dressed quickly and decided to walk down the hall to the Hospital Commissary to pick up a newspaper. He then saw Carrie Sinclair.

She was at the newsstand paying for newspapers. As Kwame approached her, Carrie turned around. She turned as if she could sense him coming. She spoke first.

"Hello Kwame. How are you? Are you feeling better?"

She looked tired and stressed. Kwame remembered that look from when they were going through their breakup and divorce. But it was also a look that reminded him of the reason that he was in the hospital. He felt guilty again for not checking in on Donald Alexander earlier.

"I'm doing just fine, Carrie. How are you? And Donald? I was going to check in on him."

"Thank you, Kwame. He's still in a coma. The doctors are very concerned. The good news is his vital signs are better, but there was so much brain hemorrhaging from the oxygen loss that the doctors don't know if there will be any brain damage. The other good news is that the surgery has repaired all the internal bleeding. All we can do now is pray."

Carrie continued, "This entire ordeal is amazing, the shooting, the press stories and bizarreness is right out of a murder mystery."

"You are so right Carrie. We have to stay prayerful that he will come out of this fully recovered."

Kwame looked at his watch and realized that he had some time before Tom was to arrive. He then offered to grab coffee with Carrie. She looked as if she could use the company.

"Carrie, have you had breakfast yet?"

"No, I was just going to get coffee from the cafeteria and head back to Donald's room."

"Well, why don't we go together, Tom is coming to meet me in about 45 minutes, if you wouldn't mind me joining you, I could use some coffee as well."

"Oh Tom," Carrie smiled weakly, "I saw him down the hallway for a minute yesterday. He didn't see me. Two women were with him. It looked like the same old Tom."

Carrie sighed and looked up in the air. It was a look he knew well. It was reflective of their past and her distrust of his best friend. She snapped out of it and looked at Kwame and flashed a half-smile.

Kwame read it as a look that Tom's womanizing with my man is not my problem anymore. He was right, and it was an even more significant realization for Carrie because she didn't care. For her, it was a moment of proof that she needed to have, to know that she moved on.

She then turned to Kwame, her face suddenly sunnier and said, "Let's go Kwame, a cup of coffee sounds like a good idea. I could use the company."

For a second, Kwame questioned if having a cup of coffee and spending time with Carrie was a good idea. He didn't know about the realization she had seconds earlier. But he forged ahead, after all, he asked her to have coffee.

He stopped reading into it and said, "Great Carrie, I could use the company too."

They hadn't had many conversations since their divorce. They were cordial and kind to each other at Donald's Hampton's party, but they didn't have more than a cordial conversation that day and for the entire weekend. They also hadn't spent any significant time together since the divorce.

Now, the reason that they were both at the hospital brought them together in an unimaginable way.

"He might even become her next husband," Kwame thought. "If so, this could be a big breakthrough meeting. They weren't married any longer and weren't in love anymore, but their worlds were now linked and maybe forever through Donald Alexander and the tragic murder of Gill Harris."

Kwame and Carrie made their way to the cafeteria and had their best conversation in years. As they talked, Carrie first shared that she was happy and progressing in her new career as a photojournalist.

"I have many new projects that I am very excited about. In particular, I just signed on to do a four-part series for your magazine, World Media on United Nations economic and agrarian development programs in eastern European and southern African countries. It is a two-year project, and I'll be living out of a suitcase again, but I love the work, so I think it will be a lot of fun."

"That sounds like amazing and significant work Carrie. But you know I'm not surprised. I'm delighted to hear this news and can't wait to see the end product."

"Thank you, Kwame. That means a lot coming from you."

He smiled and said, "you're welcome."

"Now tell me about coming back to New York?" she asked. "It must be exciting."

"Carrie, this is such a fantastic opportunity for me. I feel blessed working for Donald. He's a brilliant, talented, and highly respected media executive and beyond that such a great person. Of course, I don't have to tell you that he is a great guy. You know him better than I do. The role is a once in a lifetime opportunity, and I intend to take full advantage of it."

"He is quite fond of you and wants you to do well Kwame." She then smiled and giggled. "You know, I can't help but wonder how small this world is and how my ex and my current guy are now teaming up as leaders in this industry. I am a lucky woman to have had both of you guys as important men in my life."

"I think Donald would agree that we're the lucky ones Carrie."

"That's sweet of you Kwame, very kind of you to say." She then steered the conversation to their relationship. "You were always so kind, even when we were at war with each other. I must tell you that I had a lot of regret and grief because I wanted to hate you so much. But you were always so damn nice."

"Carrie, just so you know, those were my Mother's orders," he said with a smile and a look that she knew well. Carrie always called it the 'Stop With The Stories' look. Kwame forgot that she could read him, and he continued with the story. She let him set his own trap.

"She was crazy about you, and stayed on me about doing right by

THE PUBLISHER'S DILEMMA

you."

Carrie then stopped him, "Kwame, you know I can still tell when you're making stuff up. It hasn't been that long. That look Man, it's Your Tell."

He didn't even bother to protest. He knew he was caught and said, "I guess I'm busted, huh?"

"Yes, you are busted Brother, but I do know your Mom loves me. You don't know this, we still talk regularly. It's always been our secret."

"So, you know then that I didn't totally make it up. Mom's orders were clear. Treat Carrie right or else. I knew she was right, even when I wanted to be mean. And look how things have turned out, you are doing just fine without me."

His ex-wife looked at him, shook her head in approval of Kwame's last point. She then flashed a huge smile and said, "Yeah, Donald is a nice upgrade, huh. I'm not doing so bad after all."

"All right now. I'm going to tell my Mom that you were mean."

"You better not," Carrie shot back with a big smile, "I'll deny I said it, and since she always agrees with me, you'll lose again."

Kwame and Carrie both knew their past as lovers, husband, and wife was over. They also knew this conversation which turned out to be more positive than they both could imagine was needed. It was the closure conversation they never had.

"I'm glad we're having this talk, especially with Donald Alexander now in our lives. There's a good chance we'll be spending a lot of time together, so why not be friends, right?"

"I agree Kwame. We're both in good places now, and it would be awesome if we can be friends."

As they finished their coffee, Kwame, who was seated with his back to the entrance of the cafeteria, saw Carrie look to the entrance and smile. He turned around and saw Tom walking towards them. Michelle Nubani was with him.

"Hi Tom, how are you?" Carrie spoke first, and her tone sounded genuine. Tom needed to hear Carrie say that, as she always unnerved him. He knew she had a real problem with him because of his womanizing past.

His response was nervous, it was clear that he was unsettled by having to talk to Carrie, but he tried to act unbothered.

"Hey Carrie, how are you, sweetie? It's been a while."

Kwame chose to bail his buddy out, first by interrupting this awkward moment and changing the focus to reintroducing Michelle and Carrie.

"Hey honey. Come over and meet Carrie again. We were having some coffee, and she was giving me an update on Donald."

Kwame then leaned over to Carrie and whispered, "You got to stop messing with Tom."

Carrie looked to Tom and said, "You think?" She had a mischievous look on her face. Kwame remembered it was her prankster look.

"Yes, please stop. Look at Tom. He's looking pitiful."

"You are so right, the brother is looking kind of weak." Carrie stood up and walked over to Tom and whispered in his ear.

He smiled, and as the tension eased off his face, he said, "Absolutely, I'd like that."

Tom later told Kwame that Carrie said, "I've put our past behind me, and I am hopeful that we can have a warm friendship."

Carrie then turned to Michelle Nubani and said, "Michelle, it's not the best of circumstances, but it's good to see you again. Kwame has been telling me that things are going well. I hope we all get to be friends."

"I hope so as well Carrie. The Hamptons party was just a disastrous first meeting for all of us."

"Oh yes it was Michelle. I look forward to having laughs about that moment for many years to come."

THE PUBLISHER'S DILEMMA

"Me too Carrie, that would be great."

As he watched Carrie, Kwame was having such positive thoughts about his ex-wife. He was so impressed with her right now. She was the warm, sensitive woman that he fell in love with a long time ago, and she was doing it under pressure. He was very proud of her, but his love for Michelle Nubani was so much more intense than any feeling he'd had for Carrie. He walked over to Michelle and kissed her on the cheek.

"I am so crazy about you."

She smiled broadly. It was just what she needed to hear at this awkward reunion. Michelle whispered in his ear, "Thank you, I love you honey. I'm so happy to be with you."

Kwame then turned to Carrie and said, "Thank you for the coffee, and thank you even more for the friendship. I don't know what tomorrow will bring for us, but I hope we can build on this."

"Me too Kwame, thank you." Carrie smiled broadly and her face glowed through the smile.

Kwame then asked, "We're going to leave in a few, but would you mind if I check on Donald before I head home?"

"Oh absolutely, you must Kwame," Carrie said. "He owes his life to you. You don't have to ask me for permission."

As they walked out of the cafeteria and towards Donald's room, they saw Charlie Humphrey at the main hospital reception area. His large figure was animated. He was pointing and screaming at three people. They all had note pads in their hands.

"Oh crap," Carrie said.

The tall, blonde male spotted them and yelled, "Kwame Mills, one question, just one question."

They were trying to get past Humphrey, who stood between them and the hallway to get to the cafeteria.

DARIUS MYERS

"Shut up, McFlemming, I'm warning you," Humphrey screamed at them.

The shorter, dark-haired guy got past Humphrey and started to run down the hall towards them. He yelled, "Desanctis, I'll kick your ass if you don't get back here right now."

Charlie Humphrey turned around, pointed at the crew of Carrie Sinclair, Michelle Nubani, Tom Wilson, and Kwame Mills, and shouted, "Get back in the cafeteria and shut and lock the door."

Kwame and the group turned around and headed for the door. Two hospital police officers ran from behind them and towards the commotion between Charlie Humphrey and the Celebrity Hack Patrol. Humphrey's deep voice was booming throughout the hallway. Desanctis, now with the police rushing towards him, turned around and headed back towards the main reception area. He did not want to have anything to do with the police. McFlemming and Jennifer Kung, when they saw the police, headed towards the exit.

Mike Desanctis now had to get back past Humphrey. And he had to do it fast as the hospital cops are gaining on him. As Desanctis approached, Humphrey tried to corner him. He couldn't catch him, but he was able to take a swing at him. Desanctis ducked, and it was a good thing because Charlie Humphrey spun in a circle. Had he connected, he would have knocked Desanctis out.

The press trio now stood at the hospital exit doors. They all had cameras, and although the Police Officers were still running towards them, they were still trying to get a shot of Kwame Mills. Humphrey turned to Kwame Mills and Carrie, who had stopped to watch the commotion.

"Please, I need you all to turn around and get in the Cafeteria and lock the door right now."

Kwame grabbed Carrie's arm and spun her around, Tom and Michelle

THE PUBLISHER'S DILEMMA

Nubani were already inside the cafeteria. They all heard the click of the cameras and the police screaming at the Celebrity Hacks. After they were safely in the cafeteria, they stood by the door straining to listen to what was going on. Seconds later, they heard a knock on the window in the cafeteria. They turned to see the Celebrity Hacks. They had walked to a courtyard and were standing at a gigantic window that gave them full of the cafeteria. They had their cameras flicking and took pictures of all four of them.

"Oh Damn, let's get out of here," Tom said, and he began to unlock the door. "Let's go back into the hallway."

Tom saw Humphrey and yelled, "They are at the window in the cafeteria taking pictures."

Charlie Humphrey and the police officers ran to the Courtyard and started screaming and chasing them again.

Finally, the press guys ran off, and Kwame Mills, Tom Wilson, Carrie Sinclair, and Michelle Nubani stood in the hallway stunned.

Charlie Humphrey came in from outside. He was breathing hard and irritated.

"What in the hell just happened?" Tom asked.

"Damn Hacks. If they got a good picture, tomorrow you all are going to be Celebrities and not the right kind of Celebrities. Your lives are going to be different for a long time."

"Tell me about it," Kwame said. "I guess they'll have another picture of me for tomorrow's paper?"

Humphrey, still breathing hard, said, "Don't be surprised Kwame. These guys are scrambling to get any news they can."

After they calmed down, Kwame's thoughts turned from the press to the police. He remembered he had to talk more with Teddy Walker.

"Charlie, I know that the police still have lots of questions for me, and based on the way those two guys were harassing me the first night, the police might consider me to be a suspect."

"Don't you worry, you're not a suspect, you're a witness. Nevertheless, Walker still wants to talk to you again. He wants you to call him as soon as you get home. I'd do that immediately."

"Should you be there with me? I don't know the protocol for dealing with Police investigations. I do know from the night of the shooting and Teddy Walker's first visit that you know how to handle them."

"I'll join you. Just set up something for late afternoon and call me as soon as you do and I'll be there. Okay?"

Kwame wanted Charlie Humphrey around for his interviews and nodded his head in acknowledgment.

"I'll call you as soon as I set up a meeting."

Humphrey then said, "Now, I need you guys to get out of here. You're going to be a target for the media over the next couple of days. We've got you staying at the Walnut Hotel under secret names. Don't even bother to go home. Unfortunately, until this press hysteria dies down, you'll continue to be a target, and not just you Kwame, that goes for you two as well. I'll set up rooms for you guys also," Humphrey said as he pointed to Tom and Michelle Nubani.

"Carrie, I know you're going to be here for a while looking over Donald, but when you leave, please let me know as I have you at the Walnut Hotel as well."

Chapter Twenty-Two

Walt Bigelow got Luke McFlemming on the phone. He called in the afternoon at The News and to his surprise, caught him at his desk.

"McFlemming here."

Luke McFlemming always answered his phone in a voice accented with an Irish brogue. It was another fabricated part of his act. If you were meeting him for the first time, you might think he was really from Ireland, not the west side of Manhattan. As he answered the phone, Walt Bigelow could hear the chaotic background noise of the newsroom. It was the usual buzz of yelling, screaming, and banging sounds on keyboards. McFlemming lowered his head and pressed the phone to his head tightly so he could hear the Asst. Chief of Detectives.

"Hey Luke, Walt Bigelow here. How are you?"

"Oh, just dandy. But I can't rest on my laurels. Yesterday's story is old news. I got to get some more scoop on this Harris Simmons stuff. I'm just finishing a story that will run tomorrow. Got any juice for me, buddy?"

Walt Bigelow liked what he heard from McFlemming. He was thinking about how cocky and arrogant McFlemming could be and looked forward to taking him down a peg with this scuttle story. But before he used him, he had to admonish him for his antics at the hospital last night and this morning.

He started with his beat down, "You should be lucky that you're not in jail after that stunt you and your parking lot cronies pulled at the hospital cafeteria yesterday. And I got a call from Charlie Humphrey he told me you guys were there again this morning acting a fool."

DARIUS MYERS

"Yeah right, Bigelow. That would make your day," McFlemming said with his usual arrogance.

"It absolutely would make my day Luke. You should know that Teddy Walker suggested I lock you and your crew in a room with Humphrey. Man, that would not be good because he wants a piece of you, really bad. He was threatening to come down to your office himself. All I can say is that it's not exactly the safest story for you to cover. You better be careful. Stop antagonizing that guy."

Bigelow hoped that he was getting through to McFlemming. After all, Charlie Humphrey was not the guy to have on your enemy list. McFlemming was silent, which meant that Bigelow's tactic might be working, now he was ready to charm him and reel him in.

"But don't worry, if you don't make that mistake again, everything will be fine. Now Luke, humor me, I was wondering how you always get the scoop on the big story."

"Walt, it's not a big secret. I'm a snoop just like you," McFlemming said with a little less bravado. The threat of a Charlie Humphrey beat down had some effect. However, it was humility that only lasted for a few seconds; McFlemming couldn't help himself.

"I have great detective skills Walt. You know I am great at what I do. Do you think I could've been a good detective? I think I'd be good, world-class in fact, but I love the limelight of the Press too much."

"No, you're right, you've picked the right line of work McFlemming. Vanity will get you shot in my business. The wise guys don't like fancy cops, speaking of which real cops don't like fancy cops. And you're really fancy. You're a martini guy. You know cops drink scotch and beer."

McFlemming snapped back, "Martini my ass, I'm bourbon and scotch, and yes, fancy scotch if you count single malt. It's Brown liquor or no liquor at all for me. Vodka and Gin are for wimps."

"Okay, okay," Bigelow said. He realized that he made his point and realizing and this conversation was going down the testosterone path where they could be for hours. He needed to get down to business. McFlemming, however, beat him to the punch.

"What are you calling for Walt? To bust my hump on getting the scoop, or for taking some photographs? Well, you did that already?"

"Absolutely. I told you Walker is pissed. He thinks you're a real pain in the ass."

"So, Teddy thinks I'm a pain in the ass, huh?" McFlemming responded. "That's an honor Walt. You think I should give him a call to tell him."

"Well, if you do, then I really might have to shoot you," Bigelow said with a half-serious laugh. "But I wouldn't do that even for Teddy because I don't like going to jail, I like putting the bad guys there."

And then Walt Bigelow jumped in with the scuttle bait.

"So, what's the follow-up to yesterday's story Luke? What you got Luke?"

"I've been waiting for you to ask. Not a big story, we're trying to do a chronology piece on the shooting and our story yesterday, which was nothing more than a guess on who is likely to end up in control. We don't have any real facts to run with a story. Anything you want to give me?"

McFlemming had his primary contact at the NYPD on the line. He figured he might as well ask.

"You know I can't do that Luke." Bigelow chose to play a little hard to get. He didn't want to reveal too easily. It was a smart move as McFlemming got antsy and began to beg.

DARIUS MYERS

"What do you mean, Walt? Come on man, give me something off the record. You know you're my guy. This murder and shooting is the story of the year. I might even be able to get a book deal. Come on man. I need the extra money."

"You're my Guy? Since when did we become best friends?"

"Then why are you calling me Walt? If you don't have anything, I got to go. I am on deadline and need to put my story to bed."

"Okay McFlemming calm down, I'm feeling generous today. You're right. This is a big story, so why don't we share?" Bigelow lowered his voice as if to be covert.

McFlemming nearly dropped his phone. He was shocked.

"Say what? What did you say?"

He couldn't believe that Walt Bigelow was going to let him in on the biggest murder mystery of the year.

"You heard me," Bigelow's voice was still lowered. "I said, let's share, but we can't do it over the phone. Meet me at Billy's Bar at Chelsea's Pier in an hour."

"But my deadline is 8:00 pm, just four hours from now? I've got to put this story to bed."

"Trust me McFlemming. Meet me, and you'll have a much bigger story for tomorrow."

"Ah, hell man. You should have called me earlier."

"Do you want the story or not? I can always call the other guys."

The threat of the competition getting his story terrified McFlemming. Suddenly, all talk of deadlines and putting stories to bed ended. Walt Bigelow had Luke McFlemming eating out of his hand.

THE PUBLISHER'S DILEMMA

"No, no, I'll meet you in an hour, at Billy's Bar at Chelsea's Pier, right?"

"Yep. See you there in an hour."

At the same time, Teddy Walker was having a similar conversation with Mike Desanctis from The Post. Except that he was more direct.

When Desanctis answered his phone, he had just handed in his story for the day, a biography piece on Gill Harris with a short sidebar on Donald Alexander. The last few days were pretty traumatic, with the freshness of this story. He knew he was lucky to get the picture of Kwame Mills, and today was a long day, especially after being nearly knocked out this morning by Charlie Humphrey. He was ready to go home.

It was a kick of adrenaline when he answered his phone, and he heard the Chief of Detectives say, "Teddy Walker here."

Desanctis's heart began beating like a rabbit's. He knew this was no buddy call. To steal a couple of minutes to gain his composure, he asked Teddy Walker for a second to get rid of another call.

"Hey, Chief Walker, let me put you on hold for a second. I've got to get rid of this call."

Desanctis, true to his more conservative nature, did not attempt to be too familiar with Chief Walker. Good thing for Desanctis because it was the way Teddy Walker liked things. He didn't care for big-time personalities like McFlemming. Desanctis's direct and straightforward style was what Walker preferred.

"Sure Desanctis, no problem," Walker said. He smiled as he knew his surprise phone call to Desanctis caught him off guard.

Desanctis was so shocked that it took him a full minute to get his wits together. He was still unnerved when he pressed the line that was holding

DARIUS MYERS

Teddy Walker's phone call.

"Chief Walker, what can I do for you?"

Desanctis was trying to be as cool as possible, but even still, his voice was staccato and dry. He was, after all, the accountants son.

Walker was direct and to the point, "Well, first I want to congratulate you on getting the scoop on the shooting. What an event, huh?" He didn't bother to go into the cafeteria snooping that got him the scoop or this morning's run-in with Humphrey. He didn't want to intimidate Desanctis too much.

"Congratulations? What an event?" Desanctis thought to himself. "What in the hell is going on here?"

He got lost in his thoughts about Walker's comments long enough for Teddy Walker to repeat himself.

"I said the shooting was some event, and congratulations on a good story."

Desanctis finally calmed himself, "Oh yeah, thanks. Yeah, it was something." And then he added, "This story is a real cliffhanger."

"I'd say," Walker responded, and then he made his move. He didn't spend as much time buttering up his bait as Walt Bigelow did with McFlemming. Besides, he knew Desanctis was still in shock.

"Look Mike, this a big murder story, and I want the best guys telling the right stuff. Meet me in an hour at Kipp Meenans's on 23rd street. I'll give you an update that you can have for tomorrow's paper. Do you think you can do that?"

Mike Desanctis's brain was spinning. He could barely contain himself. Here he was, a senior reporter at the largest daily newspapers in New York City, and about to get the inside scoop on the biggest murder story of the year, maybe in New York in 20 years. Desanctis didn't beg for more time but had to control himself and asked for another moment to regain his composure.

"That's my other line again," the newsroom was buzzing with the sounds of phones ringing, and the usual high-pitched and stressed banter a few hours before closing. "Let me put you on hold for a second, don't go away. I'll be back in ten seconds."

"Go ahead Mike, I'll wait," Walker said. He knew that Desanctis wouldn't refuse his request, and the phone call wouldn't last much longer after he returned.

Desanctis put the call on hold and screamed, "Oh my God, I've got Teddy Walker on the freaking line, and he wants to give me the scoop on yesterday's shooting."

The scream from Desanctis shocked the newsroom. He was smiling and shaking at the same time, and the newsroom went silent with his announcement. His buddy, Reggie Goodman, who sat two desks down, ran over to his desk as did Pete "Press" Colon, the legendary editor of The Post. The scream seemed to relieve Desanctis, and he stood up, took a deep breath, and pressed the line holding Teddy Walker's call.

"I'll see you in an hour, Kipp Meenans's at the bar, right Chief Walker."

"That's right, in an hour, don't keep me waiting."

Desanctis hung up the phone and slapped high-five with Reggie Goodman. Everyone in the newsroom laughed at the untypical display of emotion by Desanctis. Pete Colon gave him a high-five also. Colon knew that Teddy Walker was a hard nut; everyone knew of his reputation to only deal with the news-press during press conferences. A small crowd gathered around his desk. The room was buzzing, they all wanted to know about the call. Desanctis replayed to them their conversation minus all the bouts of nervousness.

"It was pretty short, he told me he thought I did a great story on the shooting and he wants to meet tonight to give me a scoop."

Pete Colon, was chewing on a half-smoked lit cigar. He took a big draw from it. Everyone turned to him, waiting for some sage comment from their bigger than life editor. He had uncovered and reported on many big news stories. Colon was very liberal with advice and like many old news guys, didn't mind dispensing it. He also swore too much. After blowing out the smoke from the big cigar pull, he looked at Desanctis, smiled, and said in a tired, smoke filtered voice, "And I thought you were a tight ass. Today you are The Man. Go get 'em Tarzan."

The larger than life editor called all his favorites, The Man and Tarzan. It was one of the rare times he called Desanctis either, and today he got a double dose.

The newsroom erupted in laughter after Colon's joke. Mike Desanctis, bait victim #2 was on a cloud and in 15 minutes, would leave to get a beer and the scoop on the biggest murder story of the year.

As he made his way to the elevator, Desanctis had a pep in his step. He was excited and thinking, "I'm going to beat McFlemming's ass finally."

Chapter Twenty-Three

On day three after the shooting, the Scuttle Story hit the newsstands, and Teddy Walker and Walt Bigelow were ecstatic.

"We got those suckers," Bigelow said as they gathered in Walker's office to discuss their subterfuge. He had copies of the papers and was excited and ready to brag and boast. "I love these headlines," Bigelow then them to an equally pleased Walker.

"The News's headline read Exclusive by Luke McFlemming: Evidence of Shooting At Harris Simmons Lies With Video. The Post's headline was almost identical, There Is Video Evidence of Shooting At Harris Simmons: Exclusive Only By The City Post."

Teddy Walker smiled, "These headlines and stories will help our plan work to perfection."

He then picked up the papers and said to Bigelow. "The story says we confiscated video cameras in the main elevators and freight elevators and the Visitor Sign-In Books at Harris Simmons. But readers and the bad guys don't know that we purposely did not share that we have video from the private elevator. By saying we have a video of two young white males leaving via the freight elevators at about 7:00 pm can be big."

Bigelow nodded in agreement and said, "Yes Teddy, they may think now that there is no video of the private elevator and they are safe, which is what we want."

"Exactly Walt, now that we've set the trap let's see where this takes us. We did plant the correct time in the story by saying that the suspects left the building at 7 pm. Maybe someone saw these two leaving the building and will want to correct the reporting. I want the old man and the girl for questioning, and to keep this videotape a secret for now. If they are local and don't think there's a video, they won't feel a need to leave the city, and we might be able to back our way into finding them."

Bigelow shook his head in agreement. "This is a brilliant plan Teddy, that's why you're the boss."

Walker then commended the victimized Celebrity Hack Patrol members, "McFlemming and Desanctis for their part. They may be pissed off at the news conference tomorrow because we didn't give them an exclusive and a full account of what we know, but it all wasn't a lie."

"I'm sure they won't see it that way," Bigelow said and grinned, knowing that he played McFlemming.

"Such is life Walt, McFlemming's a big boy. He knows the game. Sometimes you win, sometimes you lose. We've got a murder mystery to solve, that's my only concern. Besides, these stories are going to sell a lot of newspapers today."

Walker and Bigelow were right. Desanctis and McFlemming were both disappointed with the Detectives for telling them that they were getting exclusives. The executives and editors at their papers didn't mind, online views and newsstand sales were up 50% for both papers.

Pete Colon was happy that they were one of the two chosen papers. While Desanctis was fuming over being played by Walker, Colon offered a sage's point of view.

"Let's be happy about this one. You got one of the two stories. Now everyone will be looking at us for follow-up. At least, we didn't get beat on this one."

"And remember, he called you. Your parking lot buddy, Jennifer Kung, didn't get pulled in on this. You'd be looking for a new job if she and that hound, McFlemming got this story, and you didn't."

"Don't sweat it, kid." It was another of Colon's nicknames. "You did a good job, he called you once, chances are he'll call you again."

THE PUBLISHER'S DILEMMA

Pete Colon was right too, Jennifer Kung got reamed for not getting called on the story.

Across town, McFlemming had a tougher time dealing with sharing the story with his rival. He knew the game, he was in the information business, and people got used all the time for what they knew. Newspaper reporters made their names and reputation on getting people to give them information.

Zach Goldberg, McFlemming's editor, was just as philosophical as Pete Colon. First, however, he used the opportunity to beat up the often uncontrollable McFlemming. At the 11 am editor and reporters meeting, Goldberg gave McFlemming the business. He held up for everybody to see a copy of The News with the front-page story that read, "Exclusive by Luke McFlemming: Evidence of Shooting At Harris Simmons Lies With Video."

"Ladies and gentlemen," he said to the 20 reporters crammed into the news writers bullpen. "Another excellent piece of undercover, first-rate journalism by our man with contacts into the deepest reaches of the NYPD, Mr. Luke McFlemming."

McFlemming squirmed in his seat. He knew it was coming, the buildup before the teardown. Goldberg then picked up a copy of The Post with the front page that also had in red ink headline and the words EXCLUSIVE by Mike Desanctis.

"Oops," Goldberg said, and laughed. It turned into a moment of loud laughter as the other writers at The News most who despised hot-shot Luke McFlemming bellowed.

After the laughter, Goldberg turned to McFlemming and said, "Got used, huh?"

McFlemming, humbled, looked up to Goldberg with a weak smile. He knew he got used, and it was right there in big red type.

"Yep, he got me. I got licked like a five-cent chocolate-filled lollipop."

DARIUS MYERS

Everybody in the room laughed. McFlemming, even in defeat, usually had the last laugh.

"You're right." Goldberg then used this as a teaching opportunity for the younger reporters and writers in the newsroom. "But even those five-cent lollipops can have delicious chocolate fillings. McFlemming, this was a good story. You got beat on the exclusive, but you still got the story, and it was a good one, you didn't let down the readers. Next time, be a little more careful."

McFlemming breathed a sigh of relief. He was a high stakes reporter, he often took risks to get the big story, and he often fought with Zach Goldberg about his columns. Goldberg's philosophy, be careful first and dogged for the truth second, if you take care of those two fundamentals, you'll never get burned.

At the end of the meeting, Goldberg pulled McFlemming to the side and said, "Good job Luke."

McFlemming looked at him and said, "Thanks, Zach." He then started to walk away.

Goldberg then grabbed him by the arm, stopped him, and said, "Stay after this one Luke, so what, you made a mistake. This story is bigger than your ego and certainly bigger than this paper. This may be the story of the year, maybe even your Harlowe Writing Award."

Part Three

Chapter Twenty-Four

Seven days after the shooting, Donald Alexander was still in a coma. Kwame Mills had a 7 am appointment with Teddy Walker and Charlie Humphrey at Police Headquarters. It was his second visit with Walker since leaving the hospital.

At the beginning of the meeting, Walker said to Kwame, "Please know that we have cleared you as a suspect, but we still need to keep track of your whereabouts in case the killer would attempt to make a hit on you. I know from Charlie Humphrey that Harris Simmons has a security detail on you. But know that we're also keeping a tail on you with marked police officers to dissuade any bad actors. I hope you understand that it is for your safety, and you'll be okay with this. We're going to keep you safe."

"I understand, and I appreciate it, Chief Walker. Thank you very much," Kwame said.

"You're welcome Kwame," Walker said and continued, "and, so you know, we don't know what is going on with the shooter. We do have a lead that we think is very interesting, but it is far from solid and hope we can smoke it out."

"Is there anything you can share with me about the lead Chief Walker?"

"Well yes, I can. We have identified a tall black woman who was seen

THE PUBLISHER'S DILEMMA

leaving the building with a smaller white man on the private express elevator. They both were hiding from the video camera and so the pictures were not very revealing. Charlie Humphrey has surrendered the video to my team."

Humphrey said, "I've seen this video and can't make out who they are. They knew how to shield themselves from the video camera."

"We want you to see the video today and see if anything makes sense. We've got it set up. It's only a few seconds, so please take a quick look."

Walker then turned on a monitor with the video as Kwame agreed to review it.

"Of course, I am happy to take a look Chief Walker."

The video was only 25 seconds long. Kwame looked at it five times. "I can't make any of these people out. I'm sorry, Chief Walker."

As they sat looking at the video with the unidentifiable assailants, Kwame, Walker, and Humphrey had no idea just how close Kwame came to seeing the assailants as they boarded the elevator.

After his meeting at Police Headquarters, Kwame Mills returned to work. It was his first day back and he was eager to get back in his groove.

As he walked into the building, he could feel the gaze of co-workers. It was as if every eye was on him. It was a notoriety that he did not enjoy, and as he walked in the lobby, he increased his gait to get to the elevator quicker. He entered into the first open elevator headed to the 37th floor and was somewhat relieved when he saw the familiar face of Wynne Shields' secretary, Sandi Wilson.

"Hi Kwame," Sandi said and smiled. It was the first time he saw her since his interview with Wynne. Sandi, he guessed, had to be about 55 or so, she still had a striking face, the curves, and long blonde hair that made her a knockout in her youth. She also had a pleasant personality and was delightful to be around. Everyone in the building wondered why she would work for a tyrant like Wynne Shields. She would always defend him by saying, "He was like that little brother that I always had to care for."

There was some truth in that comment as Sandi Wilson did have four younger brothers. She was the oldest and assumed a lot of responsibility for her kid brothers.

"I had four maniac little brothers, and if they broke something or did anything wrong, I often got yelled at too," she once shared with Sheila Duncan. "I admit Wynne can be a bit of a knucklehead, but I was raised to handle guys like him."

Kwame felt the tension lessen when Sandi said, "Good Morning Kwame."

He looked at her smiled and returned the greeting, "Good morning, Sandi. It's good to see you."

"Good to see you too, Kwame. It's great to have you back."

"Thank you so much Sandi. I'm glad to be back."

As the elevator made its way to his floor, he looked at his watch, and then he turned over The Post to the back page to see the sports headlines. He did not dare turn to the front cover. He also wanted to say more to Sandi Wilson but didn't know what to say.

Suddenly, he felt a hand on his shoulder. He turned around to see that the person who touched him was a young black male. Kwame recalled him as one of the summer interns from Harlowe College. He was also a college tennis player and working for Deirdre Francis at her Tennis property.

"Mr. Mills, it's good to see you. We've been praying for you and Mr. Alexander. It's great to have you back."

Kwame smiled and said, "Thank you so much. I appreciate those kind words and your prayers."

The young man then stepped back, and one by one, the other people on the elevator let Kwame Mills know that they were happy to see him. The concern and gratitude warmed him tremendously. He felt somewhat guilty about the attention but was thankful for the concern shared by his co-workers.

Kwame's spirits were lifted tremendously as the elevator made its way to the 37th floor.

Sheila, his secretary, was seated at her desk. She rose when she saw him walking towards her and smiled brightly. Before she could speak, Kwame said, "Hi Sheila, thank you for everything while I was away. Thanks for holding everything down."

"Welcome back Kwame. I'm just glad that you're okay and it's good to have you back."

Sheila then told him his first day back would be quite hectic. "Kwame it's now 8:45. Take 15 minutes to catch your breath. You need to go upstairs to Cornwall Harris's office on the 38th floor at 9:00. He called a half hour ago and said they want to see you as soon as you arrive."

"Who are they?"

"Cornwall, Wynne Shields, and Charlie Humphrey. Cornwall called himself."

He was curious about the purpose of the meeting and began to get tense, but called on his faith and it lessened his stress. "Jesus take the wheel," he whispered to himself. He then turned to Sheila and said, "How are they doing? I hope everyone is managing okay?"

Kwame knew that Cornwall was Wynne's protector, and now with Donald Alexander in a coma and Gill Harris dead, he could do whatever he wanted. The fate of the company was now in his hands.

"It's pretty sad up there. Everyone is saying that Cornwall is devastated by the events. He cried last week when he convened the company in the cafeteria to break the news. They had a memorial service at

DARIUS MYERS

Jefferson Center, and it was packed. The funeral was Saturday at The Unity Church. There were dignitaries, celebrities, politicians there, and the President even sent a telegram."

"I have to imagine that it's been hard on Cornwall, but how about Gill's Father Oliver, Jr., his wife and kids? They must be devastated?"

"Yeah, but that's not what everyone is talking about." This statement unnerved Kwame, who was still standing in the hallway. "What do you mean, Sheila? What is everyone talking about?"

"Everyone wants to know who is going to take charge."

Kwame looked at Sheila, who had now sat down at her desk. "I don't know Sheila, but I would guess Cornwall is going to take over for now and probably name Wynne as his second if Donald can't come back. And if Donald doesn't come back, maybe Wynne will be in charge."

"That's what I fear Kwame, and I have to say that I am not alone." Sheila Duncan's face took on a distressed look. "That would be devastating. The people here hate Wynne."

Sheila broke the vow she made to herself to be professional about her disdain for Wynne Shields. But as unprofessional as this comment was, by coming out, Kwame found in her an ally. Here he was with just a few months on the job, his mentor and protector in a coma, and his tyrant of a boss very likely to take control of the company. Sheila Duncan was right, and she was not alone in her fears. Kwame was equally concerned about who would take over, and he could only imagine that the rest of the company was a bit petrified as well.

He looked at his watch. His 15 minutes to get his head cleared were about over. He needed to get upstairs to see Cornwall, Wynne, and Charlie Humphrey.

"Well, its time. I'll head upstairs and see what's up."

"You'll do fine Kwame. I know you will. Just be yourself and know that

THE PUBLISHER'S DILEMMA

I'll be praying for you."

"Thanks Sheila, please do. I have no idea what's ahead."

As he headed to the elevator, Kwame had one searing thought. If Wynne would take charge, he probably would shortly after that fire him. He never expected what was going to be next.

When he got upstairs to the 38th floor, a security guard met him at the elevator and walked him back to Cornwall Harris's office. As a retired CEO, Cornwall and Gills' dad, Oliver, Jr., kept offices there as they ran their charitable operations from the Harris Simmons headquarters.

The security guard announced Kwame to Mary Kennedy, Cornwall's secretary. He walked Kwame to Cornwall's office. Mary called Cornwall immediately, and they didn't make him wait.

"Hi Kwame. Glad to have you back. Go right in, they're expecting you."

The first person he saw was Wynne. He was standing in the far corner with his arms crossed and dressed nattily as always. Kwame thought to himself. "This guy is a jerk, and he certainly looks the part."

Wynne smiled. It was the first time that Kwame saw him do so. He then said, "Hello Kwame, it's good to have you back."

Kwame mustered up a fake smile and said, "Thank you Wynne, very much. I'm glad to be back."

The office was markedly smaller than the offices on the 39th floor. It was, however, larger than Kwame's and filled with the artifacts of his time as CEO and now as a philanthropist. Kwame quickly scanned the room filled with photos of a young Cornwall with politicians and various captains of industry.

Cornwall was seated behind a large oak desk in an oversized dark brown leather chair. Kwame noticed how much smaller, grayer, and old he looked. As Cornwall stood up from behind his desk to greet him, Kwame could see that he was pained. His face wore a look of stress and exhaustion. Like Wynne, he smiled and attempted to present a pleasant face.

"Good morning, and welcome back Kwame. I'm thrilled to see you, and thanks for taking some time to visit with us this morning." He then reached out his hand for a handshake.

"Thank you Cornwall." Kwame approached Cornwall's desk and shook his hand. His grip was weak.

Cornwall then said, "Do you mind if I sit?"

As he did, Kwame noticed how relieved he appeared to sit down. Wynne walked over from the corner to shake hands as well. He then turned and went back to his space where he was standing. And then Charlie Humphrey walked into the room. The whole scene seemed scripted. Humphrey smiled broadly at Kwame. His look was more genuine than the others, but the entrance was too well timed. He began to wonder what was going on, especially when Humphrey started to talk.

"Kwame Mills, twice in one morning," Humphrey said, referring to their meeting earlier that morning at Police Headquarters with Chief Walker. "It's great to see you back on campus. What a crazy last week, huh?"

"I'd say," Kwame answered, and he looked at Wynne, Cornwall, and Charlie. He had a strong feeling in his gut, he didn't trust these guys and didn't know what to do or say.

Kwame watched Humphrey walk across the room and take a seat on the windowsill. He stood in the center of the office until Cornwall instructed him and Wynne to sit down. He sat in one of the two large armchairs opposite his desk. "Please sit down Kwame. You too Wynne."

He pointed to the other large chair. Wynne obediently walked from the corner where he was standing and sat down.

As Kwame sat, he noticed copies of the morning's Post and News sitting on Cornwall's desk. Cornwall saw Kwame looking at the papers and covered them immediately.

He then said, "Kwame, I wanted to spend some time with you this morning. I know you've been out for a few days. I want to put some eyes on you to make sure you are okay."

"Thank you Cornwall. It has been crazy. I still don't know what to make of everything, but I'm doing much better. I thank you for your concern."

"You're welcome. I also want you to know that this shooting is a tragedy that none of us in a million years could imagine we'd be dealing with, but here we are."

As he talked, Kwame noticed how his voice matched his physical appearance. It was tired and strained. He straightened up, and it looked like it was painful to do so. He then smiled at Kwame and said, "From what Charlie and the police have told us. You were cool under pressure. We lost Gill, but if not for you, we may have lost Donald too. You're a real hero."

Kwame didn't know what to say. He knew he was not a hero, and he was uncomfortable with being portrayed as one. All he did was call security.

He chose only to say thank you Sir. He also did not want to act too familiar as it was the first time he met Cornwall, so he called him Sir.

"Sir, I'm not a hero. These shootings are a horrible moment in all of our lives. I'm sorry for your loss, and I'm sorry that I couldn't do anything to help Gill."

"We know you did all that you could," Wynne said as Cornwall sat silently.

Charlie Humphrey chimed in, "You helped save Donald. If you hadn't been here, we would've lost him too."

Kwame began to squirm in his seat. This sucking up was making him very uncomfortable and a bit angry. He wanted to yell out. "I'm no hero. What are you guys talking about?"

DARIUS MYERS

Cornwall looked at Kwame hard and long. He had an unfriendly and penetrating gaze, one that made Kwame squirm even more.

Finally, he said in a very matter of fact tone, "Kwame, you may be right, but this is how it turned out. This tragedy chose you, and the press will portray you as the hero."

He pushed the copies of the Post and News to the front of his desk. "Have you seen the morning papers yet?"

Kwame had purposely not read the morning papers, and when he saw the covers for both, his stomach turned. They both featured a photo of him. The News's headline read, "The Hero Who Saved A Media Empire." The Post's Headline read, "The Man Who Saved The World." The Posts headline was a play on World Media.

"Oh Man. What is this?" He grabbed the newspapers to see the front cover stories by Luke McFlemming of The News and Mike Desanctis of The Post when the phone rang. He figured the front cover stories were part of the continued coverage of the shooting and assumed this would be his new standard until the crime was solved.

Cornwall Harris answered the phone and after a second, turned to Charlie Humphrey. "This is Teddy Walker from the NYPD. He wants to talk to you."

Humphrey quickly jumped up from the windowsill and grabbed the phone.

"Yeah, Humphrey here. What's up, Teddy?"

The conversation stopped as everyone waited to hear why Teddy Walker called. As he listened, Humphrey's facial expression changed from concern to a broad smile.

"That's great news. I'm in a meeting with Kwame Mills, Cornwall Harris, and Wynne Shields now. I'll tell them the news and meet you at the hospital in a half-hour."

THE PUBLISHER'S DILEMMA

When Charlie Humphrey hung up the phone, his smile got bigger. "That was the best call we could get, an hour ago, Donald Alexander came out of his coma. The doctors have run brain tests. He's alert and has suffered no permanent brain damage. The only bad news is that he has no recollection of the shooting."

Kwame jumped up and hugged Charlie Humphrey. "Thank you, Jesus, thank you, Jesus," he yelled out loud and without a care to Cornwall and Wynne.

Wynne Shields and Cornwall Harris both smiled. As he released Charlie Humphrey from the hug, Kwame looked at Cornwall. He noticed that Cornwall had painfully pumped his fist and mouthed the words, "Thank God."

He next looked at Wynne, whose big smile suggested that he also was relieved by the good news.

"We're back in business," Cornwall said.

"Praise God for miracles," Kwame said.

"Praise God," Wynne said. Kwame looked at him. His smile seemed genuine. It was a smile that made Kwame think, "this guy may have a heart after all."

Chapter Twenty-Five

After a month of recuperation, Donald Alexander went back to work. By late September, there was no progress on the shootings at Harris Simmons, and Alexander still had no recollections of the incident. The detectives were officially at a loss over the Gill Harris murder.

Teddy Walker told Walt Bigelow in his frustration, "Walt, a month is a long time without any developments. We can't let this murder and shooting become a cold case."

"I know Teddy, this is a big one, and we've got to figure it out."

Walker continued, "What we know is Gill was a well-liked society guy, as is Donald. The Harris Simmons security team at first wanted to believe that this was some inside job, a disgruntled employee perhaps, but all of the evidence suggests differently. The disconnect is the videotape with the tall, black woman. We have her exiting via the Private Elevator shortly after 7 pm. I'm guessing she can't be an employee. If she were, we'd have a lead by now. This woman is a ghost, even the Celebrity Hack Patrol, McFlemming, Desanctis, and Jennifer Kung haven't been able to pull up anything on her."

"I agree she's the missing link. We can solve this case Teddy, I know we can. I feel like it's right in front of us."

"I can feel it too Walt. It's going to break for us. We have to stay after it."

The next evening Walker took action. He had a number with a direct line into Donald Alexander's office. He dialed, and Alexander picked up the phone himself as it was 6:30, and his secretary had gone home for the day.

"Donald Alexander here."

"Hi Don, this is Teddy Walker. Listen, I'm still trying to figure this darn

THE PUBLISHER'S DILEMMA

thing out. I know there's an answer here. Can you meet me outside of the office? I want to try something different. I want to meet without the aid of Charlie Humphrey and any press around. Let's brainstorm on this thing once again, and maybe we'll get a fresh perspective. Can we meet tonight for an hour at Caffe Cielo and bring Kwame along if you can?"

Donald thought for a moment. Humphrey would be livid if he knew that he had a conversation with Teddy Walker without him. But he trusted Teddy. They had become friends since he regained consciousness, as close as could be given the circumstances. During his recovery, they'd spent countless hours going over the details of this case and still couldn't piece it together.

"Let me see if Kwame is still around Teddy, hold on a second." He then called Kwame's office. He didn't know if he'd still be there as it was already 6:30 pm. When his phone rang, Kwame picked up the line. He knew from the internal caller ID that it was Donald calling.

"Hi Donald, what's up."

"Kwame, I've got Ted Walker on my other line. He wants to meet without Charlie Humphrey at 8:00 pm. I know it's a last-minute request, can you join me?"

This was different, Kwame thought, but he trusted Donald's judgment. "What about the security guy?"

Humphrey had assigned Donald Alexander a 24-hour bodyguard. His name was Satchel Jones, and he was a six foot eight, 340-pound former pro football tackle.

"I'll find a way to get rid of Satch. Just be at my office at 7:45."

"Okay, Donald, I'll be there."

Donald returned to Teddy Walker. "I'll see you at 8:00, but I won't have my bodyguard. He works for Charlie Humphrey and won't allow us to meet you."

DARIUS MYERS

"Okay, be careful Donald. Don't trust anyone."

Alarmed, but eager to find the killer and his shooter too, Donald ended the phone call. "We'll see you shortly, Teddy."

At 7:15 pm, Donald put his departure plan in motion. He called Miki Nomura's restaurant and ordered some takeout. At 7:30, he called Satchel Jones to his office.

"Hey Satch, I'm going to be here for a few more hours, I ordered a bunch of takeout for you and me. Would you mind going to Nomura's to pick up the take out?"

Satchel Jones was an ex-jock, but he was no idiot. "Boss, you know I can't leave you alone, even for 15 minutes. Charlie Humphrey would be livid if he found out if I left you even for five minutes."

"Oh, don't worry, I'll handle Charlie. Remember, I'm the boss." Satchel continued to protest, "Mr. Alexander, I could lose my job over this."

"Ah, Satch, it is not a problem. Nobody is getting fired. I got your back. I'm hungry, and the Doctors have told me that I have to eat before 8 pm. I just forgot about the time."

Donald threw that part about the Doctor telling him to eat in for good measure, as he did not want to give Satch any reason to suspect his deceit.

"Just lock the door and post someone at the lower elevator."

They continued to argue for several moments until finally, Satchel Jones relented with several caveats.

"I'll have to bring one of the guys downstairs and post him outside your office. You have to promise to lock the door and only answer for me. I'll call you when I return from my cell phone. Don't answer any internal phone lines."

"Okay. I can do that," Donald promised. With Satchel Jones agreeing to get the takeout, the first part of the escape plan was hatched.

THE PUBLISHER'S DILEMMA

At 7:40, just minutes before Kwame was to arrive, Satchel Jones left to pick up the takeout. The security guard posted outside the door knew Kwame and let him into Donald's office.

When Kwame walked in, Donald was dressed in a warm-up suit. He had in his hand a second warm-up suit and a pair of running shoes.

He handed all the gear to Kwame, "I hope these shoes fit. They are size 11."

"That's my size Donald, perfect."

"Okay, then change quick, Satchel will be back in a few minutes." Kwame ran into Donald's private bathroom and changed. While he changed, Donald opened a locked drawer in his desk and pulled out a small revolver.

After Kwame changed, Donald went to his private bathroom and lit a match directly under the smoke and fire sensor. In just seconds, the smoke alarm was blaring. As the alarm went off, the guard posted outside the door of Alexander's office barged into the office. Donald and Kwame pointed to the bathroom.

"Fire, in there," Donald said.

When the guard noticed that they were both dressed in warm-up suits, he did a double-take for a moment and then ran into the bathroom.

Simultaneously, he turned on his walkie talkie and began yelling, "Fire in Alexander's office. Clear the premises."

When the guard went into the bathroom, Donald and Kwame ran to the hallway and hit the private express elevator, and to their good luck, it was on the 39th floor. "Let's get on quick," Donald said.

As they entered the elevator, the security guard came running out of Donald's office. He yelled to them, "Mr. Alexander, where are you going? Please get off the elevator."

"Tell Satch, I'm sorry and don't worry, everything will be all right," Donald said to the security guard as he ran towards them and the closing elevator doors.

As the elevator descended, Alexander pulled out the small revolver. "I've never used this thing and hope I won't need to this evening."

"Donald, I pray that won't be necessary too."

When he checked and saw that the gun was loaded, Donald said, "its good Kwame, I pray we won't need to use it too."

As soon as he put the gun safety on and in his pocket, the elevator hit the ground floor, and they exited the building from the private entrance.

"Where are we going?" Kwame asked once they were outside.

"Caffe Cielo, we've got a light jog in front of us. We're going a couple of blocks away. Follow me."

It was twilight now, and they began to jog towards Caffe Cielo. Satchel Jones was walking back towards the building. He did not know yet about Donald Alexander and Kwame Mills escaping. When he saw two men running from the private entrance of the building in warm-up suits, he dropped the takeout and took off after them.

Donald and Kwame spotted Satch chasing them. "I don't think he recognizes us, he may think we're bad guys."

They cut down an alley and finally, after two blocks, were able to elude him.

"It's a good thing that Satch isn't too fast anymore because my cardio is still rather weak following the shooting," Donald said. The rest of their escape was more fast walk than jog to Caffe Cielo, and unbeknownst to them, they had only momentarily lost the former pro athlete.

When they got to Caffe Cielo, Teddy Walker was already there. He was seated at the bar with the owner, Joe Gambado. "Let's get downstairs fast," Walker said.

The owner ushered them into the kitchen and downstairs. When they got downstairs, he opened a secret doorway. The doorway opened up to a large cavernous room. They were in a place that could have easily been a Speakeasy 75 years ago.

After they settled down, Gambado said, "Let me go upstairs and check things out. Can I get you guys anything?"

"How about a menu?" Walker asked.

"Okay, Teddy, I'll be right back."

Two minutes later, they hear yelling outside the wall that separated them from the restaurant's basement and the private room. Satchel Jones had made his way downstairs. He was hot and screaming at Gambado.

"I know that they're here, and you better hope I don't find them." He then yelled, "If you're down here, Donald and Kwame, please come out. I am here to protect you. This is not how we do things."

"I don't know what you're talking about. Look around," Gambado said.

If Satchel Jones knew that there was a secret doorway, he would have knocked it down and knocked Gambado out.

Jones had made contact with the security staff and Charlie Humphrey, and he knew that Alexander and Mills had concocted an escape. After a couple of minutes, the arguing ceased, and they heard Satch make his way back upstairs. A minute later, a beautiful exotic looking waitress with a Caribbean accent named Ami came into the room with menus.

"Man, oh, Man. There's this huge guy upstairs, and he's mad as hell. He said he's going to kick some ass."

"Joe will handle him," Walker said. He seemed unbothered with Satchel Jones.

"I hope he can," Donald said. "I wouldn't want that guy angry with me."

Ten minutes later, Gambado came back and said, "He's gone, and I'm glad, he promised to tear the whole place down. He's certainly big enough."

"That doesn't make sense. Are you sure? I wonder why he left?" Walker asked.

"He left because his boss came, some guy named Charlie Humphrey, he's at the bar now, drinking cranberry juice."

"Oh, wow, they brought out the big boss to yell at you guys," Walker said. He knew they were likely to have someone posted at the bar all night, and there weren't any private exits for them to escape. He was just surprised that it was Humphrey.

"I guess we'll be here for a while now. So much for good plans."

Kwame, Donald, and Walker then sat down and talked about the case over a meal of fried calamari, green salads, and pasta.

After an hour of going over the details, they were no closer.

"Something is missing," Walker said. "For the last couple of days it's been torturing me, the answer is right in front of me. I can feel it. It's right here, guys."

Joe Gambado had been in and out of the room with the food and listening to their conversation. He then offered up a critical tip that had never crossed their minds.

"Did you ever think about blackmail Teddy?"

"Yes Joe, but what do you have in mind?"

"Well, did you know that Cornwall Harris had an illegitimate child. This is just rumor, but she is supposedly a drop-dead gorgeous knockout. She is black, and you know who she was reported to be carrying on with?"

"Who, Joe, who?" Walker asked, this was news to everybody.

"That asshole Wynne Shields."

Kwame, Donald, and Teddy Walker were shocked, and their jaws dropped in unison.

"Jesus, Joe. Where do you get this stuff from?"

THE PUBLISHER'S DILEMMA

"Come on Teddy. Everybody in town knows about the girl and Wynne. Get with the program."

Caffe Cielo was a hangout for big wigs in the media industry. Joe Gambado had enough dirt on most of the regulars at Caffe Cielo to become an even bigger Celebrity Hack reporter than McFlemming, Desanctis, and Kung combined. Teddy Walker just stared into space thinking, as Kwame and Donald sat dumfounded. He knew that Joe Gambado was a credible source, and this blackmail piece could be the missing link, but what did Wynne and a beautiful black woman have to do with this case? After all, there were thousands upon thousands of beautiful black women in New York.

Finally, with his head spinning with blackmail theories, Walker turned to Joe, "Is Charlie Humphrey still upstairs?"

"Yes, he is."

"Well, do you think you can bring him down here?"

"Sure, just give me a moment."

As Joe went upstairs to retrieve Charlie Humphrey, Teddy Walker reached for his holster and pulled out his gun. This move alarmed both Kwame and Donald.

"Sit here and don't say a word. I'm going to get to the bottom of this."

Teddy Walker walked out of the Speakeasy room and stood in a crawl space behind the stairs and waited for Humphrey to come down. He knew that Alexander and Mills were in the restaurant. He didn't know where and that Teddy Walker was with them.

When Joe and Charlie reached the bottom of the stairs, Teddy emerged from behind the stairs and cocked his gun to the back of Charlie's head. Humphrey recognized Teddy Walker's voice, and he was not surprised.

DARIUS MYERS

"Alright, disarm Hump and no funny business."

Humphrey didn't say a word. He just raised his hands slowly and took out both of his guns, a sidearm, and an ankle pistol and laid them gently on the ground.

Joe Gambado was standing nearby. Walker said to him, "Joe, pick up the guns and empty the clips and chambers."

"No problem," Gambado said, he emptied the guns and placed them in a box behind the stairs.

Walker then turned his attention back to Charlie Humphrey, "Hands behind the back Hump."

Charlie Humphrey put his hands behind his back. Teddy Walker handcuffed him and sat him down, violently in a chair, right by the stairs.

"What is this, Teddy? Why the cuffs and the rough stuff?"

"Charlie, I'm in a pickle man. I don't know if you have been holding back information on me and I am not in a trusting way right now. So, I suggest you be quiet while I figure out what to do with you."

Walker then turned to Gambado, "Listen Joe, I need you to go upstairs and don't come back unless I call you. And let me know if that big guy shows up again."

Joe Gambado smiled. He enjoyed helping Teddy Walker out. He was also thinking about how news of the murder being solved at his restaurant would boost his business.

"Sure thing. You know this is going to be good for business. So, you better get a confession here tonight."

Teddy Walker glared at Gambado. "Just get out of here."

Gambado didn't say another word. He didn't want to piss off Teddy Walker. He bounced up the stairs to run cover and be on the lookout for Satchel Jones.

Meanwhile, in the Speakeasy room, Kwame and Donald remained quiet

THE PUBLISHER'S DILEMMA

as Teddy Walker began his interrogation of Charlie Humphrey.

"Hump, I don't know what you've been withholding here, but this is already a murder felony, and if you are involved, it's over for you, so you better come clean now."

"Teddy, I am not withholding anything. I don't know what you're talking about."

"Look, Hump, I know you know everything about the strange happenings at Harris Simmons. What can you tell me about this illegitimate child?" He was standing over Humphrey with his gun pointed directly at him.

"Teddy, I don't know," Humphrey's answer was interrupted by a scream. Walker kicked Humphrey hard on his right shin. The crack sound of the kick made Kwame and Donald shriek. It was clear that this guy meant business.

"Now Hump, let's try this once more. I need you to tell me about the illegitimate child. Next time, I'm kicking you in the balls."

Humphrey was breathing heavy. He looked at Walker with a mixed look of confusion and contempt. Humphrey knew deep inside that he had to choose the right road, and he needed to do it now.

Teddy Walker decided to expedite Humphrey's deliberation and kicked him again just where he promised.

Humphrey screamed again. Kwame and Donald kept their silence.

"Hump, let me say it again. This isn't just withholding evidence, it's a murder case. If you think those blue suits are going to be easy on you after all your years of you showing them up, you got another thing coming. I'm your only hope."

"Look Teddy. All I know is that something was going on with Cornwall, Wynne, and the girl."

"What do you mean?" Walker then pulled up a chair and sat down so he could face both Humphrey. Humphrey began to tell all that he knew.

DARIUS MYERS

"Wynne was sleeping with her, and the old man found out. A bit of bad judgment on her part. She's a dynamic young lady. Except, she showed some bad judgment when getting involved with Wynne. She kind of slipped into this relationship with him, and Gill found out about them."

"How, what are you talking about Charlie?"

"Satch found them."

"What, come on Hump, make it plain because nothing you are saying is making any sense."

Walker was perplexed now, as were Donald and Kwame.

"This is getting crazier and crazier," Donald whispered to Kwame.

Humphrey continued, "Okay, on occasion, we have to do lifestyle monitoring on employees who have sexual harassment files. It's an insurance requirement. Anyone in our organization found guilty of a sexual harassment complaint must agree to monitoring, or else."

"Or else what?" asked Walker.

"We'll be sued and likely be held accountable for damages, and we have to fire them to keep the insurance premiums down."

"So, are you telling me that Wynne Shields had problems keeping his zipper up?"

"Oh yeah. Wynne had a couple of cases on him. Margot Thomas, Associate Publisher, got paid two years back. She was a Wynne Shields victim. With her $5 million settlement, she may never work again. And this was his second offense. Three years ago, he assaulted a college intern."

"So, Gill must have been livid that Wynne was still messing around?"

"Oh yeah, Wynne's a first-rate predator."

Charlie Humphrey was telling all that he knew. "Once you settle on one of these cases, it amounts to a conviction with the insurers. If you keep the accused employee on staff, he has to agree to a fidelity clause that affects the company's premiums significantly."

THE PUBLISHER'S DILEMMA

Donald's jaws dropped, he whispered to Kwame, "I knew nothing of this."

Teddy Walker was still bearing into Charlie Humphrey, who was speaking freely now.

"What do you think Gill was going to do?"

"Fire his ass, at least, that's what I recommended. He cost the company millions. He should have been fired years ago."

"Why didn't he fire him?"

"Cornwall wouldn't let him, and although he was no longer CEO, he was Chairman Emeritus, and he promised to make things difficult for Gill. Cornwall protected Wynne, and he let Gill know that he was not going to let him fire Shields. Gill didn't want to fight him, but he had his plans for Shields."

"Who are these investigators?" Walker asked. He now had a thousand questions.

"Our insurer and Satchel Jones work together to put tails on suspected employees. These investigators are all on a private payroll, and they report to Satch and Gill. Donald Alexander doesn't even know. I don't even know who they are. I'm an officer of the company and, as such, subject to investigation as well. Therefore, these investigators report to a non-officer, Satchel. They also have a special contact number for confidential access to the most senior ranking corporate officer, Gill. I don't even know how they got paid. I suspect it was built into our insurance premium. It's a common policy, and most FORTUNE 500 companies have it."

"This is amazing. Do you at least know who are the investigators?"

"Moldovan & Lanza," Humphrey said.

"Alright," Walker said. "I know these guys, and John Moldovan is a buddy. He's a retired secret service agent that I know from the D.C. area. Moldovan was a good security and surveillance guy in his day and known for

239

the highest level of integrity. His involvement is a good thing."

"That's all I know, Teddy. I'm not holding anything back."

"Okay, here's what's going to happen next. You're going to get to me from Satchel all your files on this stuff and arrange a meeting with me and John Moldovan immediately."

"Not a problem."

"Now, who is the girl?"

"Her name is Samantha Rivers. Cornwall met her mother about 25 years ago. Her name is Betty Rivers. Betty was a Broadway dancer, a beautiful and elegant woman," and he paused, "she's black. Cornwall denied her because he thought it would hurt his public standing. But everyone in the family and at the helm of the business knew about her. Except for Donald."

"Gill too?"

"Yes, Gill loved the girl and took care of her and her mother. He supported them both. He put the girl through college, even set aside a small percentage partnership share for her in the company. Cornwall, the dirty bastard, never cared for the girl much until recently."

"What do you mean? Why so?"

"Cornwall's dying, he's got liver cancer and probably six months left. Gill despised his evil ways but loved his Uncle unconditionally. He set up the introduction between Samantha and Cornwall."

Teddy Walker was shocked. He took a step back and scratched his head. "Now the videotape is starting to make sense. But I am not going to do anything before I speak to John Moldovan."

"Jesus," Donald said and looked at Kwame.

"Wow," Kwame whispered, "That Cornwall guy is crazy."

Chapter Twenty-Six

Following the reveal of all this new information at Café Cielo, Charlie Humphrey set up a meeting the next day for Ted Walker with John Moldovan at Police Headquarters.

Also at the meeting were Walt Bigelow and Satchel Jones. The meeting was scheduled for 10:00 am. Satch came in early at 9:00 to meet with Walker and Bigelow.

"Can you help us find the girl? She can answer a lot of questions," Bigelow asked Jones.

"I have an address in my file, but it's an old one. Rivers moved a couple of months ago and left no forwarding address. We know that she's in the city. Our tails on her have not been able to identify and verify an address. She's pretty slippery for sure. I guess you can say she is hiding in plain sight."

"We've got to locate her," Bigelow said. "I'll put a team together to work with your guys and intensify the efforts to find her."

"I like that idea, it should help," Jones said.

"I agree, let's find her," Teddy Walker chimed in. He then changed the discussion to Wynne Shields.

"I called John Moldovan and asked him to bring all the videotapes and photos he has of Shields accumulated by his firm. I'm curious too about the girl, but I think this case is pointing at Wynne Shields. I also want to know why this guy has so much protection from Cornwall."

Walker continued, "Let's look at the facts, he's a notoriously bad manager. He's a womanizer whose philandering cost the company millions. He was sleeping with Cornwall's illegitimate daughter, against the expressed wishes of Gill. He sounds like a guy with a criminal nature."

He then apologized to Satchel Jones for the ruse. "Satch, apologies for deceiving you as we did last night. I know our subterfuge pissed you off, but we did not know anyone's role in all of this. We are glad for your help and being on our side."

"You're welcome Teddy, I am glad to help. If I were in your shoes I would have done the same thing. No apologies are necessary." He then asked about his boss. "Is Charlie Humphrey in trouble?"

"Humphrey will be fine," Walker answered, "but I told him not to leave town. If we can solve this case with his help from last night, I'll likely look the other way. Also, since we never looked at him as a conspirator and he did come clean, there was little likelihood of any obstruction or withholding information charges sticking."

Both Satchel Jones and Walt Bigelow nodded their heads after this statement from Walker.

Walker continued, "I know Humphrey is a good guy, but my goodness, he creates a lot of stress for me with my detectives and the street cops. Everybody knows that Hump and I are good friends, and they complain to me when he is a hard ass. I do need him to be better with my force. Maybe now he'll be a little nicer to my guys."

Satchel said, "You're right Humphrey is a good guy. He can be tough, I know, but he is not a crook. I like working for him, as does the rest of the security team at Harris Simmons. I'm sure any concealment on his part was not to deceive you because he has a lot of respect for you. I hope we can get the answers on this and solve this fast."

"I agree," Bigelow said as he echoed his fondness for the Head of Security at Harris Simmons, "Charlie Humphrey is great. Mean to our guys at times, but he's a great cop, and when you get him away from work, just a world-class dude."

Walker then changed the subject to the blackmail conspiracy. "Guys, I want to get to the bottom of this blackmail. The facts are Cornwall is dying and only has months to live. Cornwall has also got this illegitimate daughter who he's known about of her life but disavowed until recently. Cornwall is Wynne's protector. And Wynne is sleeping with the girl. Wynne, Man, Jesus, he's just a first-rate creep."

They all nodded their heads in agreement, and Bigelow said, "Yes, Wynne seems like the kind of guy who would be running a blackmail scheme. He's a privileged golden boy creep. I wouldn't mind locking his ass up."

Satchel Jones then said, "Off the record, I wouldn't mind kicking his ass too. And so would most of the guys on the security team."

At 9:55, John Moldovan arrived, he was a spit-shine former top cop. Moldovan, 45, was a no-nonsense guy who ran his investigations business by the book. He came with two large briefcases filled with files from his work at Harris Simmons. After they exchanged greetings, he said to Walker, "Teddy, I won't bother to ask for a warrant. Charlie Humphrey has told me to cooperate fully, and I know that you'd get one anyhow, so I'll hand this stuff over."

"Thanks John. I appreciate you being forthright. We can use your help."

As Walker suspected, John Moldovan kept meticulous notes. His first file on Wynne Shields dated back three years and was tabbed, Lisa Farren. Walker looked through the files and began to read aloud. "Lisa Farren came to Harris Simmons as an intern during her junior at Lynn College. She was a high honors student. She spent ten weeks at Harris Simmons and worked in the editorial department. She did a few small sidebar stories and was given high marks for her work that summer."

"Read the next file on her," John Moldovan said.

There was another file with L. Farren, and it was marked "Sexual Battery, Paid." Walker opened it and said out loud, "Okay, this page has Complaint in bold stamped across the front. It's probably going to be interesting. I see photos of Farren, and I'm not liking what I see. These are photos of this girl, Farren, with two black eyes and a swollen lip. She was beaten up like she was in a bar fight."

He passed the photo to Bigelow, who, after a quick look, shouted, "I really hate this guy."

The next page was a police report filed by Farren. Walker read the filing complaint.

"October 15th. A white female age 21, identified as Lisa Farren, of 121 W. 72nd Street, Manhattan, NY and 42 Wink Street in Lynn, MA filed a sexual assault complaint against Gill Harris, Cornwall Harris, and Wynne Shields. Warrants issued for questioning and possible arrest of all three individuals."

Bigelow then said, "Jesus, all of these guys are predators. Gill too?" Shocked, Walker turned to Moldovan and Satchel Jones. "What do you know about this case?"

Satchel was just as surprised, looked back at Walker, and shrugged his shoulders.

"Nothing, absolutely nothing. I wasn't with the company three years ago."

Moldovan said to Walker, "Didn't you know about this?"

Walker, exasperated with all the twists and turns of this case, looked

THE PUBLISHER'S DILEMMA

at Moldovan, "No, I didn't. Humor me?"

Moldovan said, "I think you better get adjusted in your seat."

For the next 15 minutes, John Moldovan told him more than he could imagine. He began with Lisa Farren's story.

"Gill Harris met Lisa Farren at the company's summer picnic. The young college girl attracted Gill with her wit and beauty. She was also impressed with him and later admitted to a sexual attraction. 'I suppose it was his power, and he is a fun, handsome guy with a lot of style,' she told her lawyers. After the picnic, they commenced a steamy summer romance they both agreed would end once she returned to Lynn. It all seemed innocent enough. She had a boyfriend back at Lynn, and when the summer ended, she would return to her college life in New England. Gill had no intention of ending his marriage for a summer of folly."

Moldovan continued, "The plan all seemed fine until the fall of that year when Lisa called Gill in hysterics. It seemed that Wynne learned of their affair and had her summoned to New York under the guise of doing a project for some editorial bylines and extra college credit. As a fledgling writer, Lisa Farren jumped at the opportunity. She came down to New York for a late afternoon meeting. After a meeting with World's editor, she was scheduled to meet with Wynne for a final interview. This meeting was no big deal at World, given Wynne Shields's autocratic management style."

"I don't like where this is going," Teddy Walker said.

"No, you won't Teddy," Moldovan said. "After the meeting, he ordered some sandwiches and beers and suggested that she stay and have a quick bite before heading to the hotel that the company put her up for the evening. Although Lisa Farren had plans to meet friends for drinks, she thought it best to accommodate the request of her new boss. After the sandwiches arrived, Wynne called Cornwall Harris, who just happened to be in the office that evening."

DARIUS MYERS

"According to Farren, no sooner had the old man arrived had the situation become filled with sexual innuendos and advancements. They began to grab and fondle her breast, and when she tried to leave, Cornwall smacked her hard, bloodying her nose, busting her lip, and blacking her eyes. Wynne grabbed her, he shook her real hard, ordering her to shut up. He shook her so hard that he dislocated her shoulder. She began to scream, and when security arrived, they let her go. Wynne told security that she tried to attack him and to escort her from the building."

Walker, Bigelow, and Satchel Jones are listening with looks of shock on their faces.

Moldovan continued, "After the incident, Lisa Farren went immediately to her parent's home in Manhattan. The next morning, the police arrested Wynne and Cornwall. The arrests were at their homes, and they successfully kept it out of the news. As the police investigated the case, Gill and Lisa Farren's affair came to light. Under the advice of their attorney, the family pressed charges against the entire company, which led to Gill being named a claimant on the sexual assault charges. The case got settled out of court for $3 million. And based upon our records, it's when the real family fighting or blackmail began."

"Damn, these guys are evil," Walker said.

"Teddy," Moldovan continued, "I thought this was one you knew about because of the arrests and the settlement. I know files get sealed, but this case was one newsflash from being a blockbuster story. These guys are powerful and used it all to keep it out of the news."

Walker looked at his Bigelow and asked, "Did you know about this one?"

Bigelow shook his head angrily, "No and I should have known about this Teddy. You know we have some detectives a few levels down that do favors for friends. I'm going to find these guys and I suspect that is why. I

THE PUBLISHER'S DILEMMA

will strongly let them know that they should have stepped up and let us know."

"Hell yeah Bigelow. We can't have guys on our team playing with information like this, put them on warning and let them know if they do this again, they're gone. This incident is a textbook example of how certain guys exploit privilege. I will not tolerate this on my watch."

"Done Teddy," Bigelow said. "I'm pissed and embarrassed. There's going to be more than warnings. If I don't like what I hear, there will be suspensions or worse."

"Do what you need to do. I want the message to be loud and clear. There will be no more privilege in this department. The days of the rich and powerful getting passes around here are over."

Walker and Bigelow both shook their heads in anger. Walker then said, "Now, this is coming together. Gill's involvement with Farren explains the blackmail angle."

"Exactly," Moldovan said. "The level of craziness is off the charts. This incident ruined any opportunity for Wynne Shields to become CEO of Harris Simmons. Gill Harris saw this as an intentional attack by Wynne and Cornwall that was meant to extort and force Gill's acceptance of Wynne as the next firm President. They were now all tangled in a nasty legal incident that, while kept out of the news, labeled all three of them as impenitent abusers of power and sexual predators. If leaked to the public, it could result in irreparable personal embarrassment for Gill, his family, and the company."

"Gill hated him for it and told Wynne that this act was unforgivable and that he could not extort his way to the top job."

"He told him, 'You just signed your death certificate here. You will never move beyond your current job at World Media. You can forget it,' were Gill's exact words. Three months later, when Donald Alexander was going to leave, and Gill had to choose to promote Alexander or Shields, Gill kept his word and named Alexander. This choice infuriated Cornwall even more as he hoped that Gill would have gotten over his anger and still selected Wynne for the President's post."

Walker and Bigelow were stunned as they listened to John Moldovan. Walker turned to Bigelow and said, "These guys are unbelievable."

Satchel Jones just shook his head in shock and disbelief.

After Moldovan finished with the Lisa Farren episode, he put the folder on the bottom of the pile. Teddy Walker sat back in his seat and sighed.

He then looked at John Moldovan and said, "So what about Margot Thomas?"

"The same situation," Moldovan answered.

"So, what happened?" Walker asked.

"It was Wynne and Cornwall again and pretty much the same situation. They slapped her around, and she filed charges. She got Five million dollars. Gill was livid. But he had his own past. He was in counseling with his wife Colleen over the Lisa Farren incident and trying to put his marriage back together. He didn't want any of these events going public."

"Gosh," Satchel Jones said, "and they say pro athletes are predators. These guys deserve ten minutes in the woodshed."

"You're right," Moldovan said. "If either of these girls were my daughters, I'd have dragged their asses outside and issued some knuckle judgment."

"So, what about the estranged daughter, Samantha Rivers?" Walker asked.

"Another innocent," Moldovan answered.

"What do you mean by innocent?" asked Walker.

"The girl was charmed by Gill. He would have dinner with her often and have her travel with his family. She spent holidays at Gill's house. His

THE PUBLISHER'S DILEMMA

wife, Colleen, had taken her in as family, and the three had a great relationship. They treated her as their daughter."

Walker stood up and placed his hands on his temples and rubbed them. He closed his eyes as he was processing all that he just learned. He turned to Moldovan and asked, "John, what do you think happened at Harris Simmons?"

"I don't know Teddy. All I can tell you for sure is that those two guys are ruthless."

"Ruthless enough to commit murder?"

Moldovan looked to the floor and nodded his head affirmatively. He then looked up to Walker and said, "They certainly think they are above the law."

Walker looked at Moldovan and said, "Not on my watch."

He then turned to Bigelow and said, "Let's see if we can draw them out and make them sweat a little."

"What do you have in mind?" Bigelow asked.

"We'll start by getting some arrest warrants for these two fools, and then I'm going to go visit my friends at the press."

Chapter Twenty-Seven

Following his meeting with John Moldovan and Satchel Jones, Walker knew there was more to know from Wynne Shields and Cornwall Harris. He called his friend Assistant DA Brian Gath and asked for help.

Gath answered his phone on the second ring. "ADA Gath here."

"Hey Brian, its Teddy Walker. I need 15 minutes of your time. Can I come by now, I'm in my office across the street at Police Headquarters?"

ADA Gath looked at his watch and his calendar, "I'll be good in 15 minutes. Just finishing up something. Can you come, then?"

"Great, I'll be there in 15. I appreciate this."

Walker set up the meeting to show Gath the files. He knew the files had enough evidence to get a warrant, and Gath would ask for them. Bringing the files would save everyone time.

Fifteen minutes later, Walker enters ADA Gath's office and hands him the files.

"I need you to see this. I think we've got the culprits in the Gill Harris murder, and they are powerful. I need your help. A confession won't come easy."

As Gath reviewed the files, Walker continued, "We've got to learn why Wynne Shields and Cornwall Harris are so tightly aligned and why their behavior has been so deviant. All the evidence is pointing to them as shooters and or conspirators in this murder."

ADA Gath agreed after a quick review of the files. "I hate these guys already. They are by the evidence in these case files sexual predators. I want their sex cases unsealed, and I'll get you the warrants for the murder. Let them defend themselves in court. I'll get you the warrants you need

250

THE PUBLISHER'S DILEMMA

today."

"Thanks so much Gath, I appreciate it. You are the Man."

Gath smiled as Walker walked out the door, "We'll have them by three today. I'll see to it myself."

After the meeting, Walker called Bigelow and told him to organize a meeting with the Celebrity Hack Patrol.

"Can you get a hold of the Celebrity Hack guys? This time, let's be honest with them and be sure to include Jennifer Kung. Tell them we need their help to expose our main suspects in the Harris Simmons murders as this case may be won in the court of public opinion. Let them know we dearly need their help. I'm sure that will appease their egos, especially McFlemming. Let's see if we can get them in here today after lunch."

"Great idea, Teddy," Bigelow said. "I think I can have them all here by 3:00. Does that work for you?"

"My calendar is cleared for the remainder of the day if necessary," Walker answered. "Let's crack this nut."

Bigelow called Luke McFlemming first, Mike Desanctis second, and Jennifer Kung last. McFlemming was first because Bigelow knew he would be whining about the scuttle story.

He called McFlemming on his cell phone. As expected, he was having lunch. He did not know his lunch date was Jennifer Kung at Miki Nomura's midtown restaurant.

He answered his phone, "Luke McFlemming here."

"Luke, Walt Bigelow here. I don't have a lot of time, so first things first, I'm calling to say sorry on the scuttle story, but you know how it goes in this game."

McFlemming attempted to protest to Bigelow. He started with, "I'm angry, I'm a star, and you don't treat me this way."

Bigelow interrupted him and yelled into the phone. "Look stupid. I'm calling you because Teddy Walker wants you and your crew of Celebrity Hacks to come down to headquarters by 3:00. I'm calling you first, and I have to get through to Desanctis and Kung, so I don't have time to mess around."

McFlemming stopped complaining but did not let on that Jennifer Kung was seated right across from him. Instead, he attempted to press Bigelow on the purpose of the meeting. "Why a meeting? What do you want?"

"We are piecing together the suspects for the shooting. Our hunch is still extremely circumstantial, and we need you guys to help us out. I'll see you at 3:00, okay?"

"Okay," McFlemming answered, "I'll see you at 3:00." McFlemming ended the call and raised his hand to ask for the check.

A couple of minutes later, after Bigelow finished talking to Mike Desanctis, he called Jennifer Kung. She answered her phone by stating her initials, she said, "J.K. here."

Bigelow didn't mince words with Jennifer Kung either, he said, "Jennifer, this is Walt Bigelow from the NYPD Detective Bureau. Teddy Walker and I need you to make it downtown to our office by 3:00." Kung's heart began to race.

"What is this about?"

"The Harris Simmons murders. We want you and your buddies from the Celebrity Hack patrol to help us out with the investigation."

At this point, it clicked with her that Bigelow called McFlemming less than five minutes earlier. She got upset that he did not share this news.

"Do you mean my so-called colleague, Luke McFlemming, who's also my lunch date, sitting right across from me. You did tell him that you wanted me to be at this meeting?"

Kung glared across the table at McFlemming.

THE PUBLISHER'S DILEMMA

"Don't tell me he's sitting there?" This detail pissed Bigelow off, too, but he didn't have time for McFlemming's games.

"Jennifer, I've got to go, be here by 3:00 please, and tell McFlemming that I said he's not only an asshole, but he's a whole ass."

McFlemming, who was also notoriously cheap, was paying his half of the check with some coins as Jennifer Kung ended her call. After she hung up, she glared at him. "Do you have some kind of birth defect? How could you be so evil?"

"Hey baby, I'm not your Secretary, if he wanted you, he knew how to find you. He found you, didn't he?"

She shook her head, stood up, opened her purse, pulled out two $20 bills, and dropped them on the table.

"You are so overrated. It must be torturous to know that you are such a loser. By the way, Bigelow told me to tell you that he's going to kick your tight white ass," Kung exaggerated Bigelow's statement to put a little fear in him. "It would bring me so much joy to see that."

"Whatever T.V., I'll see you at 3."

"See you at 3, you moron," Kung said as she got up from the table. "I need to catch a cab and head back to my office and prepare."

McFlemming sat back in his seat and waited for Kung to walk out of the door. He picked up one of the $20.00 bills. She was so angry that she didn't realize the entire lunch bill was $25. McFlemming then took back the $14 that he previously put on the table. He added seven dollars and fifty cents for a total of $27.50.

"Lunch was almost free today. Thank you T.V.," McFlemming said to himself.

By 3:00 pm, all three members of the Celebrity Hack Patrol were at Police headquarters and waiting in the lobby. Bigelow and Walker had put together a flow chart that included the Lisa Farren and Margot Thomas

DARIUS MYERS

sexual assaults. Samantha Rivers as the illegitimate child of Cornwall Harris. Wynne Shields as the lustful parasite exploiting Samantha Rivers and other pertinent information from the John Moldovan files.

Bigelow met the Celebrity Hack Patrol in the lobby and escorted them to a second-floor conference room. He introduced himself to Desanctis and Kung but refused to shake McFlemming's hand. Instead, he just glared at him and said, "Luke, you need to grow up."

He then turned to Kung and Desanctis and said, "Follow me."

Kung smiled at McFlemming as she envisioned, Bigelow roughing up her partner. McFlemming smirked, her smile was pissing him off.

He whispered under his breath, his bravado false. "You think I'm scared?" Loud enough only for Kung to hear.

"Yeah, I do, Luke. You just went from white to pale Bro."

They both knew it was a statement he wouldn't dare make loud enough for Bigelow to hear. And he hated that Kung knew it.

When McFlemming, Desanctis, and Kung arrived at the conference room, Teddy Walker was standing and facing the window. He turned around and before introducing himself, instructed them to sit down at three specific seats. On the conference table in front of three chairs, Walker had placed manila folders.

"Take a seat in front of a manila folder. All of the files are the same, so don't fret. You can compare them later if you like."

As the Celebrity Hack patrol members opened the files, he spoke. "My name is Teddy Walker, and I'm Chief of Detectives for the NYPD. You all know Walt Bigelow, my assistant." As they looked to Bigelow, he nodded to the Celebrity Hack patrol.

"Before I start, I want to apologize to Mike Desanctis and even you McFlemming for the scuttle story we duped you guys on. That was in response to you guys getting the scoop in the hospital cafeteria the night of the shooting. You got in the way of our investigation, and we had to get control of the story."

He then looked at Jennifer Kung, "We apologize for not dealing you in, but you are here today, and as far as Walt and I are concerned, we have a clean slate. Right, Walt?"

Bigelow looked first to Walker and then to all three of the Celebrity Hack Patrol team and nodded affirmatively.

For confirmation that everybody was fine, Walker asked them to assure him that they were okay with the past scuttle story.

"Are we good?" he asked, followed by a hard stare at McFlemming. They all nodded to Walker and Desanctis spoke up saying, "Thanks for the apology Teddy, now tell us why we're here."

"Okay guys, you'll see in these folders that we have some pretty heavy stuff on Cornwall Harris and Wynne Shields at Harris Simmons. These guys have been carrying on like sexual predators and white-collar gangsters, as far as our records show, for at least five years. We suspect that they are co-conspirators in the murder of Gill Harris, along with a woman named Samantha Rivers. We are attempting to find her, as we think she is the woman in the videotape."

Walt Bigelow then turned on a monitor with the video of the tall black woman and old white man in the elevator. "We think these may be the shooters. Cornwall Harris and Samantha Rivers."

Teddy Walker then walked to the far end of the conference table. There was an easel with a large board turned backward. Walker turned the board around that revealed the flow chart with names and pictures of Cornwall Harris, Wynne Shields, Samantha Rivers, Gill Harris, Donald Alexander, and Kwame Mills.

On the top of the chart in bold letters, Walker had typed, Harris Simmons Murder. Right underneath was the subtitle, Shooting Victims, under which were the names of Donald Alexander and Gill Harris. On a diagonal line to the right was the subtitle, Suspects under which were the names of Cornwall Harris, Samantha Rivers, and Wynne Shields. Parallel to this line on the left side of the chart was the subtitle, Witness, and underneath was the name of Kwame Mills.

Teddy Walker stood at the easel and said, "Lady and gentlemen, this chart will tell you all that we know." Walker then stepped back to allow them to review.

The Celebrity Hack Patrol was silent and stunned. They all knew that this was a significant coup, and they were bursting with excitement. McFlemming was the first to break the silence. He looked at Walker. "This is phenomenal, what do you want us to do with this?"

"We're going to bring in Wynne Shields and Cornwall Harris tomorrow morning for questioning. We're in the process of getting a warrant to bring them in, but they don't know yet. I don't care what you write or how you write it, but these are the facts."

He then added for emphasis, "These facts are unofficial, of course, based on our suspicion of the shooting crime. On the other hand, the stuff in those manila folders about sexual harassment and abuse at Harris Simmons is all true."

Jennifer Kung asked, "Is there going to be a perp walk?"

Walt Bigelow answered this question. "No, not yet, there won't be any photo ops, but we do want you guys to play up that Shields and Cornwall Harris will be brought in for questioning."

Desanctis then asked Walker, "What do you hope to come out of this Teddy? Do you think us leaking this news will get these guys to confess? Based on the stuff I'm looking at in these files, these guys won't be afraid of a news story."

He pondered Desanctis's question for a second. Bigelow was silent as

THE PUBLISHER'S DILEMMA

this was a question the Chief of Detectives should answer.

Walker turned back to the board and pointed to the topline to the caption that read Harris Simmons Murders. He then said, "Lady and Gentlemen, someone was shot and killed, another person was critically wounded. We think two extremely rich, self-absorbed, power-hungry egomaniacs are involved. We need all the help we can to break them. You can help us wear them down and destroy some of this glamorous glow that adorns them. Hell, if you all milk this right, each of you can probably get a book deal."

Walker smiled as he knew the prospects of a book deal would appease their egos.

Bigelow ended the meeting asking, "Can we count on you for good stories for tomorrow morning?"

He then scanned the room and looked at McFlemming, Desanctis, and Kung.

"Oh, yeah, I'm in," Jennifer Kung said as she got up out of her chair and began to pack her manila folder into her bag.

"You bet," Desanctis added.

"You got anything else for me?" McFlemming asked sarcastically. He then added, "I want first dibs on the book deal."

Mike Desanctis and Jennifer Kung rolled their eyes in contempt at McFlemming.

Teddy Walker shut him up by yelling from the front of the conference room table, "Hey big time, let's get through tomorrow. If you guys don't write good stories, this investigation might be like Gill Harris, dead."

As the Celebrity Hacks prepared to leave, Walker said to Bigelow, "Go across the street and pick up the warrants from Gath and let's find Wynne Shields and Cornwall Harris and issue their warrants by 4 pm. Let them know that if they don't come in by 11 am, we're doing a perp walk by noon."

"Oooh, that would be awesome, Perp Walk," Jennifer Kung said excitedly. "Will you let us know if there will be a perp walk?"

Walker then smiled and said to Bigelow, "Be sure to let them know that we'll have the press on notice if we have to find them."

Walker then turned to the Celebrity Hacks and said, "How's that? They are both so arrogant that they may object. We'll keep you aware. Okay?"

"Right on," Jennifer Kung shouted. "You know what Teddy Walker, I used to think you were a dick, but you're pretty cool."

Everyone in the room laughed, even Teddy Walker.

.

Chapter Twenty-Eight

The next day Wynne Shields arrived at the Police Station at 10:45 am. Cornwall Harris had yet to arrive, but he still had an hour and 15 minutes before the threat of a perp walk was to be executed.

After the warrants were issued, Wynne and Cornwall's lawyer, Hollis Tassie of the prominent law firm Bolton & Vassell, called Walt Bigelow. "It's four o'clock in the afternoon Bigelow. There's no way we'll get these guys in by 11 tomorrow."

Bigelow made Teddy Walker's promise to the Celebrity Hack Patrol clear to Hollis Tassie. "If they are not here by 11, we are going to do a perp

THE PUBLISHER'S DILEMMA

walk by 12. I promise you that. Get their asses here on time."

John Moldovan and Satchel Jones arrived at police headquarters at 10 am and were hanging out in Bigelow's office. They all got a big kick out of the news stories in the three major daily newspapers. As Walker and Bigelow hoped, the press had come through. They all had front page stories that dominated the front sections of their papers with exhausting accounts of the activities of Cornwall Harris and Wynne Shields.

The stories reported that Cornwall Harris and Wynne Shields were to show up at police headquarters for questioning as suspects. As a result, the entrance lobby and courtyard outside of Police Headquarters was jam-packed with news and gossip reporters. Every news team in the tristate area had a press contingent on hand. The crowd was so massive that it forced Wynne Shields to duck in through the back entrance at headquarters.

As a reward for their great stories, Bigelow sought out McFlemming, Desanctis, and Kung and moved them into the front of the press scrum.

Wynne Shields showed up at 10:45, escorted by his attorney, Hollis Tassie. Teddy Walker greeted them and escorted them both to an interrogation room. John Moldovan, Satchel Jones, and Walt Bigelow sat in a viewing room. A one-way mirror concealed their presence. All three were eager to see how this interview unfolded. For now, even though Cornwall Harris had yet to arrive, the day was working out fine. They would interview Cornwall alone later. In the interview room, Teddy Walker sat opposite Tassie and Shields.

Over the last couple of days, Walker had begun to despise Wynne for what he now knew. Like John Moldovan, Walt Bigelow, and Satch Jones, he would love to take his badge off and tear Shields's head off. He began the interview with a bad attitude.

Walker leaned across the table and barked at Wynne, "Do you know why you're here?" his eyes locked on Wynne in a piercing stare.

DARIUS MYERS

"Yes, we think so, but why don't you tell us?" Tassie interrupted. Hollis Tassie was familiar with Walker and his intimidating interrogation tactics. He was there to take the heat, not his client. Wynne did not respond to Walker as he was following orders from Hollis Tassie.

"Was I talking to you?" Walker said. He shot a caustic look at Tassie.

Tassie moved back from the table instinctively. He realized it would be smart to be out of striking range of Teddy Walker.

This beginning of the interview left Shields's heart pounding. With this one comment, he was no longer the hard-core, cantankerous predator. Walker had stripped him of any of his legendary toughness before he answered a question.

However, he was not prepared to cave in. After a few seconds of silence, he mustered up his composure. He looked back across the table and answered Teddy Walker's question.

"It's about Gill. What a tragic loss."

"Spare me the dramatics," Walker responded coldly, bluntly. He was still leaning forward with his eyes fixed on Shields.

"Tell me what happened that night."

Back in the surveillance room, Bigelow got up and whispered to Satchel Jones and John Moldovan and said, "Now we play hardball." He picked up one of John Moldovan's files, turned to Satchel Jones and said, "I'll show you some real dramatics, watch my entrance."

"Gee Whiz Bigelow, was what we just saw only a warm-up?"

Bigelow smiled and said, "You'll see. Hold onto your seat."

Two seconds later, he entered the interrogation room, slammed the file down on the desk right in front of Walker. He then sauntered across the room and stood next to the window. His body cut off the light and cast a sinister darkness over the room. It was a dramatic entrance without question.

THE PUBLISHER'S DILEMMA

"I, I, don't know what you're talking about," Shields said. Unnerved by the entrance and mass of the big man. Walt Bigelow wasn't nearly as big as Satch Jones, but at six feet three and 260 pounds, he was quite imposing.

"Well, let's start from the top then," Walker said. "Were you in the building the night of the murder?"

"Well, uh, no."

"Come again?" Walker snapped back immediately.

"You heard him. He said no," Hollis Tassie snapped back. Tassie knew his client was intimidated, and this was what he got paid to handle. He was trying to take as much of the heat as possible.

The early part of the interview was working for them. Walker and Bigelow knew they could break Wynne. They had already robbed him of his famed defiance, but that wouldn't mean anything if they couldn't beat Hollis Tassie.

Hollis Tassie was one of the best and brightest criminal defense attorneys in the business. Teddy Walker realized that he couldn't outsmart him or intimidate him. But by being relentless, he could probably scare Shields enough to where he would let something slip. That was his plan, and he kept turning up the heat.

For his next move, Walker stood up and said very sarcastically, "Tell me then Wynne, what do you think happened that night? Two people shot, one murdered. One left for dead. What do you think happened?"

Wynne Shields was fighting a valiant fight to keep his composure. Inside, he was a bundle of nerves. Wynne was a master salesman and summoned those skills to get through this interview. He took a deep breath to calm himself.

Bigelow was one step ahead of him. "Go ahead, take a deep breath, calm yourself, and get your story together. You only got one shot."

DARIUS MYERS

Hearing this from the large man almost wrecked Shields's resolve. "Control, control," he thought to himself.

He then said, "All I know is what everybody else knows. Somebody entered into our executive suite at about 7:00 and shot Donald Alexander and killed Gill Harris." These words seemed to steady him because he then said calmly, "I didn't do it."

Hollis Tassie didn't like the way this interview was going. Tassie was concerned, Walker and Bigelow were tough, and his client might incriminate himself under this duress. Tassie hoped to end the interview with Shields's statement. He stood up and yelled across the table. "There you have it, a statement by my client, unless you are prepared to make an arrest, we are going to leave right now."

"Sit down and shut up," Bigelow said.

"Hollis, you know we have a warrant to question your client. Otherwise, you wouldn't be here," Walker said. "So, to repeat the statement of my esteemed colleague here. Sit down and shut up."

Just then, there was a knock at the door. Detective Doug Melendez was standing outside. He didn't speak. He waived for Walker and Bigelow to come to the door.

"Relax and make yourself at home, we'll be right back," Walker said. Wynne Shields was relieved for the momentary break in the action. Tassie did not want to use the break to talk out loud. He didn't know who might be in the observation room, so he walked over and whispered to Wynne. Tassie thought this might be a tactic, as did John Moldovan and Satchel Jones, but it wasn't.

At the doorway, Melendez said, "Cornwall Harris and Samantha Rivers just arrived and are asking for Chief Walker. Charlie Humphrey is with them."

It was a few minutes after 11, and having Samantha Rivers there was

THE PUBLISHER'S DILEMMA

big news for Walker and Bigelow. They could finally put eyes on her.

Melendez continued, "the old man seems to be a bit eccentric. I asked them all to wait quietly, but the Girl and Humphrey could not calm Cornwall Harris down."

"Let's look into this Walt," Walker said to his partner.

"We'll be right back," he said to Wynne Shields and Hollis Tassie. Walker didn't close the door, it was an unintentional move, but one that set off a chain of events. Teddy Walker and Walt Bigelow walked down the hall to introduce themselves to Samantha Rivers and Cornwall Harris. Cornwall appeared disturbed as Melendez stated. His hair was disheveled, and his appearance was also in disarray. His jacket collar was mussed up, and his shirt untucked. He was also angry and demanded to know what was going on.

"Hi, I am Teddy Walker, Chief of Detectives, and this is my second-in-command Walt Bigelow. Thanks for coming down this morning," Teddy Walker said. His greeting was pleasant and warm.

"I know who you are. Why am I here?" Cornwall Harris snapped.

Walker, surprised by the behavior and antics of the old man, looked at Charlie Humphrey for help. Humphrey, now knew that he had been duped by the evil doers at Harris Simmons and might even be implicated as a conspirator.

Humphrey said meekly, "he wants to know what is going on Teddy."

Walker didn't want to lose control of his station and the situation. He looked at Cornwall and said sternly, "Sir, we'd like to ask you some questions. Please sit down, and we'll be right with you."

Cornwall looked at Walker with rage. It was a look that even unnerved the very calm and unshakeable Walker.

Samantha Rivers stroked Cornwall Harris on the back of the head. "Relax please, you need to relax."

DARIUS MYERS

He was old for sure, stooped over and small looking, but mean. Teddy Walker then began to wonder if he was mean enough to kill his nephew. He then politely said to Cornwall.

"We will be with you in a second. Can you give us a few minutes?"

Cornwall snapped back at Walker again, "I wait for nobody. You don't tell me what to do."

These words and attitude angered Walker. He then responded as he didn't want to do, he momentarily lost control.

Walker looked down at old, stooped-over Cornwall Harris and yelled, "Sit down old man and shut up."

His demand angered Cornwall even more. He yelled back to Walker even louder, "Do you know who I am?"

John Moldovan, Satchel Jones, Hollis Tassie, and Wynne Shields finally realized what was going on, Cornwall Harris was in the police station. Wynne Shields bolted through the doorway and into the hallway and the commotion. He yelled, "What's going on?"

At that moment, Cornwall made a move that stopped everyone in their tracks. He was now standing behind his daughter, with his back to the wall and using her as a shield. He also had a gun to her head.

He yelled at the top of his lungs, "I'll kill her."

Cornwall had reached down his pants leg and pulled out a small plastic gun.

He was wobbly and holding her against him, not aggressively, or firmly. He was too weak. She probably could have broken free with little effort, but if she made a move, he probably would have shot her accidentally.

She was also shocked. She saw her Father shoot her cousin Gill so she knew what he was capable of and she didn't move. Teddy Walker and all of the cops immediately drew their firearms and in seconds, had Cornwall covered.

Walker quickly assessed what kind of gun could make it through the metal detector. He then attempted to take control of the situation. "Folks, this is real. He has a fiberglass gun, and the fiberglass bullets will kill at this close range, so I need everyone to be cool."

He then turned to Cornwall Harris, "Sir, I need you to relax and put the gun down."

Cornwall didn't acknowledge Teddy Walker. He started sobbing. He looked to Shields, who was standing feet away.

"Why? Why? I did it all for you," he said to Wynne.

"I know, I know," Wynne said.

"Did you tell them? Did you tell them?" Cornwall asked through tears.

"No, I didn't, no, I didn't." Wynne also started crying. Samantha Rivers began to cry too.

"I'm a dead man, Wynne, all you had to do was hold on."

In that instance, overcome by her fear, Samantha Rivers fainted and fell to the ground. Her deadweight knocked the rickety old man off-balance, and his gun went off. He sent a single shot to the direction of the young detective Melendez.

Instinctively, Melendez responded with a series of four shots. They all missed Cornwall Harris.

However, Wynne threw his body at Cornwall Harris and the last shot hit him in the back and pierced his heart. He collapsed in Cornwall Harris's arms. Cornwall looked down on Shields, who was fighting for his breath.

His last words as Cornwall held him were, "I'm sorry, daddy. I'm sorry, daddy. I didn't tell."

Cornwall held Wynne and whispered, "I know, I believe you, my son. I believe you, my son." Cornwall held Wynne Shields, patting his head furiously, as his son, the illegitimate, rebel died in his arm

Chapter Twenty-Nine

Cornwall Harris died six months after the police shooting that took the life of his illegitimate son, Wynne Shields. He stood trial as the shooter in his nephew's, Gill Harris's death but died before he was sentenced. Because of his illness he never spent a day in jail.

A major investigation followed the police station incident filled in all of the blanks of the Harris Simmons affair. It was a story carried in all three of the city papers. An excerpt of Mike Desanctis's story in the Post:

"The results of our investigation revealed that Cornwall Harris shot and killed his nephew in an angry rage when he learned of Gill Harris's plan to send Wynne away. It was a plan to rehabilitate his reputation. The investigation also revealed that there was no illicit romance between Wynne and Samantha Rivers. The truth was that Gill Harris had united them.

He learned of the illegitimacy of Wynne from Cornwall after the Margot Thomas incident. After that incident, he was planning to fire Wynne regardless of the embarrassment it might bring to the firm. But this news brought him around.

It endeared a great deal of compassion for Wynne. While he knew about Samantha Rivers for years, Gill now saw Wynne as a lost soul. Once he learned the

THE PUBLISHER'S DILEMMA

whole story, he went as far as to set up a reunion between Wynne and his long-lost half-sister, Samantha Rivers.

Quietly, thanks to the snooping of the private detective, John Moldovan, Gill was kept aware of their regular meetings. He was going to send Samantha to London with hopes that their sibling relationship would grow. Gill never told John Moldovan that Samantha was Wynne's sister. This omission was the reason Moldovan thought Samantha and Wynne were involved in another illicit affair. Meanwhile, Gill was gaining comfort in knowing that they had created a bond as long-lost brother and sister."

Luke McFlemming had a more revealing story in the News that delved into Cornwall Harris's deeply disturbing and cantankerous past, an excerpt of Harlowe Award-nominated expose was as follows:

"Wynne Shields was conceived during an affair Cornwall had with Wynne's mother, Gloria. It was a birth not known to the man who raised him as his Father, Monroe Shields. It was an affair and illegitimate birth that took 20 years to be exposed.

Monroe Shields and Gloria divorced after young Wynne went to college. It was at this time that Wynne learned his birth father was not Monroe Shields, the noted Wall Street executive. Monroe Shields, an investment banker, was wealthy, handsome, gregarious, and unfailingly faithful to Gloria. His power, wealth, and aristocratic bearings made him the mark of many young and beautiful women.

During Wynne's second year in college, Monroe and Gloria hosted a summer party for his investment bank's staff at their Hamptons house. A young associate and admirer of Monroe for some time had too much to drink. She openly and embarrassingly pursued Monroe in front of all the guests.

Monroe, being the gracious host, excused the behavior of the young associate to too much liquor and escorted her off the grounds under the pretense that she needed some fresh air. Once they got outside the yard, he firmly let her know that she was embarrassing him, his wife, and their guests. She ignored his reprimand, and drunkenly attempted to kiss him and grab his crotch. Gloria, who was standing 20 feet away, watched this whole display and lost her cool.

Gloria Shields walked across the yard, pulled the woman away from Monroe.

DARIUS MYERS

She then yelled, 'That's my husband, you need to get the hell out of here now.' As she pulled the woman away from Monroe, the associate fell to the ground. She was stumbling drunkenly and trying to stand up, Gloria then grabbed her arm and began to drag her across the lawn and towards the front of the house.

While dragging her along, Gloria passed by a table, paused for a moment, picked up a full water pitcher and poured it on the head of the young associate. 'That'll cool your hot ass down.' She said and started to drag her again until two young male associates from the bank interceded.

As they separated the two women, Gloria yelled, 'Get that tramp out of here,' and tried to kick her while she was on the ground. She missed the girl, but the kick landed instead on the shin of one of the young associates.

Gloria Shields's rage didn't end there. When she kicked the associate, she ended up breaking her big toe. The immediate pain increased her anger even more. She next turned her fury to Monroe.

'You bastard,' she yelled at Monroe, who was standing alone in the middle of the yard. All the guests had now moved to the outer reaches of the yard, away from Monroe, and out of striking range of Gloria.

'You dare invite that tramp to my house!' she screamed. Gloria's sister, Tina, then ran in and interceded. She was able to pull a weeping and hysterical Gloria into the house.

This episode ruined the afternoon. After Tina got her sister, Gloria inside, Monroe addressed the guests. 'Well folks, this is not quite what we had in mind for this afternoon. I'm sorry to all of you who drove out here today just for this party. Today was supposed to be a great day. Unfortunately, it didn't turn out that way. If you all will excuse me, I have to attend to my wife. Feel free to enjoy the food and stay as long as you'd like. I'll see you all at the office next week.'

Of course, all the guests left immediately, and when Monroe went in to check on his wife, she exploded again. 'You bastard, you embarrassed me,' it was then in a rage that she revealed the lie that had been her secret and Cornwall Harris's for 20 years.

Monroe was devastated by the news. His good friend of more than 40 years, Cornwall had perpetrated the most serious offense, other than murder, that one

THE PUBLISHER'S DILEMMA

could do to a friend.

This news and the eventual divorce turned out to be the significant influence of Wynne's evil nature and selfish ways. Devastated by this affair, he lost faith and trust in everyone and was particularly disdainful to women and authority figures. Gloria turned to liquor and became an alcoholic as she tried to drink her way past her humiliation.

Monroe Shields, after the divorce, never remarried. Cornwall Harris was plagued by his guilt and involvement with Gloria and the effect it had on the Shields clan. It was this guilt that gave him the unconditional loyalty and responsibility for Wynne. He was also burdened by the heartache and devastation that his deviance caused for his childhood friend, Monroe Shields, who the young Wynne idolized. Not surprisingly, the two men's friendship ended that day, despite scores of overtures for forgiveness on Cornwall's part. Cornwall's guilt left him powerless to what Wynne would become, a wild and cantankerous miscreant in his adult years with a sense of entitlement at Harris Simmons. It was also the reason that Wynne had no children of his own.

Cornwall, Monroe, Gloria, and Wynne decided to continue to live a lie. They agreed that no one could benefit from such a nasty scandal. The truth hurt for sure, but no one else needed to know. Gill only recently learned that Wynne Shields was his cousin. He learned after the Margot Thomas sexual assault.

Monroe filed for divorce under irreconcilable differences, and Gloria, who had family money of her own, did not contest the divorce. Monroe kept the Hamptons house, and she kept the Manhattan apartment.

After the divorce, Monroe attempted to continue to play a role in young Wynne's life. He was the only father Wynne knew, but as time went on Wynne's behavior became increasingly deviant and defiant. As he began to climb the ranks at Harris Simmons, and closer to Cornwall, Monroe Shields began to distance himself from Wynne. By the time of Wynne Shields' death, twenty plus years after the fateful Hampton's party, Monroe and Wynne's relationship had deteriorated. It was limited to the exchange of holiday and birthday cards. They had not seen each other in five years.

When Wynne and Samantha Rivers finally met, it was as if he met someone who could finally understand his situation, to share in his pain. While Samantha's mother never married, and she was not the product of such a scandalous affair, she did have to live secretly estranged from her father. Samantha and Gill bonded in the knowledge and commonness of their lineage. They both were living lives veiled in deep cloaks of secrecy.

It also turned out that the plan of Gill to send Wynne to London to oversee Harris Simmons's international operations was agreed to by Wynne. Gill and Wynne saw it as a way to put the turmoil and revelations of the last couple of years behind them. He hoped to draw some attention away from the media circus following the company and to give Wynne a fresh start.

Gill saw Wynne as the prodigal son, and he wanted to do what was necessary to welcome him back home. He pledged to make it right and give him his due as a Harris Family scion. Wynne was warmed by the gesture and leniency offered by his older cousin and agreed to do whatever it took to win Gill's favor."

Luke McFlemming had hit the jackpot with this story. It took him three weeks to report and was as his editor said, 'a huge story and possibly his Harlowe Writing Award.'

Even Jennifer Kung did well. Kung was lucky enough to get an exclusive with Samantha Rivers. They started a friendship that continues to this day.

After they became friends, Samantha shared with her why she went to the Ron Cherry party.

"Gill loved Donald, he thought he was so cool, and so I thought you know, let me check this guy out and see what he was all about. I learned about the Ron Cherry party in the society pages and just went, nobody asked me who I was, and so I just hung out. I checked him out a little and then left."

"You did that," Kung said, "you got balls Sister."

"I know that was kind of crazy," Rivers said. "He is what everybody says and really good looking too, but not my type. You should check out his buddy Miki Nomura though. He's hot and he's got this crazy Power Moves

THE PUBLISHER'S DILEMMA

rap that he puts on the ladies. He's pretty cool too. I would date him in a second. I'm going to get Donald to introduce him to me."

Samantha gave Jennifer Kung the play by of grand jury testimony that turned into a big winner for her and The Ledger. An excerpt, that was written as a first-person story, under the headline, The Harris Simmons Lost Child:

"Gill came up with this plan for Wynne to go to Europe. Wynne agreed wholeheartedly. They even set a timetable for him to come back. If he did everything right, he would come back as a Vice-Chairman. But there were things that Wynne did that didn't help him, like the Val Tolliver affair and the sexual assaults. Wynne didn't get it that he couldn't bully or blackmail Gill. Finally, after Gill dressed him down right before the Kwame Mills was hired. Wynne began to get with the program. He realized that the blackmail story was Cornwall's dirt, not Gill's. Unfortunately, Cornwall didn't see it that way."

The story also included a conversation Samantha Rivers had with her Uncle Gill after the infamous sales meeting on the day of the shooting.

"Even after Gill got pissed off at Wynne during the sales meeting, he called me and told me what happened and that he was still pulling for Wynne. He told me that the goal was for Donald to run the company as President and eventually as CEO. Still he was not cutting him out of the company. Gill felt like we needed to know each other; he had a deep sense of history and respect for this family.

It was a great gesture on Gill's part, given the history of those two. He had such strong sympathy for Wynne and his situation. I don't think he would have ever fired him.

Then, holding back tears and turning back to the London plan, she continued, 'Gill thought it was best to take the plan to Cornwall for his approval. They even had a role for me. I was going to join Wynne in London. We were getting to know each other and were getting along quite well,' she smiled as she recalled the time spent with her new-found half-brother. 'I was going to work for Wynne. The plan was for me to report to him, and he was going to show me the ropes of the business, and if everything worked out, we both would play a big role in the future

DARIUS MYERS

of the company. But we didn't know my father had cancer and a short time left to live. I'm sure Gill wouldn't have made the plan to send Wynne to London had he known.' As she finished this statement, she began to cry uncontrollably."

This was the same testimony that Samantha Rivers made at the jury trial and when Cornwall Harris, heard it, he began to cry. Samantha Rivers looked at him in this broken state, as did the Assistant District Attorney Gath leading the prosecution, Cornwall's attorney, Hollis Tassie, and the Judge.

Cornwall was a wreck of a man. He looked back to her as she walked from the witness stand. As Samantha Rivers made her way slowly past her Father, she reached in the air towards him, hoping to touch his hand. He reached out to her reflexively, sobbing and putting his head down in grief as she took her seat in the courtroom.

After Cornwall Harris regained his composure, he was the next to testify. "I killed him, and I shot Donald Alexander because I just lost my mind over how he was passing the company out of family hands."

"Yes, it's true that they came to me with the plan. But I was just too stubborn. I had only recently found out about my cancer, and I knew that I had just a short time to live. But I didn't want sympathy."

"You have to understand," he said to the Judge, "I've never had to ask anyone for anything. I didn't know how. This whole affair was all my fault." Samantha Rivers started to cry again. Her sobbing was tearing Cornwall up.

He continued talking to the Judge, "If only I shared with Gill and my kids what was going on, I know he would have made it right. You see, the truth was that my nephew was a good man, I was so proud of him, but in many ways envious and I couldn't humble myself. I just wanted my son and my daughter to be with me at the end." Then he broke down uncontrollably.

All this crying moved the Assistant District Attorney Gath. He felt compassion for the sad demise of this once-proud leader of such an esteemed company and family, a family whose legacy was tarnished forever. He asked for a recess. The Judge agreed.

THE PUBLISHER'S DILEMMA

After the recess, Cornwall gave a detailed account of the shooting.

"When they came to me with the plan, I went wild. I didn't want to hear it. So, I slammed Gill's coffee pot on the floor and walked out of his office. I went downstairs to my office and got a gun I kept in my desk and went straight to Donald Alexander's office and shot him. Gill and Samantha ran down to Donald's office. Gill went back to his office to call the police. He had no choice but to call the police. I told him to put the phone down, and when he didn't, I shot him too."

The D.A. asked, "So what happened next?"

"After that, my daughter, my sweet baby girl," Samantha Rivers began to cry again. Samantha longed for so many years for Cornwall to accept her. "She grabbed me and took me down the elevator and out of the building."

"You may not believe this, but I liked the job Donald Alexander was doing for the company. He's a good man and a great media executive. In my opinion, he's the right man to run this company, but in my rage, all I could think was that he was so young and so good and that my son would never have a chance to run Harris Simmons. My Brother Oliver, Jr., I have appointed him CEO along with his President's title of the company. I know he will run it greatly in the future."

Cornwall concluded his testimony with this final statement. "I'm not asking for any mercy from the Judge. I'm a condemned man. My fate is sealed, but I had a momentary lapse, a mad moment. I lost my mind in my rage."

Cornwall straightened up in his chair and looked again to the Judge and the Assistant District Attorney Gath. "I have no reason to lie, especially now, as I prepare to face a trial and fate at an even higher court."

Samantha Rivers was cleared of any wrongdoing, even though she aided Cornwall Harris as he left the scene of the crime.

As he testified, before his death, Cornwall Harris and his older Brother and Gill's Father voted Donald Alexander as Chairman, CEO, and President of The Company.

After Cornwall's death, Oliver, Jr., said to Alexander, "Donald, I know Gill was a big fan of yours, and you know when he was alive, all we asked is that you produce. Now I want you to be fearless in your leadership and take the company in the direction you choose. You will always have my support and trust for as long as I live."

He then smiled and said, "And you earmark enough money for my pet projects."

Donald, sensed that Oliver, Jr., being facetious, so he said, "Like Alaskan fruit flies, Oliver?"

"Oh, forget about those damn Alaskan fruit flies," he said as a huge smile and reflective look crossed his face.

"I know those crazy projects were stupid, but I use to support stupid stuff like that to get under Gill's skin. I was only doing that so he would make time for me. Now that he's gone, I'll give that up and put my money to better work."

He then said, "I hope you won't mind if this old guy calls or visits now and again when he's bored."

"Oliver," Donald said. "I will always have time for you." He then made an offer to Oliver that made him very happy and commenced a warm friendship between the two of them. "I'd like it if you and I can have a regular lunch or breakfast monthly. It's still your company, and I was such a fan and friend of Gill that it would be nice for me to get to know the man that helped make him so great. I wouldn't be here without him, and I attribute that to you being such a great Father and leader."

"Thank you, Donald, that would make me very happy, and I look forward to spending time with you."

Donald and Oliver's friendship lasted until Oliver's death. He died six

THE PUBLISHER'S DILEMMA

years after his son of natural causes. During that time their fondness of each other continued to grow. So much so that Oliver began to redirect his annual pet project money at Donald's direction to Historical Black Colleges and Universities. It was also because Donald was driving the company to record performance. Four years after Gill's death, they were delivering $4 billion in annual revenue, a 5x growth of cash since the death of Gill and Wynne Shields. It grew another billion to $5 billion by the time of his death.

Oliver, Jr., championed the diversity initiative at Harris Simmons, which led to Kwame Mills eventually rising to become the President of Harris Simmons International, and one of the top five executives in the company. Oliver, Jr., jumped in and played a significant role in mentoring his grandniece Samantha Rivers, who turned out to be an outstanding media executive. At his death, she was the Head of Sales and Operations for all the women's fashions and lifestyle properties at Harris Simmons.

A month before he died, he gathered Donald Alexander, Samantha Rivers, and Kwame together during a lunch that they would have during Kwame's quarterly visits to New York.

Oliver, Jr., said at their last lunch, "I never knew that I would have such a rewarding final act. Working with you guys has been such a joy. My final days have so much meaning, thanks to all of you. I appreciate you all more than you'll ever now."

After his death, he left instructions for Donald to sell the company and divert a considerable stake to his remaining family and charities. The company sold for $75 billion, a staggering 15x multiple of cash flow. Oliver, Jr., made his niece Samantha Rivers very rich with $100 million, she received $50 million from the family trust and another $50 million in stock as a company executive. Donald Alexander, the leader, and architect of the dramatic growth pocketed $2 billion, Kwame Mills took $500 million. They were all named Directors of The Oliver Harris Diversity Education

DARIUS MYERS

Foundation, which was designed to support HBCU's and scholarships for ethnic minorities and women. For this Foundation, he left three billion dollars.

Oliver, Jr.'s final words read to them through the executor at his Will was "you've all worked hard and are deserving of this, now go out, enjoy life and use this money to do some good."

The End